I0548859

Tales of a Time and Place

Louisiana Bayou History and Heritage in Five Stories

By Grace King

Published by Pantianos Classics

ISBN-13: 978-1-78987-104-3

First published in 1892

Contents

Bayou l'Ombre

Of course they knew all about war — soldiers, flags, music, generals on horseback brandishing swords, knights in armor escalading walls, cannons booming through clouds of smoke. They were familiarized with it pictorially and by narrative long before the alphabet made its appearance in the nursery with rudimentary accounts of the world they were born into, the simple juvenile world of primary sensations and colors. Their great men, and great women, too, were all fighters; the great events of their histories, battles; the great places of their geography, where they were fought (and generally the more bloody the battle, the more glorious the place); while their little chronology — the pink-covered one— stepped briskly over the centuries solely on the names of kings and sanguinary saliencies. Sunday added the sabbatical supplement to week day lessons, symbolizing religion, concreting sin, incorporating evil, for their better comprehension, putting Jehovah himself in armor, to please their childish faculties — the omnipotent Intervener of the Old Testament, for whom they waved banners, sang hymns, and by the brevet title, "little *soldiers* of the cross," felt committed as by baptism to an attitude of expectant hostility. Mademoiselle Couper, their governess, eased the cross-stitching in their samplers during the evenings, after supper, with traditions of "le grand Napoléon," in whose army her grandfather was a terrible and distinguished officer, le Capitaine Césaire Paul Picquet de Montignac; and although Mademoiselle Couper was most unlovable and exacting at times, and very homely, such were their powers of sympathetic enthusiasm even then that they often went to bed envious of the possessor or so glorious an ancestor, and dreamed fairy tales of him whose gray hair, enshrined in a brooch, reposed comfortably under the folds of mademoiselle's fat chin — the hair that Napoleon had looked upon!

When a war broke out in their own country they could hardly credit their good-fortune; that is, Christine and Régina, for Lolotte was still a baby. A wonderful panorama was suddenly unfolded before them. It was their first intimation of the identity of the world they lived in with the world they learned about, their first perception of the existence of an entirely novel sentiment in their hearts— patriotism, the *amour sacré de la patrie,* over which they had seen mademoiselle shed tears as copiously as her grandfather had blood. It made them and all their little companions feel very proud, this war; but it gave them a heavy sense of responsibility, turning their youthful precocity incontinently away from books, slates, and pianos towards the martial considerations that befitted the hour. State rights, Federal limits, monitors

4

and fortresses, proclamations, Presidents, recognitions, and declarations, they acquired them all with facility, taxing, as in other lessons, their tongue to repeat the unintelligible on trust for future intelligence. As their father fired his huge after-dinner bombs, so they shot their diminutive ammunition; as he lighted brands in the great conflagration, they lighted tapers; and the two contending Presidents themselves did not get on their knees with more fervor before their colossal sphinxes than these little girls did before their doll-baby presentment of "Country." It was very hard to realize at times that histories and story-books and poetry would indeed be written about them; that little flags would mark battles all over the map of their country — the country Mademoiselle Couper despised as so hopelessly, warlessly insignificant; that men would do great things and women say them, teachers and copy-books reiterate them, and children learn them, just as they did of the Greeks and Romans, the English and French. The great advantage was having God on their side, as the children of Israel had; the next best thing was having the finest country, the most noble men, and the bravest soldiers. The only fear was that the enemy would be beaten too easily, and the war cease too soon to be glorious; for, characteristic of their sex, they demanded nothing less than that their war should be the longest, bloodiest, and most glorious of all wars ever heard of, in comparison with which even "le grand Napoleon" and his Capitaine Picquet would be effaced from memory. For this were exercised their first attempts at extempore prayer. God, the dispenser of inexhaustible supplies of munitions of war, became quite a different power, a nearer and dearer personality, than "Our Father," the giver of simple daily bread, and He did not lack reminding of the existence of the young Confederacy, nor of the hearsay exigencies they gathered from the dinner-table talk.

Titine was about thirteen, Gina twelve, and Lolotte barely eight years old, when this, to them, happy break in their lives occurred. It was easily comprehensible to them that their city should be captured, and that to escape that grim ultimatum of Mademoiselle Couper, "*passées au fil de l'épee*," they should be bundled up very hurriedly one night, carried out of their home, and journey in troublesome roundabout ways to the plantation on Bayou l'Ombre.

That was all four years ago. School and play and city life, dolls and fetes and Santa Claus, had become the property of memory. Peace for them hovered in that obscurity which had once enveloped war, while "'61," "'62," "'63," "'64," filled immeasurable spaces in their short past. Four times had Christine and Régina changed the date in their diaries — the last token of remembrance from Mademoiselle Couper — altering the numerals with naïve solemnity, as if under the direction of the Almighty himself, closing with conventional ceremony the record of the lived -out twelve months, opening with appropriate aspirations the year to come. The laboriously careful chronicle that followed was not, however, of the growth of their bodies advancing by inches, nor the expansion of their minds, nor of the vague forms that began to people the shadow-land of their sixteen and seventeen-year-old hearts. Their own budding and leafing and growing was as unnoted as that of the trees and weeds about them. The progress of the war, the growth of their hatred of the enemy, the expansion of the *amour sacré* germ — these were the confidences that filled the neatly -stitched foolscap volumes. If on comparison one sister was found to have been happier in the rendition of the common sentiment, the coveted fervor and eloquence were plagiarized or imitated the next day by the other, a generous emulation thus keeping the original flame not only alight, but burning, while from assimilating each other's sentiments the two girls grew with identity of purpose into identity of mind, and effaced the slight difference of age between them.

Little Lolotte responded as well as she could to the enthusiastic exactions of her sisters. She gave her rag dolls patriotic names, obediently hated and loved as they required, and learned to recite all the war songs procurable, even to the teeming quantities of the stirring "Men of the South, our foes are up!" But as long as the squirrels gambolled on the fences, the blackbirds flocked in the fields, and the ditches filled with fish; as long as the seasons imported such constant variety of attractions — persimmons, dewberries, blackberries, acorns, wild plums, grapes, and muscadines; as long as the cows had calves, the dogs puppies, the hogs pigs, and the quarters new babies to be named; as long as the exasperating negro children needed daily subjugation, regulation, and discipline — the day's measure was too well filled and the night's slumber too short to admit of her carrying on a very vigorous warfare for a country so far away from Bayou l'Ombre — a country whose grievances she could not understand.

But— there were no soldiers, flags, music, parades, battles, or sieges. This war was altogether distinct from the wars contained in books or in Mademoiselle Couper's memory. There was an absence of the simplest requirements of war. They kept awaiting the familiar events for which they had been prepared; but after four years the only shots fired on Bayou l'Ombre were at game in the forest, the only blood shed was from the tottering herds of Texas beeves driven across the swamps to them, barely escaping by timely butchery the starvation they came to relieve, and the only heroism they had been called upon to display was still going to bed in the dark. Indeed, were it not that they knew there was a war they might have supposed that some malignant fairy had transported them from a state of wealth and luxury to the condition of those miserable Hathorns, the pariahs of their childhood, who lived just around the corner from them in the city, with whom they had never been allowed to associate. If they had not so industriously fostered the proper feelings in their hearts, they might almost have forgotten it, or, like Lolotte, been diverted from it by the generous overtures of nature all around them. But they kept on reminding each other that it was not the degrading want of money, as in the Hathorns' case, that forced them to live on salt meat, corn -bread, and sassafras tea, to dress like the negro women in the quarters, that deprived them of education and society, and imprisoned them in a swamp-encircled plantation, the prey of chills and fever; but it was for love of country, and being little women now, they loved their country more, the more they suffered for her. Disillusion might have supervened to disappointment and bitterness have quenched hope, experience might at last have sharpened their vision, but for the imagination, that ethereal parasite which fattens on the stagnant forces of youth and garnishes with tropical luxuriance the abnormal source of its nourishment. Soaring aloft, above the prosaic actualities of the present, beyond the rebutting evidence of earth, was a fanciful stage where the drama of war such as they craved was unfolded; where neither homespun, starvation, overflows, nor illness were allowed to enter; where the heroes and heroines they loved acted roles in all the conventional glitter of costume and conduct, amid the dazzling pomps and circumstances immortalized in history and romance. Their hearts would bound and leap after these phantasms, like babes in nurses' arms after the moon, and would almost burst with longing, their ripe little hearts, Pandora-boxes packed with passions and pleasures for a lifetime, ready to spring open at a touch! On moonlit nights in summer, or under the low gray clouds of winter days, in the monotony of nothingness about them, the yearning in their breasts was like that of hunting dogs howling for the unseen game. Sometimes a rumor of a battle "out in the Confederacy" would find its way across the swamps to them, and months afterwards a newspaper would be thrown to them from a passing skiff, some old, useless, tattered, disreputable, journalistic tramp, garrulous with mendacities; but it was all true to them, if to no one else in the world — the factitious triumphs, the lurid glories, the pyrotechnical promises, prophecies, calculations, and Victory with the laurel wreath always in the future, never out of sight for an instant. They would con the fraudulent evangel, entranced; their eyes would sparkle, the blood color their cheeks, their voices vibrate, and a strange strength excite and nerve their bodies. Then would follow wakeful nights and restless days; Black Margarets, Jeanne d'Arcs, Maids of Saragossa, Katherine Douglases, Charlotte Cordays, would haunt them like the goblins of a delirium; then their prayers would become imperious demands upon Heaven, their diaries would almost break into spontaneous combustion from the incendiary material enmagazined in their pages, and the South would have conquered the world then and there could their hands but have pointed the guns and their hearts have recruited the armies. They would with mingled pride and envy read all the names, barely decipherable in the travel-stained record, from the President and Generals in big print to the diminishing insignificance of smallest-type privates; and they would shed tears, when the reaction would come a few days later, at the thought that in the whole area of typography, from the officers gaining immortality to the privates losing lives, there was not one name belonging to them; and they would ask why, of all the families in the South, precisely their father and mother should have no relations, why, of all the women in the South, they should be brotherless.

There was Beau, a too notorious guerrilla captain; but what glory was to be won by raiding towns, wrecking trains, plundering transports, capturing couriers, disobeying orders, defying regulations? He was almost as obnoxious to his own as to the enemy's flag.

Besides, Beau at most was only a kind of a cousin, the son of a deceased step-sister of their father's; the most they could expect from him was to keep his undisciplined crew of "'Cadians," Indians, and swampers away from Bayou l'Ombre.

"Ah, if we were only men!" But no! They who could grip daggers and shed blood, they who teemed with all the possibilities of romance or poetry, they were selected for a passive, paltry contest against their own necessities; the endurance that would have laughed a siege to scorn ebbing away in a never-ceasing wrangle with fever and ague — willow-bark tea at odds with a malarious swamp!

It was now early summer; the foliage of spring was lusty and strong, fast outgrowing tenderness and delicacy of shade, with hints of maturity already swelling the shape. The day was cloudless and warm, the dinner -hour was long past, and supper still far off. There were no appetizing varieties of menu to make meals objects of pleasant anticipation; on the contrary, they had become mournful effigies of a convivial institution of which they served at most only to recall the hours, monotonously measuring off the recurring days which passed like unlettered mileposts in a desert, with no information to give except that of transition. To-day the meal-times were so far apart as to make one believe that the sun had given up all forward motion, and intended prolonging the present into eternity. The plantation was quiet and still; not the dewy hush of early dawn trembling before the rising sun, nor the mysterious muteness of midnight, nor yet the lethargic dulness of summer when the vertical sun-rays pin sense and motion to the earth. It was the motionless, voiceless state of unnatural quietude, the oppressive consciousness of abstracted activity, which characterized those days when the whole force of Bayou l'Ombre went off into the swamps to cut timber. Days that began shortly after one midnight and lasted to the other; rare days, when neither horn nor bell was heard for summons; when not a skiff, flat-boat, nor pirogue was left at the "gunnels;" [1] when old Uncle John alone remained to represent both master and men in the cares and responsibilities devolving upon his sex. The bayou lived and moved as usual, carrying its deceptive depths of brackish water unceasingly onward through the shadow and sunshine, rippling over the opposite low, soft banks, which seemed slowly sinking out of sight under the weight of the huge cypress-trees growing upon it. The long stretch of unfilled fields back of the house, feebly kept in symmetrical proportion by crumbling fences, bared their rigid, seedless furrows in despairing barrenness to the sun, except in corner spots where a rank growth of weeds

8

had inaugurated a reclamation in favor of barbarism. The sugar-house, superannuated and decrepit from unwholesome idleness, tottered against its own massive, smokeless chimney; the surrounding sheds, stables, and smithy looked forsaken and neglected; the old blind mule peacefully slept in the shade of his once flagellated course under the corn-mill. Afar off against the woods the huge wheel of the draining-machine rose from the underbrush in the big ditch. The patient buzzards, roosting on the branches of the gaunt, blasted gum-tree by the bayou, would raise their heads from time to time to question the loitering sun, or, slowly flapping their heavy wings, circle up into the blue sky, to fall again in lazy spirals to their watch-tower, or they would take short flights by twos and threes over the moribund plantation to see if dissolution had not yet set in, and then all would settle themselves again to brood and sleep and dream, and wait in tranquil certainty the striking of their banqueting hour.

The three girls were in the open hall-way of the plantation house, Christine reading, Régina knitting, both listlessly occupied. Like everything else, they were passively quiet, and, like everything else, their appearance advertised an unwholesome lack of vitality, an insidious anamorphosis from an unexplained dearth or constraint. Their meagre maturity and scant development clashed abnormally with the surrounding prodigality of insensible nature. Though tall, they were thin; they were fair, but sallow; their gentle deep eyes were reproachful and deprived looking. If their secluded hearts ventured even in thought towards the plumings natural to their age, their coarse, homely, ill-fitting garments anathematized any coquettish effort or naïve expression of a desire to find favor. Like the fields, they seemed hesitating on the backward path from cultivation. Lolotte stood before the cherry-wood armoire that held the hunting and fishing tackle, the wholesome receptacle of useful odds and ends. Not old enough to have come into the war with preconceptions, Lolotte had no reconciliations or compromises to effect between the ideal and the real, no compensations to solicit from an obliging imagination, which so far never rose beyond the possibilities of perch, blackbirds, and turtle eggs. The first of these occupied her thoughts at the present moment. She had made a tryst with the negro children at the draining machine this afternoon. If she could, unperceived, abstract enough tackle from the armoire for the crowd, and if they could slip away from the quarters, and she evade the surveillance of Uncle John, there would be a diminished number of "brim" and "goggle-eye" in the ditch out yonder, and such a notable addition to the plantation supper to-night as would crown the exploit a success, and establish for herself a reputation above all annoying recollections of recent mishaps and failures. As she tied the hooks on to the lines she saw herself surrounded by the acclaiming infantile populace, pulling the struggling perch up one after the other; she saw them strung on palmetto thongs, long strings of them; she walked home at the head of her procession; heard

Peggy's exclamations of surprise, smelt them frying, and finally was sitting at the table, a plate of bones before her, the radiant hostess of an imperial feast.

"Listen!" Like wood-ducks from under the water, the three heads rose simultaneously above their abstractions. "Rowlock! Rowlock!" The eyes might become dull, the tongue inert, and the heart languid on Bayou l'Ombre, but the ears were ever assiduous, ever on duty. Quivering and nervous, they listened even through sleep for that one blessed echo of travel, the signal from another and a distant world. Faint, shadowy, delusive, the whispering forerunner of on-coming news, it overrode the rippling of the current, the hooting of the owls, the barking of dogs, the splash of the gar-fish, the grunting of the alligator, the croaking of frogs, penetrating all turmoil, silencing all other sounds. "Rowlock! Rowlock!" Slow, deliberate, hard, and strenuous, coming upstream; easy, soft, and musical, gliding down. "Rowlock! Rowlock!" Every stroke a very universe of hope, every oar frothing a sea of expectation! Was it the bayou or the secret stream of their longing that suggested the sound today? "Rowlock! Rowlock!" The smouldering glances brightened in their eyes, they hollowed their hands behind their ears and held their breath for greater surety. "Rowlock! Rowlock!" In clear, distinct reiteration. It resolved the moment of doubt.

"Can it be papa coming back?"

"No; it's against stream."

"It must be swampers."

"Or hunters, perhaps."

"Or Indians from the mound."

"Indians in a skiff?"

"Well, they sometimes come in a skiff."

The contingencies were soon exhausted, a cut off leading travellers far around Bayou l'Ombre, whose snaggy, rafted, convoluted course was by universal avoidance relegated to an isolation almost insulting. The girls, listening, not to lose a single vibration, quit their places and advanced to the edge of the gallery, then out under the trees, then to the levee, then to the "gunnels," where they stretched their long, thin, white necks out of their blue and brown check gowns, and shaded their eyes and gazed down-stream for the first glimpse of the skiff — their patience which had lasted months fretting now over the delay of a few moments.

"At last we shall get some news again."

"If they only leave a newspaper!"

"Or a letter," said Lolotte.

"A letter! From whom?"

"Ah, that's it!"

"What a pity papa isn't here!"

"Lolotte, don't shake the gunnels so; you are wetting our feet."

"How long is it since the last one passed?"

"I can tell you," said Lolotte — "I can tell you exactly: it was the day Lou Ann fell in the bayou and nearly got drowned."

"You mean when you both fell in."

"I didn't fall in at all; I held on to the pirogue."

The weeping-willow on the point below veiled the view; stretching straight out from the bank, it dropped its shock of long, green, pliant branches into the water, titillating and dimpling the surface. The rising bayou bore a freight of logs and drift from the swamps above; rudely pushing their way through the willow boughs, they tore and bruised the fragile tendrils that clung to the rough bark, scattering the tiny leaves which followed hopelessly after in their wake or danced up and down in the hollow eddies behind them. Each time the willow screen moved, the gunnels swayed under the forward motion of the eager bodies of the girls.

"At last!"

They turned their eyes to the shaft of sunlight that fell through the plantation clearing, bridging the stream. The skiff touched, entered, and passed through it with a marvellous revelation of form and color, the oars silvering and dripping diamonds, arrows and lances of light scintillating from polished steel, golden stars rising like dust from tassels, cordons, buttons, and epaulets, while the blue clouds themselves seemed to have fallen from their empyrean heights to uniform the rowers with their own celestial hue — blue, not gray!

"Rowlock! Rowlock!" What loud, frightful, threatening reverberations of the oars! And the bayou flowed on the same, and the cypress-trees gazed stolidly and steadfastly up to the heavens, and the heavens were serenely blue and white! But the earth was sympathetic, the ground shook and swayed under their feet; or was it the rush of thoughts that made their heads so giddy? They tried to arrest one and hold it for guidance, but on they sped, leaving only wild confusion of conjecture behind.

"Rowlock! Rowlock!" The rudder headed the bow for the gunnels.

"Titine! Gina! Will they kill us all?" whispered Lolotte, with anxious horror.

The agile Lou Ann, Lolotte's most efficient coadjutor and Uncle John's most successful tormentor, dropped her bundle of fishing-poles (which he had carefully spread on his roof to "cure"), and while they rolled and rattled over the dry shingles she scrambled with inconceivable haste to her corner of descent. Holding to the eaves while her excited black feet searched and found the top of the window that served as a step, she dropped into the ash-hopper below. Without pausing, as usual, to efface betraying evidences of her enterprise from her person, or to cover her tracks in the wet ashes, she jumped to the ground, and ignoring all secreting offers of bush, fence, or ditch, contrary to her custom, she ran with all the speed of her thin legs down the shortest road to the quarters. They were, as she knew, deserted. The doors of the cabins were all shut, with logs of wood or chairs propped against them. The chickens and dogs were making free of the galleries, and the hogs wallowed in peaceful immunity underneath. A waking baby from a lonely imprisoned cradle sent cries for relief through an open window. Lou Ann, looking neither to the right nor the left, slackened not her steps, but passed straight on through the little avenue to the great white-oak which stood just outside the levee on the bank of the bayou.

Under the wide-spreading, moss-hung branches, upon the broad flat slope, a grand general washing of the clothes of the small community was in busy progress by the women, a proper feminine consecration of this purely feminine day. The daily irksome routine was broken, the men were all away, the sun was bright and warm, the air soft and sweet. The vague recesses of the opposite forest were dim and silent, the bayou played under the gunnels in caressing modulations. All furthered the hearkening and the yielding to a debonair mood, with disregard of concealment, license of pose, freedom of limb, hilarity, conviviality, audacities of heart and tongue, joyous indulgence in freak and impulse, banishment of thought, a return, indeed, for one brief moment to the wild, sweet ways of nature, to the festal days of ancestral golden age (a short retrogression for them), when the body still had claims, and the mind concessions, and the heart owed no allegiance, and when god and satyr eyes still might be caught peeping and glistening from leafy covert on feminine midsummer gambols. Their skirts were girt high around their broad full hips, their dark arms and necks came naked out of their low, sleeveless, white chemise bodies, and glistened with perspiration in the sun as if frosted with silver. Little clouds of steam rose from the kettles standing around them over heaps of burning chips. The splay legged battling boards sank firmer and firmer into the earth under the blows of the bats, pounding and thumping the wet clothes, squirting the warm suds in all directions, up into the laughing faces, down into the panting bosoms, against the shortened, clinging skirts, over the bare legs, out in frothy runnels over the soft red clay corrugated with innumerable toe-prints. Out upon the gunnels the water swished and foamed under the vigorous movements of the rinsers, endlessly bending and raising their flexible, muscular bodies, burying their arms to the shoulders in the cool, green depths, piling higher and higher the heaps of tightly-wrung clothes at their sides. The water-carriers, passing up and down the narrow, slippery plankway, held the evenly filled pails with the ease of coronets upon their heads. The children, under compulsion of continuous threats and occasional chastisement, fed the fire with chips from distant wood-piles, squabbling for the possession of the one cane-knife to split kindlers, imitating the noise and echoing with absurd fidelity the full-throated laughter that interrupted from time to time the work around the wash-kettles.

High above the slop and tumult sat old Aunt Mary, the official sick-nurse of the plantation, commonly credited with conjuring powers. She held a corn-cob pipe between her yellow protruding teeth, and her little restless eyes travelled inquisitively from person to person as if in quest of professional information, twinkling with amusement at notable efforts of wit, and with malice at the general discomfiture expressed under their gaze. Heelen sat near, nursing her baby. She had taken off her kerchief, and leaned her uncovered head back against the trunk of the tree; the long wisps of wool, tightly wrapped in white knitting cotton, rose from irregular sections all over her elongated narrow skull, and encircled her wrinkled, nervous, toothless face like some ghastly serpentine chevelure.

"De Yankees! de Yankees! I seed 'em — at de big house! Little mistus she come for Uncle John. He fotched his gun — for to shoot 'em,"

Lou Ann struggled to make her exhausted breath carry all her tidings. After each item she closed her mouth and swallowed violently, working her muscles until her little horns of hair rose and moved with the contortions of her face.

"An' dey locked a passel o' men up in de smoke-house— Cornfedrits."

The bats paused in the air, the women on the gunnels lifted their arms out of the water, those on the gang-plank stopped where they were; only the kettles simmered on audibly.

Lou Ann recommenced, this time finishing in one breath, with the added emphasis of raising her arm and pointing in the direction from whence she came, her voice getting shriller and shriller to the end:

"I seed 'em. Dey was Yankees. Little mistus she come for Uncle John; he fotched his gun for to shoot 'em; and they locked a passel o' men up in de smoke-house — Cornfedrits."

The Yankees! What did it mean to them? How much from the world outside had penetrated into the unlettered fastnesses of their ignorance? What did the war mean to them? Had Bayou l'Ombre indeed isolated both mind and body? Had the subtle time-spirit itself been diverted from them by the cut-off? Could their rude minds draw no inferences from the gradual loosening of authority and relaxing of discipline? Did they neither guess nor divine their share in the shock of battle out there? Could their ghost seeing eyes not discern the martyr-spirits rising from two opposing armies, pointing at, beckoning to them? If, indeed, the water-shed of their destiny was forming without their knowledge as without their assistance, could not maternal instinct spell it out of the heart-throbs pulsing into life under their bosoms, or read from the dumb faces of the children at their breast the triumphant secret of their superiority over others born and nourished before them?

Had they, indeed, no gratifications beyond the physical, no yearnings, no secret burden of a secret prayer to God, these bonded wives and mothers? Was this careless, happy, indolent existence genuine, or only a fool's motley to disguise a tragedy of suffering? What to them was the difference between themselves and their mistresses? their condition? or their skin, that opaque black skin which hid so well the secrets of life, which could feel but not own the blush of shame, the pallor of weakness.

If their husbands had brought only rum from their stealthy midnight excursions to distant towns, how could the child repeat it so glibly — "Yankees — Cornfedrits?" The women stood still and silent, but their eyes began to creep around furtively, as if seeking degrees of complicity in a common guilt, each waiting for the other to confess comprehension, to assume the responsibility of knowledge.

The clear-headed children, profiting by the distraction of attention from them, stole away for their fishing engagement, leaving cane -knife and chips scattered on the ground behind them. The murmuring of the bayou seemed to rise louder and louder; the cries of the forsaken baby, clamorous and hoarse, fell distinctly on the air.

"My Gord A'mighty!"

The exclamation was uncompromising; it relieved the tension and encouraged rejoinder.

"My Lord!— humph!"

One bat slowly and deliberately began to beat again — Black Maria's. Her tall, straight back was to them, but, as if they saw it, they knew that her face was settling into that cold, stern rigidity of hers, the keen eyes beginning to glisten, the long, thin nostrils nervously to twitch, the lips to open over her fine white teeth — the expression they hated and feared.

"O-h! o-h! o-h!"

A long, thin, tremulous vibration, a weird, haunting note: what inspiration suggested it?

"Glo-o-ry!"

Old Aunt Mary nodded her knowing head affirmatively, as if at the fulfilment of a silent prophecy. She quietly shook the ashes out of her pipe, hunted her pocket, put it in, and rising stiffly from the root, hobbled away on her stick in the direction of her cabin.

"Glo-o-ry!"

Dead-arm Harriet stood before them, with her back to the bayou, her right arm hanging heavy at her side, her left extended, the finger pointing to the sky. A shapely arm and tapering finger; a comely, sleek, half-nude body; the moist lips, with burning red linings, barely parting to emit the sound they must have culled in uncanny practices. The heavy lids drooped over the large sleepy eyes, looking with languid passion from behind the thick black lashes.

"Glo-o-ry!" It stripped their very nerves and bared secret places of sensation! The "happy" cry of revival meetings — as if midnight were coming on, salvation and the mourners' bench before them, Judgment-day and fiery flames behind them, and "Sister Harriet" raising her voice to call them on, on, through hand clapping, foot stamping, shouting, groaning, screaming, out of their sins, out of their senses, to rave in religious inebriation, and fall in religious catalepsy across the floor at the preacher's feet. With a wild rush, the hesitating emotions of the women sought the opportune outlet, their hungry blood bounding and leaping for the midday orgy. Obediently their bodies

14

began the imperceptible motion right and left, and the veins in their throats to swell and stand out under their skins, while the short, fierce, intense responsive exclamations fell from their lips to relieve their own and increase the exaltation of the others.

"Sweet Christ! sweet Christ!"

"Take me, Saviour!"

"Oh, de Lamb! de Lamb!"

"I'm a-coming! I'm a-coming!"

"Hold back, Satan! we's a-catching on!"

"De blood's a-dripping! de blood's a-dripping!"

"Let me kiss dat cross! let me kiss it!"

"Sweet Master!"

"Glo-o-ry! Fre-e-dom!" It was a whisper, but it came like a crash, and transfixed them; their mouths stood open with the last words, their bodies remained bent to one side or the other, the febrile light in their eyes burning as if from their blood on fire. They could all remember the day when Dead -arm Harriet, the worst worker and most violent tongue of the gang, stood in the clearing, and raising that dead right arm over her head, cursed the overseer riding away in the distance. The wind had been blowing all day; there was a sudden loud crack above them, and a limb from a deadened tree broke, sailed, poised, and fell crashing to her shoulder, and deadening her arm forever. They looked instinctively now with a start to the oak above them, to the sky — only moss and leaves and blue and white clouds. And still Harriet's voice rose, the words faster, louder, bolder, more determined, whipping them out of their awe, driving them on again down the incline of their own passions.

"Glory! Freedom! Freedom! Glory!"

"I'm bound to see 'em! Come along!"

Heelen's wild scream rang shrill and hysterical. She jerked her breast from the sucking lips, and dropped her baby with a thud on the ground. They all followed her up the levee, pressing one after the other, slipping in the wet clay, struggling each one not to be left behind. Emmeline, the wife of little Ben, the only yellow woman on the place, was the last. Her skirt was held in a grip of iron; blinded, obtuse, she pulled forward, reaching her arms out after the others.

"You Stay here!"

She turned and met the determined black face of her mother-in-law.

"You let me go!" she cried, half sobbing, half angry.

"You stay here, I tell you!" The words were muttered through clinched teeth.

"You let me go, I tell you!"

"Glory! Freedom!"

The others had already left the quarters, and were on the road. They two were alone on the bank now, except Heelen's baby, whimpering under the tree; their blazing eyes glared at each other. The singing voices grew fainter and fainter. Suddenly the yellow face grew dark with the surge of blood underneath, the brows wrinkled, and the lips protruded in a grimace of animal rage. Grasping her wet bat tightly with both hands, she turned with a furious bound, and raised it with all the force of her short muscular arms. The black woman darted to the ground; the cane-knife flashed in the air and came down pitilessly towards the soft fleshy shoulder. A wild, terrified scream burst from Emmeline's lips; the bat dropped; seizing her skirt with both hands, she pulled forward, straining her back out of reach of the knife; the homespun tore, and she fled up the bank, her yellow limbs gleaming through the rent left by the fragment in the hand of the black woman.

The prisoners were so young, so handsome, so heroic; the very incarnation of the holy spirit of patriotism in their pathetic uniform of brimless caps, ragged jackets, toeless shoes, and shrunken trousers — a veteran equipment of wretchedness out of keeping with their fresh young faces. How proud and unsubdued they walked through the hall between the file of bayonets! With what haughty, defiant eyes they returned the gaze of their insultingly resplendent conquerors! Oh, if girls' souls had been merchantable at that moment! Their hands tied behind their backs like runaway slaves! Locked up in the smoke house! that dark, rancid, gloomy, mouldy depot of empty hogsheads, barrels, boxes, and fetid exhalations.

They were the first soldiers in gray the girls had ever seen; their own chivalrous knights, the champions of their radiant country. What was the story of their calamity? Treacherously entrapped. Overpowered by numbers? Where were their companions — staring with mute, cold, upturned faces from pools of blood? And were these to be led helplessly tethered into captivity, imprisoned; with ball and chain to gangrene and disgrace their strong young limbs, or was solitary confinement to starve their hearts and craze their minds, holding death in a thousand loathsome, creeping shapes ever threateningly over them?

The smoke-house looked sinister and inimical after its sudden promotion from keeper of food to keeper of men. The great square whitewashed logs seemed to settle more ponderously on the ground around them, the pointed roof to press down as if the air of heaven were an emissary to be dreaded; the hinges and locks were so ostentatiously massive and incorruptible. What artful, what vindictive security of carpenter and locksmith to exclude thieves or immure patriots!

The two eldest girls stood against the open armoire with their chill fingers interlaced. Beyond the wrinkled back of Uncle John's copperas-dyed coat before them lay the region of brass buttons and blue cloth and hostility; but they would not look at it; they turned their heads away; the lids of their eyes refused to lift and reveal the repugnant vision to them. If their ears had only been equally sensitive!

16

"And so you are the uncle of the young ladies? Brother of the father or mother." What clear, incisive, nasal tones! Thank Heaven for the difference between them of the voice at least!

The captain's left arm was in a sling, but his hand could steadily hold the note-book in which he carefully pencilled Uncle John's answers to his minute cross-examination — a dainty, fragrant, Russia leather note book, with monogram and letters and numbers emblazoned on the outside in national colors. It had photographs inside, also, which he would pause and admire from time to time, reading the tender dedications aloud to his companions.

"And the lady in the kitchen called mammy? She is the mother, I guess?"

"P-p-p-peggy's a nigger, and my mistresses is white," stuttered Uncle John.

"Ah, indeed! Gentlemen in my uniform find it difficult to remember these trifling distinctions of color."

What tawdry pleasantry! What hypocritical courtesy! What exquisite ceremony and dainty manual for murderous dandies!

"Ef-ef-ef-ef I hadn't done gone and forgot dem caps!"

Uncle John stood before his young mistresses erect and determined, his old double-barrel shotgun firmly clasped in his tremulous hands, his blear, bloodshot eyes fearlessly measuring the foe. If it were to be five hundred lashes on his bare back under the trees out there (terms on which he would gladly have compromised), or, his secret fear, a running noose over one of the branches, or the murderous extravagance of powder and shot for him, he had made up his mind, despite every penalty, to fulfil his duty and stand by his word to Marse John. Ever since the time the little crawling white boy used to follow the great awkward black boy around like a shadow, John had made a cult of Marse John. He had taught him as a child to fish, hunt, trap birds, to dress skins. knit gloves, and play cards on the sly, to fight cocks on Sunday, to stutter, to cut the "pigeon wing" equal to any negro in the State — and other personal accomplishments besides. He had stood by him through all his scrapes as a youth, was valet to all his frolics as a young man, and now in his old age he gardened for him, and looked after the young ladies for him, stretching or contracting his elastic moral code as occasion required; but he had never deceived him nor falsified his word to him. He knew all about the war: Marse John had told him. He knew what Marse John meant when he left the children to him, and Marse John knew what to expect from John. He would treat them civilly as long as they were civil, but his gun was loaded, both barrels with bullets, and —

"Ef-ef-ef-ef I hadn't done gone and forgot dera caps!"

There was his powder-horn under one arm, there was his shot-flask filled with the last batch of slugs under the other; but the caps were not in his right-hand coat-pocket, they were in his cupboard, hidden for safety under a pile of garden "truck."

The busy martins twittered in and out of their little lodge under the eaves of the smoke-house. Régina and Christine were powerless to prevent furtive glances in that direction. Could the *prisoners* hear it inside? Could *they* see the sun travelling westward, crack by crack, chink by chink, in the roof? Could they feel it sinking, and with it sinking all their hopes of deliverance? Or did they hope still?

Maidens had mounted donjon towers at midnight, had eluded Argus-eyed sentinels, had drugged savage blood-hounds, had crossed lightning-flashed seas, had traversed robber-infested forests; whatever maidens had done they would do, for could ever men more piteously implore release from castle keep than these grayclad youths from the smoke-house? And did ever maiden hearts beat more valiantly than theirs? (and did ever maiden limbs tremble more cowardly?) Many a tedious day had been lightened by their rehearsal of just such a drama as this; they had prepared roles for every imaginable sanguinary circumstance, but prevision, as usual, had overlooked the unexpected. The erstwhile feasible conduct, the erstwhile feasible weapons, of a Jeanne d'Arc or Charlotte Corday, the defiant speeches, the ringing retorts — how inappropriate, inadequate, here and now! If God would only help them! but, like the bayou, the cypresses, and the blue sky, He seemed to-day eternally above such insignificant human necessities as theirs.

Without the aid of introspection or the fear of capital punishment, Lolotte found it very difficult to maintain the prolonged state of rigidity into which her sisters had frozen themselves. All the alleviations devised during a wearisome experience of compulsory attendance on plantation funerals were exhausted in the course of this protracted, hymnless, prayerless solemnity. She stood wedged in between them and the armoire which displayed all its shelves of allurements to her. There were her bird-traps just within reach; there was the fascinating bag of nux-vomica root — crow poison; there was the little old work-box filled with ammunition, which she was forbidden to touch, and all the big gar-fish lines and harpoons and decoy-ducks. There were her own perch lines, the levy she had raised in favor of her companions; they were neatly rolled, ready to tie on the rods, only needing sinkers; and there was the old Indian basket filled with odds and ends, an unfailing treasure of resource and surprise. She was just about searching in it for sinkers when this interruption occurred.

The sky was so bright over the fields! Just the evening to go fishing, whether they caught anything or not. If the enemy would only hurry and go, there might still be time; they would leave, they said, as soon as mammy cooked them something to eat. She had seen mammy chasing a chicken through the yard. She wondered how the nice, fat little round "doodles" were getting on in their tin can under the house; she never had had such a fine box of bait; she wondered if the negro children would go all the same without her; she wondered if she could see them creeping down the road. How easy she could have got away from Uncle John! Anything almost would do for sinkers — bits of iron, nails; they had to do since her father and Uncle John made their last moulding of bullets. She thought they might have left her just one real sinker simply as a matter of distinction between herself and the little darkies. Her eyes kept returning to the Indian basket, and if she stopped twisting her fingers one over the other but a moment they would take their way to rummaging among the rusty contents.

"Glory! Freedom!"

In came the negresses, Bacchantes drunk with the fumes of their own hot blood, Dead-arm Harriet, like a triumphant sorceress, leading them, waving and gesticulating with her one "live" arm, all repeating over and over again the potent magical words, oblivious of the curious looks of the men, their own exposure, the presence of their mistresses, of everything but their own ecstasy.

"Freedom! Master! Freedom!"

Christine and Régina raised their heads and looked perplexed at the furious women in the yard, and the men gazing down to them.

What was the matter with them? What did they mean? What was it all about?"

"Freedom! Freedom!"

Then light broke upon them; their fingers tightened in each other's clasp, and their cheeks flushed crimson.

"How dared they? What insolence! What —"

The opposite door stood open; they rushed across the hall and closed it between them and the humiliating scene. This, this they had not thought of, this they had never read about, this their imagination in wildest flights had not ventured upon. This was not a superficial conflict to sweep the earth with cannons and mow it with sabres; this was an earthquake which had rent it asunder, exposing the quivering organs of hidden life. What a chasm was yawning before them! There was no need to listen one to the other; the circumstances could wring from the hearts of millions but one sentiment, the tongue was left no choice of words.

"Let them go! let them be driven out! never, never to see them again!"

The anger of outraged affection, betrayed confidence, abandoned trust, traitorous denial, raged within them.

These were their servants, their possessions! From generation to generation their lives had been woven together by the shuttle of destiny. How flimsy and transparent the fabric! how grotesque and absurd the tapestry, with its vaunted traditions of mutual loyalty and devotion! What a farce, what a lying, disgusting farce it had all been! Well, it was over now; that was a comfort — all over, all ended. If the hearts had intergrown, they were torn apart now. After this there was no return, no reconciliation possible! Through the storm of their emotions a thought drifted, then another; little detached scenes flitted into memory; familiar gestures, speeches, words, one reminiscence drawing another. Thicker and thicker came little episodes of their pastoral existence together; the counter interchanges of tokens, homely presents, kind offices, loving remembrances; the mutual assistance and consolation in all the accidents of life traversed together, the sicknesses, the births, the deaths; and so many thousand trivial incidents of long, long ago — memory had not lost one — down to the fresh eggs and the pop-corn of that very morning; they were all there, falling upon their bruised hearts.

In the hearts of the women out there were only shackles and scourges. What of the long Sundays of Bible reading and catechism, the long evenings of woodland tales; the confidences; the half-hours around the open fireplaces when supper was cooking, the potatoes under their hillocks of ashes, the thin-legged ovens of cornbread with their lids of glowing coals, the savory skillets of fried meat, the — Was it indeed all of the past, never again to be present or future? And those humble, truthful, loving eyes, which had looked up to them from the first moment of their lives: did they look with greater trust up to God Himself? It was all over, yes, all over! The color faded from their faces, the scornful resolution left their lips; they laid their faces in their hands and sobbed.

"Do you hear, Titine?" Lolotte burst into the room. "They are all going to leave, every one of them; a transport is coming to-night to take them off. They are going to bundle up their things and wait at the steamboat-landing; and they are not going to take a child, and not a single husband. The captain says the government at Washington will give them the nicest white husbands in the land; that they ought to be glad to marry them. They carried on as if they were drunk. Do you believe it, Titine? Oh, I do wish Jeff Davis would hurry up and win!"

The door opened again; it was Black Maria, still holding the cane knife in her hand. She crossed the room with her noiseless barefooted tread, and placed herself behind them. They did not expect her to say anything; Black Maria never talked much; but they understood her, as they always did.

Her skirts were still tied up, her head-kerchief awry; they saw for the first time that the wool under it was snow-white.

Black Maria! They might have known it! They looked at her. No! She was not! She was not negro, like the others. Who was she? What was she? Where did she come from, with her white features and white nature under her ebon skin? What was the mystery that enveloped her? Why did the brain always torture itself in surmises about her? Why did she not talk as the others did, and just for a moment uncover that coffin heart of hers? Why was she, alone of all the negroes, still an alien, a foreigner, an exile among them? Was she brooding on disgrace, outrage, revenge? Was she looking at some mirage behind her — a distant equatorial country, a princely rank, barbaric state, some inherited memory transmitted by that other Black Maria, her mother? Who was the secret black father whom no one had discovered? Was it, as the negroes said, the Prince of Darkness? Who was her own secret consort, the father of Ben? What religion had she to warrant her scornful repudiation of Christianity? What code that enabled her to walk as if she were free through slavery, to assume slavery now when others hailed freedom, to be loyal in the midst of treason?

"Look!" Lolotte came into the room, and held up a rusty, irregular piece of iron. "I found this in the old Indian basket where I was looking for sinkers. Don't you see what it is? It is the old key of the smoke-house, and I am going to let those Confederates out." She spoke quietly and decidedly. There was something else in the other hand, concealed in the folds of her dress. She produced it reluctantly. It was the gun-wrench that filled so prominent a part in her active life — always coveting it, getting possession of it, being deprived of it, and accused unfailingly for its every absence and misplacement. "You see, it is so convenient; it screws so nicely on to everything," she continued, apologetically, as she demonstrated the useful qualification by screwing it on to the key. "There! it is as good as a handle. All they've got to do is to slip away in the skiff while the others are eating. And I would like to know how they can ever be caught, without another boat on the place! But oh, girls" — her black eyes twinkled maliciously — "what fools the Yankees are!"

If the Federals, as they announced, were only going to remain long enough for the lady in the kitchen to prepare them something to eat, the length of their stay clearly rested in Peggy the cook's hands, as she understood it. She walked around her kitchen with a briskness rarely permitted by her corpulent proportions, and with an intuitive faith in the common nature of man regardless of political opinion, she exerted her culinary skill to the utmost. She knew nothing of the wholesale quarrelling and fighting of a great war, but during her numerous marital experiments, not counting intermittent conjugalities for twenty-five years with Uncle John, she had seen mercy and propitiation flow more than once after a good meal from the most irate; and a healthy digestion aiding, she never despaired of even the most revengeful. The enemy, in her opinion, were simply to' be treated like furious husbands, and were to be offered the best menu possible under the trying circumstances. She worked, inspired by all the wife-lore of past ages, the infiltrated wisdom that descends to women in the course of a world of empirical connubiality, that traditionary compendium to their lives by which they still hope to make companionship with men harmonious and the earth a pleasant abiding-place. With minute particularity Peggy set the table and placed the dishes. The sun was now sinking, and sending almost horizontal rays over the roof of the smoke-house, whose ugly square frame completely blocked the view of the dining-room window. Peggy carefully drew the red calico curtain across it, and after a moment's rehearsal to bring her features to the conventional womanly expression of cheerful obtuseness to existing displeasure, she opened the dining-room door.

Gina and Lolotte stood close under the window against the dwelling, looking at the locked door of the smoke-house before them, listening to the sounds falling from the dining-room above. Once in the skiff, the prisoners were safe; but the little red curtain of the window fluttering flimsily in the

21

breeze coquetted with their hopes and the lives of three men. If the corners would but stay down a second! Titine and Black Maria were in front, busy about the skiff. Peggy's culinary success appeared, from the comments of the diners, to be complimentary to her judgment. But food alone, however, does not suffice in the critical moments of life; men are half managed when only fed. There was another menu, the ingredients of which were not limited or stinted by blockade of war. Peggy had prepared that also; and in addition to the sounds of plates, knives, forks, and glasses, came the tones of her rich voice dropping from a quick tongue the *entremets* of her piquant imagination. The attention in the room seemed tense, and at last the curtain hung straight and motionless.

"Now! now!" whispered Gina. "We must risk something."

Woman-like, they paused midway and looked back; a hand stretched from the table was carelessly drawing the curtain aside, and the window stared unhindered at the jail.

Why had they waited? Why had they not rushed forward immediately? By this time their soldiers might have been free! They could hear Peggy moving around the table; they could see her bulky form push again and again across the window.

"Mammy! Mammy!"

Could she hear them? They clasped their hands and held their faces up in imploring appeal. The sun was setting fast, almost running down the west to the woods. The dinner, if good, was not long. It all depended upon Peggy now.

"Mammy! Mammy!" They raised their little voices, then lowered them in agony of apprehension. "Mammy, do something! Help us!"

But still she passed on and about, around the table, and across the window, blind to the smokehouse, deaf to them, while her easy, familiar voice recited the comical gyrations of "old Frizzly," the half-witted hen, who had set her heart against being killed and stewed, and ran and hid, and screamed and cackled, and ducked and flew, and then, after her silly head was twisted off, "just danced, as if she were at a 'Cadian' ball, all over the yard."

It would soon be too late! It was, perhaps, too late now!

Black Maria had got the skiff away from the gunnels, but they might just as well give it up; they would not have time enough now.

"Mammy!" The desperate girls made a supreme effort of voice and look. The unctuous black face, the red bead ear-rings, the bandanna head-kerchief, appeared at the window with "old Frizzly's" last dying cackle. There was one flashing wink of the left eye.

Her nurslings recognized then her *pièce de résistance oratoire* — a side-splitting prank once played upon her by another nursling, her pet, her idol, the plague of her life — Beau.

Who could have heard grating lock or squeaking hinges through the bois-terous mirth that followed? Who could have seen the desperate bound of the three imprisoned soldiers for liberty through that screen of sumptuous flesh — the magnificent back of Mammy that filled to overlapping the insignificant little window?

They did not wait to hear the captain's rapturous toast to Peggy in sassafras tea, nor his voluble protestations of love to her, nor could they see him in his excitement forgetting his wounded arm, bring both clinched fists with a loud bravo to the table, and then faint dead away.

"I knew it!"

"Just like him!"

"Take him in the air — quick!"

"No, sir! You take him in there, and put him on the best bed in the house." Peggy did not move from the window, but her prompt command turned the soldiers from the door in the hall, and her finger directed them to the closed bed-chamber.

Without noticing Christine standing by the open window, they dropped their doughty burden — boots, spurs, sword, epaulets, and all — on the fresh, white little bed, the feather mattress fluffing up all around as if to submerge him.

"Oh, don't bother about that; cut the sleeve off!"

"Who has a knife?"

"There."

"That's all right now."

"He's coming round."

"There's one nice coat spoiled."

"Uncle Sam has plenty more."

"Don't let it drip on the bed."

"Save it to send to Washington — trophy — wet with rebel blood."

The captain was evidently recovering.

"You stay here while I keep 'em eating," whispered Peggy, authoritatively, to Christine.

Titine trembled as if she had an ague.

"How could they help seeing the tall form of Black Maria standing in the prow of the boat out in the very middle of the bayou? Suppose she, Titine, had not been there to close the window quick as thought? Suppose instead of passing through her room she had run through the basement, as she intended, after pushing off the skiff?"

Rollicking, careless, noisy, the soldiers went back to their interrupted meal, while the boat went cautiously clown the bayou to the meeting place beyond the clearing.

"How far was Black Maria now?" Titine opened the window a tiny crack. "Heavens! how slowly she paddled! lifting the oar deliberately from side to side, looking straight ahead. How clear and distinct she was in the soft evening light! Why did she not hurry? why did she not row? She could have muffled the oars. But no, no one thought of that; that was always the way — always something overlooked and forgotten. The soldiers could finish a dozen dinners before the skiff got out of sight at this rate. Without the skiff the prisoners might just as well be locked still in the smoke-house. Did he on the bed suspect something, seeing her look out this way?" She closed the window tight.

"How dark the room was! She could hardly see the wounded man. How quiet he was! Was he sleeping, or had he fainted again? In her bed! her enemy lying in her bed! his head on her pillow, her own little pillow, the feverish confidant of so many sleepless nights! How far were they now on the bayou? She must peep out again. Why, Maria had not moved! not moved an inch! Oh, if she could only scream to her! if she were only in the skiff!

"How ghastly pale he looked on the bed! his face as white as the coverlet, his hair and beard so black; how changed without his bravado and impertinence! And he was not old, either; not older than the boys in gray. She had fancied that age and ugliness alone could go with violence and wrong. How much gold! how much glitter! Why, the sun did not rise with more splendor of equipment. Costumed as if for the conquest of worlds. If the Yankees dressed their captains this way, what was the livery of their generals? How curious the sleeveless arm looked! What a horrible mark the gash made right across the soft white skin! What a scar it would leave! What a disfigurement! And this, this is what men call love of country!"

On Saturday nights sometimes, in the quarters, when rum had been smuggled in, the negroes would get to fighting and beating their wives, and her father would be sent for in a hurry to come with his gun and separate them. Hatchets, axes, cane-knives — anything they would seize, to cut and slash one another, husbands, wives, mothers, sons, sisters, brothers; but they were negroes, ignorant, uneducated, barbarous, excited; they could not help it; they could not be expected to resist all at once the momentum of centuries of ancestral ferocity. But for white men, gentlemen, thus furiously to mar and disfigure their own mother-given bodies! All the latent maternal instinct in her was roused, all the woman in her revolted against the sacrilegious violence of mutilation. "Love of country to make her childless, or only the mother of invalids! This was only one. What of the other thousands and hundreds of thousands? Are men indeed so inexhaustible? Are the pangs of maternity so cheap? Are women's hearts of no account whatever in the settlement of disputes? O God! cannot the world get along without war? But even if men want it, even if God permits it, how can the women allow it? If the man on the bed were a negro, she could do something for his arm. Many a time, early Sunday mornings, Saturday night culprits had come to her secretly, and she had washed off the thick, gummy blood, and bandaged up their cuts and bruises; they did not show so on black skin....This man had a mother somewhere among the people she called 'enemies;' a mother sitting counting day by day the continued possession of a live son, growing gray and old before that terrible next minute ever threatening to take her boy and give her a corpse. Or perhaps, like her own, his mother might be dead. They might be friends in that kingdom which the points of the compass neither unite nor divide; together they might be looking down on this quarrelling, fighting world; mothers, even though angels, looking, looking through smoke and powder and blood and hatred after their children. Their eyes might be fixed on this lonely little spot, on this room...." She walked to the bed.

The blood was oozing up through the strips of plaster. She stanched and bathed and soothed the wound as she well knew how with her tender, agile fingers, and returned to the window. Maria had disappeared now; she could open the window with impunity. The trackless water was flowing innocently along, the cooling air was rising in mist, the cypress -trees checked the brilliant sky with the filigree and net-work of their bristly foliage. The birds twittered, the chickens loitered and dallied on their way to roost. The expectant dogs were lying on the levee waiting for the swampers, who, they ought to know, could not possibly return before midnight. And Molly was actually on time this evening, lowing for mammy to come and milk her; what was the war to her? How happy and peaceful it all was! What a jarring contrast to swords and bayonets! Thank God that Nature was impartial, and could not be drilled into partisanship! If humanity were like Nature! If — if there had been no war! She paused, shocked at her first doubt; of the great Circumstance of her life it was like saying, "If there had been no God!"

As she stood at the window and thought, all the brilliant coloring of her romantic fantasies, the stories of childhood, the perversions of education, the self-delusions, they all seemed to fade with the waning light, and with the beautiful day sink slowly and quietly into the irrevocable past. "Thank God, above all, that it is a human device to uniform people into friends and enemies! The heart (her own felt so soft and loving) — the heart repudiates such attempts of blue and gray; it still clings to Nature, and belongs only to God." She thought the wound must need tending again, and returned to the bed. The patient, meanwhile, went in and out of the mazes of unconsciousness caused by weakness.

"Was that really he on this foamy bed? What a blotch his camp-battered body made down the centre of it! It was good to be on a bed once more, to look up into a mosquito-bar instead of the boughs of trees, to feel his head on a pillow. But why did they put him there? Why did they not lay him somewhere on the floor, outside on the ground, instead of soiling and crumpling this lily-white surface?"

He could observe his nurse through his half-closed lids, which fell as she approached the bed, and closed tight as she bent above him. When she stood at the window he could look full at her. "How innocent and unsuspecting she looked!" The strained rigidity had passed away from her face. Her transparent, child-like eyes were looking with all their life of expression in the direction of the bed, and then at something passing in her own mind. "Thank Heaven, the fright had all gone out of them! How horrible for a gentleman to read fear in the eyes of a woman! Her mind must be as pure and white, yes, and as impressionable, too, as her bed. Did his presence lie like a blot upon it also? How she must hate him! how she must loathe him! Would it have been different if he had come in the other uniform — if he had worn the gray? would she then have cared for him, have administered to him? How slight and frail she was! What a wan, wistful little face between him and the gloomy old bayou!

He could see her more plainly now since she had opened the window and let in the cool, fragrant air. There was no joyous development of the body in her to proclaim womanhood, none of the seductive, confident beauty that follows coronation of youth; to her had only come the care and anxiety of maturity. This — this,'" he exclaimed to himself, "is the way women fight a war." Was she coming this way? Yes. To the bed? Hardly. Now she was pressing against it, now bending over him, now dropping a cooling dew from heaven on his burning arm, and now — oh, why so soon? — she was going away to stand and look out of the window again.

The homely little room was filled with feminine subterfuges for ornament, feminine substitutes for comfort. How simple women are! how little they require, after all! only peace and love and quiet, only the impossible in a masculine world. What was she thinking of? If he could only have seen the expression of her eyes as she bent over him! Suppose he should open his and look straight up at her? but no, he had not the courage to frighten her again. He transplanted her in his mind to other surroundings, her proper surroundings by birthright, gave her in abundance all of which this war had deprived her, presented to her assiduous courtiers, not reckless soldiers like himself, but men whom peace had guided in the lofty sphere of intellectual pursuits. He held before her the sweet invitations of youth, the consummations of life. He made her smile, laugh.

"Ah!" — he turned his face against the pillow — "had that sad face ever laughed? Could any woman laugh during a war? Could any triumph, however glorious, atone for battles that gave men death, but left the women to live? This was only one; how many, wan and silent as she, were looking at this sunset — the sunset not of a day, but a life? When it was all over, who was to make restitution to them, the women? Was any cost too great to repurchase for them simply the privilege of hoping again? What an endless chain of accusing thoughts! What a miserable conviction tearing his heart! If he could get on his knees to her, if he could kiss her feet, if he could beg pardon in the dust — he, a man for all men, of her, a woman for all women. If he could make her his country, not to fight, but to work for, it..."

She came to his side again, she bent over him, she touched him.

Impulsive, thoughtless, hot-headed, he opened his eyes full, he forgot again the wounded arm. With both hands he stayed her frightened start; he saw the expression of her eyes bending over him.

"Can you forgive me? It is a heartless, cowardly trick! I am not a Yankee; I am Beau, your cousin, the guerilla."

The door of the smoke-house opened, the escaped soldiers ran like deer between the furrows of Uncle John's vegetable garden, where the waving corn leaves could screen them; then out to the bank of the bayou — not on the levee, but close against the fence — snagging their clothes and scratching their faces and hands on the cuckle-burs; Lolotte in front, with a stick in her hand, beating the bushes through habit to frighten the snakes, calling, directing, animating, in excited whispers; Régina in the rear, urging, pressing, sustaining the young soldier lagging behind, but painfully striving with stiffened limbs to keep up with the pace of his older, more vigorous companions. Ahead of them Black Maria was steadily keeping the skiff out in the current. The bayou narrowed and grew dark as it entered between the banks of serried cypress trees, where night had already begun.

Régina looked hurriedly over her shoulder. "Had they found out yet at the house? How slowly she ran! How long it took to get to the woods! Oh, they would have time over and over again to finish their dinner and catch them. Perhaps at this very moment, as she was thinking of it, some forgotten article in the skiff was betraying them! Perhaps a gun might even now be pointing down their path! Or, now! the bullet could start and the report come too late to warn them."

She looked back again and again.

From the little cottage under the trees the curtains fluttered, but no bayonet nor smooth-bore was visible.

She met her companion's face, looking back also, but not for guns — for her. "If it had been different! If he had been a visitor, come to stay; days and evenings to be passed together!" The thought lifting the sulphurous war-clouds from her heart, primitive idylls burst into instantaneous fragrant bloom in it like spring violets. He was not only the first soldier in gray she had ever seen, but the first young man; or it seemed so to her.

Again she looked back.

"How near they were still to the house! how plainly they could yet be seen! He could be shot straight through the back, the gray jacket getting one stain, one bullet-hole, more, the country one soldier less. Would they shoot through a woman at him? Would they be able to separate them if she ran close behind him, moving this way and that way, exactly as he did? If she saw them in time she could warn him; he could lie flat down in the grass; then it would be impossible to hit him."

Increasing and narrowing the space between them at the best of each succeeding contradictory thought, turning her head again and again to the house behind her, she lost speed. Lolotte and the two men had already entered the forest before she reached it. Coming from the fields, the swamps seemed midnight dark. Catching her companion's hand, they groped their way along, tripped by the slimy cypress knees that rose like evil gnomes to beset and entangle their feet, slipping over rolling logs, sinking in stagnant mire, noosed by the coils of heavy vines that dropped from unseen branches overhead. Invisible wings of startled birds flapped above them, the croaking of frogs ebbed and flowed around them, owls shrieked and screamed from side to side of the bayou. Lolotte had ceased her beating; swamp serpents are too sluggish to be frightened away. In the obscurity, Black Maria could be dimly seen turning the skiff to a half-submerged log, from which a turtle dropped as if ballasted with lead. A giant cypress -tree arrested them; the smooth, fluted trunk, ringed with whitish watermarks, recording floods far over their heads; where they were scrambling once swam fish and serpents. The young soldier turned and faced her, the deliverer, whose manoeuvres in the open field had not escaped him.

She had saved him from imprisonment, insult, perhaps death — the only heir of a heroic father, the only son of a widowed mother; she had restored him to a precious heritage of love and honor, replaced him in the interrupted ambitious career of patriotic duty; she had exposed her life for him — she was beautiful. She stood before him, panting, tremulous, ardent, with dumb, open red lips, and voluble, passionate eyes, and with a long scratch in her white cheek from which the blood trickled. She had much to say to him, her gray uniformed hero; but how in one moment express four years — four long years — and the last long minutes. The words were all there, had been rushing to her lips all day; her lips were parted; but the eager, overcrowded throng were jammed on the threshold; and her heart beat so in her ears! He could not talk; he could not explain. His companions were already in the boat, his enemies still in gunshot. He bent his face to hers in the dim light to learn by heart the features he must never forget — closer, closer, learning, knowing more and more, with the eager precocity of youth.

Bellona must have flown disgusted away with the wings of an owl, Columbia might have nodded her head as knowingly as old Aunt Mary could, when the callow hearts, learning and knowing, brought the faces closer and closer together, until the lips touched.

"I shall come again; I shall come again. Wait for me. Surely I shall come again,"

"Yes! Yes!"

Black Maria pushed the skiff off. "Rowlock! Rowlock!" They were safe and away.

A vociferous group stood around the empty gunnels. Uncle John, with the daring of desperation, advanced, disarmed as he was, towards them.

"I-I-I-I don't keer ef you is de-de-de President o' de United States hisself, I ain't gwine to 'low no such cussin' an' swearin' in de hearin' o' de-de-de young ladies. Marse John he-he-he don't 'low it, and when Marse John ain't here I-I-I don't 'low it."

His remonstrance and heroic attitude had very little effect, for the loud talk went on, and chiefly by ejaculation, imprecation, and self-accusation published the whole statement of the case; understanding which. Uncle John added his voice also:

"Good Gord A'mighty! Wh-wh-what's dat you say? Dey — dey — dey Yankees, an' you Cornfedrits? Well, sir, an' are you Marse Beau — you wid your arm hurted? Go 'long! You can't fool me; Marse Beau done had more sense en dat. My Gord! an' dey wuz Yankees? You better cuss — cussin's about all you kin do now. Course de boat's gone. You'll never ketch up wid 'em in Gord's world now. Don't come along arter me about it .' 'Tain't my fault. How wuz I to know? You wuz Yankees enough for me. I declar', Marse Beau, you ought to be ashamed o' yourself! You wanted to I'arn dem a lesson! I reckon dey I'arnt you one! You didn't mean 'em no harm! Humph! dey've cut dey eye-teeth, dey have! Lord! Marse Beau, I thought you done knowed us better. Did you really think we wuz a-gwine to let a passel o' Yankees take us away off our own plantation? You must done forgot us. We jes cleaned out de house for 'em, we did — clo'es, food, tobacco, rum. De young ladies 'ain't lef a mossel for Marse John. An' — an' — an' 'fore de good Gord, my gun! Done tuck my gun away wid 'em! Wh-wh-wh-what you mean by such doin's? L-l-look here, Marse Beau, I don't like dat, nohow! Wh-wh-what! you tuck my gun and gin it to de Yankees? Dat's my gun! I done had dat gun twenty-five year an' more! Dog-gone! Yes, sir, I'll cuss — I'll cuss ef I wants to! I 'ain't got no use for gorillas, nohow! Lem me 'lone, I tell you! Lem me 'lone! Marse John he'll get de law o' dat! Who's 'sponsible? Dat's all I want to know — who's 'sponsible? Ef-ef-ef-ef— No, sir; dar ain't nary boat on de place, nor herea-bouts. Yes, sir; you kin cross de swamp ef you kin find de way. No, sir — no, sir; dar ain't no one to show you. I ain't gwine to leave de young ladies twell Marse John he comes back. Yes, I reckon you kin git to de cut-off by to-morrow mornin', ef you ain't shot on de way for Yankees, an' ef your compa-ny is fool enough to wait for you. No, sir, I don't know nothin' 'bout nothin'; you better wait an' arsk Marse John. ... My Gord! I'm obleeged to laugh; I can't help it. Dem fool nigger wimen a-sittin' on de brink o' de byer, dey clo'es tied up in de bedquilts, an' de shotes an' de puUits all kilt, a-waitin' for freedom! I lay dey'll git freedom enough to-night when de boys come home. Dey git white gentlemen to marry 'em! Dey'll git five hundred apiece. Marse Beau, Gord'll punish you for dis— He surely will. I done tole Marse John long time ago he oughter sell dat brazen nigger Dead-arm Harriet, an' git shet o' her. Lord! Lord! Lord! Now you done gone to cussin' an' swearin' agin. Don't go tearin' off your jackets an' flingin' em at me. We don't want 'em; we buys our clo'es — what we don't make. Yes, Marse John'll be comin' along pretty soon now. What's your hurry, Marse Beau .Well, so long, ef you won't stay. He ain't got much use for gorillas neither, Marse John hain't."

The young officer wrote a few hasty words on a leaf torn from the pretty Russia-leather notebook, and handed it to the old darky. "For your Marse John."

"For Marse John — yes, sir; I'll gin hit to him soon 's he comes in."

They had dejectedly commenced their weary tramp up the bayou; he called him back, and lowered his voice confidentially: "Marse Beau, when you captured dat transport and stole all dem fixin's an' finery, you didn't see no good chawin' tobacco layin' round loose, did you? Thanky! thanky, child! Now I looks good at you, you ain't so much changed sence de times Marse John used to wallop you for your tricks. Well, good-bye, Marse Beau."

On the leaf were scrawled the words:

"All's up! Lee has surrendered. — Beau."

Bonne Maman

IT was in a part of the city once truthfully, now conventionally, called "back of town," and it had been used as an obscure corner in which to thrust domestic hearths not creditable to the respectability assumed in the front part of town; where oil-lamps could be economically substituted for gas, and police indifference for police protection.

The long rows of tallow trees, with here and there an oak, shaded an unpaved street and a seemingly unbroken continuity of low cottages, with heavy green doors and windows and little wooden steps jutting out on to the banquette. Their homely architectural physiognomies were adapted to such an isolated, dimly-lighted locality, and were frankly devoid of any beauty or picturesqueness of expression. But as the banquette, wrinkled and corrugated from the roots beneath, retarded the steps of the passer-by, faintly asserting individualities might be discerned: declensions of one -storied degrees of prosperity, comparisons of industry and cleanliness, and pretensions to social precedence inherited from the architect of a century ago, or acquired, perhaps, by the thrift of a present tenant. The steps were all scrubbed red with brick, or yellow with wild camomile, which, besides gilding, lent them a pleasant aromatic fragrance.

The quiet that reigned told that the street was still back of town in all that a corporation suggests of movement, bustle, and noise. The air of desertion which hung about the little closed cottages would have been oppressive had it not been for the children — a motley crowd, accusing an "olla podrida" parentage, chattering in tongues as varied as their complexions, and restless with the competing energies of hidden nationalities in their veins. Dressed with tropical disregard of conventionality, they were frank, impudent, irrepressible; at all times noisy and unanimous, swooping down the street at any moment in eager response to some distant alarm, or taking swarming possession of whole rows of steps with perfect disregard of any superior proprietary right.

The delusive similarity of the blocks would in time generate in the passerby the suspicion of a treadmill under foot, did not the sharp point of a triangular enclosure furnish a landmark in the region by cutting into the very middle of the street, parting the hitherto companion banquettes, and sending them on at divergent angles in ever-increasing separation, until they were finally arrested at unrecognizable distances apart by the banks of the bayou. The fence of this obtruding property may have been painted in front on the other street, but to its apex it degenerated through every stage of shabbiness and neglect. For a screen the large square house inside was mostly indebted to a hedge of orange-trees, which, raising their heads proudly in the sun, illuminated the ugly spot with their golden fruit in the winter, and sanctified it in the spring with their blossoms. The shaded banquettes along the sides of the triangle were a constant temptation to the children, alluring them, against experience, into the range of the epithets and missiles of the children-hating people within.

"Allez-vous-en!"

"Pestes de la terre!"

"Negrillons!"

"Gamins!"

"Tits démons!"

"Enfants du diable!"

The loss of a knot from one of the boards of the fence furnished a providential peep-hole into the mysteries of a "menage" from which abnormal discoveries seemed constantly expected by the children, and if persistence of attention could have been relied upon, warnings might always have been given for timely refuge on the steps of the nearest little corner cottage. These offered an ideal juvenile place of refuge, where there were no brick or camomile scrubbings to rebuke their litter, no sudden front -door openings to sweep them away in confusion, no front-window admonitions or imprecations to disturb them, and absolutely no banquette ordinances to taunt them into wilfulness, but instead an upward glance through the small opening of the bowed shutters showed them the face of "la blanche mamzelle là-yè" at her sewing.

They were too young to appreciate the fact that the batten windows were bowed only when they were there, or to wonder why they, the children, were the only ones who ever saw her; but they did know that her face was whiter, her hair straighter and finer, than human comparison for them, and so they could not keep their eyes from looking for responses from hers, nor their lips from smiling invitingly at hers, nor their tongues from sallies of wit intended for her ear alone. To-day she paid little attention to them. They could hear her "Miseres!" of impatience, and the vexatious tapping of her foot, though they could not see that she was manipulating some gaudy woollen material which gave her infinite worry with its ungracious, not to say stubborn, opposition to a necessity which ordered its stripes to go flouncing in diagonal procession round and round a skirt.

"Claire!" called a feeble voice from the back room.

She raised her head incredulously.

"Claire! Claire Blanche!"

A shade of disappointment passed over her face.

"Bonne maman!"

"Mais, Claire, fillette, where are you?"

"I am coming, bonne maman."

She caught her work together and folded it in a cloth before going into the other room.

"What are you doing, bébé?"

"But my work, bonne maman."

"Ah! I could not think where you were."

"I thought it was cooler in the other room."

"It is very warm in here."

"You are not going to get up, bonne maman? You have not finished your sleep yet."

"Have I not slept as long as usual?"

"No, indeed; only a few minutes. That was the reason I could not think it was you calling."

"Enfin, it is better for me to get up."

"But why, bonne maman .-' There is no necessity for you to get up earlier to-day than usual."

"As you say, it is warm here."

The old lady lay on her bed underneath the mosquito bar, the straight folds of her white "blouse volante" settled around her thin figure. Claire picked up a fan, and putting back the bar, commenced to fan her.

"Chère, bonne maman, try. Maybe you can sleep some more."

The coaxing, caressing voice and the soft motions of the fan had a soothing effect, and although the grandmother repeated, "Yes, decidedly I had better get up," she made no effort to move.

"The weather is so warm and tiresome," continued the girl, suggesting an excuse for lethargy.

"Yes, as you say, it is warm and debilitating."

"But, just shut your eyes, bonne maman, and try to sleep. You have not rested at all."

"Rest," she said, catching the word. "I do not need rest; I have worked very little to-day — in fact, not at all."

"Oh, but I mean rest from thinking. Mon Dieu! if I thought as much as you, I could not keep my eyes open at all."

The grandmother turned her head on the pillow, and did close her eyes.

Claire smiled with satisfaction. Her bright face showed the reflection of cheerful interpretations alone, and her quick eyes, glancing over the surface of things, gathered only pleasant sights. She was going on tiptoe out of the room.

"Why do you not bring your work in here, Claire, where I am?"

"What, not asleep? Vilaine!"

"But, my child, how you talk! Sleep? when I have so much to finish!"

"Oh, there is plenty of time for that, bonne maman. At least stay in bed a little longer."

"One would suppose that I was the grandchild and you the bonne maman."

Claire brought her work; not the gaudy stripes, but a piece of embroidery, and seated herself at some distance from the bed, in the path of a ray of light.

The old lady sighed heavily; her eyes were fixed on Claire.

"But what is the matter, bonne maman?"

"Oh, nothing, nothing, chérie — only, what makes you stoop so, Claire?"

"Ah, that ugly habit! Imbécile!"— slapping her forehead — "can't you cure yourself, enfin? I ought to be well tapped for it, as I was at the convent."

She straightened herself up to an uncomfortable degree of rectitude, which lasted as long as the remembrance of her grandmother's sigh, and she talked as if her needle could only move in unison with her tongue.

"It was funny at the convent how many bad habits I had. They seemed to grow on purpose to be corrected. And I was so young, too. Bad mark for this, en penitence for that, fool's-cap for something else, twenty-five lines by heart for something else. And all the time, 'Your grandmother never did this,' 'Your mother never did that,' 'Ah, if you had seen your tante Stephanie,' 'Look at your cousin Adelaide.' Ma foi! the first lesson I learned was that I was like no member of my family seen before. How I used to wish there had been just one lazy bad one like me! Was it that way when you were there, bonne maman?"

The old lady did not answer, but Claire showed no hesitation in summoning her thoughts from any pleasanter dallying ground.

"Hein, bonne maman?"

"What, Claire?"

"At the convent, was it that way with you? Always scolding you because you were not some one else, always punishing you because you were what you were? That was justice! And then to tell me I was lazy and could not learn! It enrages me every time I think of it. I am sure I learned very nearly the whole of the *Génie da Christianisme* in punishment. It was killing. Study! When I was thinking all the time about something else, straining my ears to listen, just to see if I could hear the cannon shooting 'way out there in the distance."

She heard another sigh, and raised her shoulders with a start.

"Pardon, bonne maman! I forget. You will see I can cure myself. Oh! I can do anything I want except be pious, as they wanted me to be at the convent. Ha! it was very easy for the Sisters to say 'Study history!' 'Study geography!' and stick *La Vie des Saints* before me. Saints! It was 'ces diables de l'enfer' out there shooting their cannons that I was thinking of! Books! I hated books, and pen and ink and paper make me ill to this day; but I could embroider; that didn't prevent listening and thinking. I was only pious when the mail came in. When I remember those days, mon Dieu Seigneur! but we were frightened then! Oh, how we loved God and the saints then! and how we used to pray to them, fast, fast, fast as we could, before the letters were brought around! Getting a letter meant almost just the same thing as killing some one in our family. Those were times — eh, bonne maman?"

"Bonne maman!"

"Fillette!"

"But, bonne maman, you don't listen to me, you don't answer me."

"But, ma petite, I thought you wanted me to go to sleep?"

"Ah, were you going to sleep? And I woke you? What a fool I am!"

"What were you talking about, my daughter? I will listen now."

"Ah, no, bonne maman, don't listen to me, I am so silly; indeed, I am not worth listening to. Try to go to sleep again. To think that I woke you, when I wanted you so much to sleep! I believe the Sisters at the convent were right. I shall never have any sense — never; only strength. Ah, yes! they told me that often enough, and tried to shame me by pointing to the good girls — the good, weak girls. Anyhow," shrugging her shoulders, "goodness doesn't stand a convent and war as well as badness. Ma chère! when I left there you would have said that a battle had been fought in the dormitory, with the guns loaded with fevers, and all aimed at the good girls. Only the fool's-cap wearers escaped. The little cemetery was full, full, full, and the graves so even and regular, all of one size, like a patchwork quilt spread out inside the four fences."

"Now, Claire, I shall get up."

"You see, if it had not been for me you would have been sleeping; and it is so hot and tiresome to-day."

Her grandmother sat up in bed.

"Just to give me pleasure, bonne maman, stay quiet a moment longer."

"To give you pleasure — ah, well, if it gives you pleasure!" and she reclined again.

"Claire!"

"Oh, bonne maman, I forget" — sitting up with innocent egoism.

"Claire, I was thinking I would like to see my little green work-table again."

"Ah, that was what you were thinking, eh? I thought it was about my shoulders."

"My little green work-table," the old lady repeated to herself.

"Which stood in the window of your room, that looked on to the gallery, over the orange-trees, over the levee, into the river —"

"To think I should forget it until to-day! To think I could forget it! — my little green worktable."

"But, bonne maman, you have so much to forget!"

"But that was my 'corbeille de noces,' ordered from Gessler, in Paris. A corbeille de noces!" talking more to herself than to the girl. "How much that means! I can see the very day, the very hour, it came. First, my vexation and disappointment; there were tears in my eyes; it was so 'bourgeoise,' a work-table, with nothing but scissors and threads and needles, instead of orange flowers and lace and fans and sentiment. Eh, mon Seigneur! what ideas I had! But Aza was there! What a devil Aza was! impertinent, pushing, and perfectly fearless. I was the only one who could manage her. They said I had spoiled

35

her, but she adored me more than she did God, and was more afraid of displeasing me, too. She followed me around like a little dog. I never could put my hand out, so, without touching Aza."

Claire nodded attention, as her fingers flew backward and forward about her work.

"It seems to me," and the soft feeble voice sounded very plaintive — "it seems to me that all the bright hopes that used to fly before me, they fly behind me now as memories."

"Well, of course that is natural," the girl answered cheerfully. "We are two crabs, you and I — we walk backward. We couldn't see anything going on before us, par exemple."

"But, Claire, I keep forgetting. I must get up and finish that embroidery."

"Oh, just one moment, bonne maman — just one moment more."

"It must be finished and returned this evening."

The needle sped faster and faster, and the soothing words fell more and more disconnectedly.

"Go and fetch it to me, Claire."

"Yes, bonne maman."

"Indeed I feel quite refreshed."

"Dieu merci!" muttered the girl, and recklessly added, "Vogue la galère!"

The grandmother got very slowly out of the bed and walked to her rocking-chair,

"It is in the basket there on the mantelpiece."

Claire went for the basket, and slipped the roll of embroidery she held into it.

"Here it is, bonne maman."

"Ah! mais, this is not my embroidery."

"Si, it is your embroidery, bonne maman."

"No, my child, you have made a mistake, and put yours in my basket. Look again, and give me mine, chère."

Claire turned her head away, that her face might not discredit her voluble tongue.

"But I tell you that is your embroidery, bonne maman."

"My embroidery! Claire, how can you say so? Come and convince yourself. See! this is all done; and mine — there was a good piece to do still."

"But—"

"A — h! I see! Claire, it is you who have finished it for me."

"Eh, why not? I had already finished mine, and I had nothing to do — absolutely nothing. Was I to sit still and hold my hands — hein? Oh, you need not examine the stitches! I know they are not so fine, nor so smooth, nor so regular as yours, but they are good enough for that old 'chouette' Varon all the same, and —"

The grandmother jumped violently at a sudden knock at the door.

"Mais, mon Dieu! what is that?"

36

"À la bonne heure!" whispered Claire to herself. "It is Betsie, bonne maman; I will see what she wants."

"Ah, that Betsie! she is so badly raised. She knocks at the door as if she were a Suisse. Now, Aza —"

Claire had already left the room, and closed the door behind her.

"Mamzelle," said Betsy, standing on the step, "there's that nigger out there come for her gownd."

"Hush, Betsie! Bonne maman is awake,"

"There's some frolic going on to-night, and she has set her heart on wearing her new gownd."

"But it is not finished."

"That's bad."

"I was still sewing on it when bonne maman awoke."

"I suspicioned you hadn't done it, and I tried my best to send her away; but. Lord! such a contrary, obstreperous nigger like that!"

"If bonne maman had only slept a little while longer—"

"You couldn't baste it up any sort of fashion, right off, and let her go?"

"But how can I, Betsie? Bonne maman —"

"Couldn't you just slip out in the kitchen with it? You could say I wanted you to look after the soup while I go in the street a minute."

"Ha! you think bonne maman would not go herself to see to it?"

"That's so; the madam would come right out there herself. But that gal is so owdacious and high-minded; she has been a-jawin' out there for an hour constant, and I've been a-answering her just as fair as I could, 'cause I didn't want no fuss. I never seen anything like her brazenness all the days of my life. A-driving of white folks like they was niggers...Couldn't you say I wanted you to cut a josie for me?"

"She would tell me to bring it to her to cut. Bonne maman is not so easy to fool, Betsie."

The bright sunlight showed lines of weariness and dejection in the girl's face which the darkness of the bedchamber had concealed. She leaned back against the closed doors and clasped her hands over her head to shelter her eyes.

"Well, I don't know. If she was not such a loudmouthed, lazy, good-for-nothing, trolloping thing. I wish we could make an end of her!" — turning to go. "Let me see what I can do with her again."

"Ask her to wait just a little while longer; perhaps —"

"Wait! Lord bless you! she 'ain't got any idea of going. Gabriel hisself couldn't drag her away for the judgment-day withouten that gownd. I ain't afeard of her going; I'm afeard she'll holler so loud the madam will hear her."

Claire peeped anxiously through the door before entering. It was all still. She walked in on tiptoe. Her grandmother sat with her eyes closed, the embroidery in her hand.

"Ah, bonne chance!" — her face was sanguine and gay again — "bonne maman has gone to sleep at last."

She hastily got her gaudy task of sewing, and followed Betsy across the yard.

The little kitchen basked in the double heat of sun and furnace, and was overcrowded with its assemblage of three. The only chair in the room was occupied by the colored votary of fashion, whose monotonous argument rolled on to an unresponsive audience.

"I was a-telling this lady here," she nodded to Claire, and pointed to Betsy — "I was a-telling her I wanted my frock for to-night, for that moonlight picnic is a-coming off to-night at last. You 'ain't heerd tell of it? Me and my society gives it, and all the members is going to go, and they is bound to go. I laid off yesterday to come and tell you, but I didn't have time; and it appears to me a week's long enough to make a frock, anyhow; and if it wasn't, you should have told me so fair and square before you ever put a needle into it. The moonlight picnic's done been put off long enough, the Lord knows! It did seem to me as how we never would be able to get it up. Something was always a-happening against it. Every blessed time we got all the money we'd look in the box, and, sure enough, there wouldn't be enough yet, and then it would be put off till another collection. And if it hadn't been for Sister Johnson's funeral last night it wouldn't come off now. But it's coming off this time, sure; 'cause if it had a-come off when we first started it, Sister Johnson herself could have gone to it; yes, indeed, as sure as you are standing there; and if it hadn't been for holding her funeral last night I don't believe we ever would have got it up. It was a-long past midnight when they come to me for my money, 'cause I never would have given it to 'em before; and after they had done got all the money, they said as how they had better wait for the moon; but the sisters, they just said, 'No, sir; you give that there moonlight picnic to-night, moon or no moon, 'cause it's a heap easier to give a moonlight picnic without a moon than without the money.' As I was a-telling this lady here, and if you had a-told me last week you wasn't a-going to give me that there frock there for the moonlight picnic, I could ha' given it to somebody else. Lord knows there's white people enough to do sewing, and glad to get it; and you knows yourself, after I done paid my money last night at Sister Johnson's funeral for a moonlight picnic, I'm bound to go, and I'm bound to wear a new frock if I've got one."

"Lord, child! don't you jaw so much. Don't you see the mamzelle's 'most done it? Who says you ain't gwine to git it done in time?"

"She's bound to git it done in time, if I stays here a week — she's bound to git it done in time."

It lay under Claire's busy hands on the table like a heap of fresh glowing vegetables. The young negress picked up the waist.

"And I hope to gracious you 'ain't made the josie too tight! I busts my josies awful. The color is real stylish, though. You 'ain't got a collar or some sort of neck fixin' you could sell me, have you? I could pay you cash down for it," rummaging in the privacy of her bosom; "you can see for yourself," untying the knot in a handkerchief. "Lord knows I had trouble enough getting this money after I had done worked for it! I had to jaw that white woman what owed it to me two hours incessant before she had the grace to pay me. But I was bound to get it for the moonlight picnic, and I wasn't going to wash and iron one day longer, neither, for anybody, and I told her so. Goodness knows, I ain't obliged to work for her nohow; and she flung it to me, and told me for God's sake to hush talking, and clear out and never let her lay eyes on me no more, and I ain't going to, neither; and if you've got any sort of collar or neck fixin' you could sell me cheap, I'd pay you cash down for it."

"Hein, Betsie?" asked Claire, putting at last the finishing stitches in her work.

Betsy answered in a quick whisper, "Ef you have got some sort of little old thing you 'ain't got any use for, you know the money'll come in mighty handy."

Claire quit the kitchen, hurried across the little yard, and went into the room with the same precautions as before. Her fingers trembled as she opened the door of the armoire so near the sleeping grandmother, and she pulled from an old pasteboard box the first piece of lace that met her eye — a large antique collar of Valenciennes, and like a thief she crept softly away with it.

"Will this do, Betsie?" she asked, entering the kitchen.

The damage done its marketable value by the deep yellow color was painfully evident to both.

"How much you want to give for it?" asked Betsy of the customer.

"Well, I can't give you more'n I've got. I'm willing to give you all I have got, and that is the best I can do. Here's the six bits for the making of the frock, fair and square as she agreed on, out of this dollar, and here's two bits besides, and that's the last cent I've got in this world, as the Lord hears me speak; and I wouldn't have had that two bits there if I hadn't been let off last night from giving it to the collection, 'cause they didn't know I had it; and they wouldn't 'a' come to me, nohow, if they hadn't found out I'd been washing by the week —"

"Six bits outen the dollar and two bits besides. How much does that make altogether?" asked Betsy of Claire.

"And that dollar there was what the white woman gave me."

"I will take it, Betsie, I will take it," said Claire, eagerly. "I assure you it is quite sufficient," putting the piece of lace into the bundle she was making

"Well, so long!" The negro girl loitered on the door -sill. "I'm just a-willing to bet, now, that that moonlight picnic is put off again. I mistrusted them brothers when they come a-knocking me up last night in the middle of the night. I don't believe in moonlight picnics, nohow, and —

She walked, talking, away.

"Eh, Betsie?" exclaimed Claire. "That is plenty of money, hein? But if bonne maman finds out!"

The old lady did not open her eyes for some time after Claire returned to the chamber, and then she resumed, as if in continuation of her thoughts: "It is curious I never thought of my little work-table until to-day. My 'corbeille de noces.' And it was Aza the first who found it out — Aza." She shook her head meditatively as she repeated the name. "She was always pushing herself forward where I was. They told me I spoiled her; perhaps so. She was more like a doll to me than a human being. Her mother gave her to me, when she was only a day old, in my arms. It felt so grand to have a live doll, just as I was beginning to tire of the others. What plans I made for her! Enfin! it was the will of God. While I was standing, with tears in my eyes, looking at the needles and thread, Aza was feeling the green bag underneath. Do you remember the green bag, Claire?"

"Do I remember it, bonne maman? But surely!"

"She gave the drawer one pull, and, voilà! it was all before me."

The grandmother's bluish hands, with their dark, knotted, angry veins, rubbed nervously up and down the arms of her chair, and she made frequent pauses by leaning back and closing her eyes, breathing heavily.

"Ma foi, if Aza had waited, she would not have had to thank me for her freedom. 'Ma fille,' I used to tell her, 'it is not only the difference in our skin, but the difference in our nature.' She would have died for me — ah, yes! — but she could not be good for me. Claire, I wish I could see my little work-table again." Her voice, usually so trained, was surprisingly plaintive to-day. "You see, so much would come back to me if I could see my little table. I think sometimes, mon enfant, that the loss of our souvenirs is the worst loss of all for us women. With them we never forget. When one is old, things get so far away. When we are young, we are like dogs: we hide away out of our provision of the present, for the future, scraps of ribbon, lace, or a glove — no matter what — and it is very hard when, old and hungry, we come to the hiding-place and find them all gone. Of course it is all sentiment; but we women, going through so much, we like to remember when everything happened for the first time — one's first copy-book, one's first communion, one's first ball, and when one gets married, and one's first child. Ah, mon Dieu! one can get reconciled to changes in life, but one cannot get reconciled to changes in one's self. Even when our souvenirs are crumbling to dust they are fresher than we women are at the end. Mon enfant, I advise you, give up everything in life except your souvenirs; keep them for your sentiments to gnaw on, as one might say, when you get old."

"Eh, grand'mère, souvenirs of what? Of the war? of the convent? Merci! I am in no danger of forgetting them. Every piece of bread I eat reminds me how hungry I used to be there, and—"

The grandmother had taken another leave of absence of mind, and Claire, having now no ulterior motive for loquacity, was silent also.

The closed eyes, however, were not, had not been, sleeping; on the contrary, under their pallid lids they were looking with tense vision, in vague fear of an indeterminate something slowly evolving out of misty uncertainty into a fatal conviction.

That the conviction had not come to her before was owing to the coercive strength of an inflexible will; that it came to her to-day with the irrefutable accumulated evidence hitherto suppressed or ignored, did not astonish, only awed, her. Women live so close to nature, they are guided from initiation to initiation in life by signals and warnings — divine, they call them — which they, and only they, can see. There can be no question with them of rebellion, no refusing of the credentials of the angels of the twilight who still knock at their doors, the bearers of God's commands, messengers of life or messengers of death.

She was failing — failing in physical, failing in mental, strength. The child Claire was managing her, doing her work for her surreptitiously. It was time for her to prepare for the future; she would do it, but why would the past obtrude upon her, turning its corpse lights into every nook and cranny of her memory? Regrets were useless; now that death was so near, but why would they come, sowing discord, corroding with tardy indecision the supreme decisions of her life, arraigning, from the vantage-ground of the present, cherished feats of spent heroism, testing the metal of her approaching martyr's crown?

"This, then, was to be the end of a life conducted on principles drawn from heroic inspirations of other times. The principles were the same, but human nature had changed since women's hearts were strong enough not to break over bullet wounds, sabre cuts, and horse-hoof mutilations, when women's hands were large enough to grasp and hold the man-abandoned tiller of the household. It had all gone wrong." The old lady spread her handkerchief over her eyes. The closed lids could not shut in all the tears. "Yes, it had all gone wrong somehow. The battle turned out a defeat, not a victory; the son came back on his shield, not with it." And she? She might perhaps have done better. Death would now have been easier for her if the times and she had been different in the past. Had it not been for overflows and disasters and disappointments, for failure of crops and epidemics of disease, for the feeding of so many useless and infirm dependents, she too might have been a successful plantation manager. As it was, when her commission merchant came to her with a statement, she frankly and firmly acknowledged that she could not rightfully claim an acre of her possessions. They came in a royal grant; they went in a royal cause. There were law quibbles; but was she one to lose a creed to grovel for coppers? She might have gone to France, as it was supposed she had done; and desert the country for which her only son had died? But after the war she was less than ever a Frenchwoman, more than ever an American. At bay, every nerve tingling with haughty defiance at the taunts and jeers of despising conquerors, every heart-throb beating accusations of womanly weakness and grief, what more effective answer to the challengers of her blood and country, what nobler one to herself, than bravely to assume the penalty she had dared? As the men had fought, let the women suffer against overpowering odds. So she left the beautiful country, her plantation, her home, her souvenirs of youth and happiness, and came to the detested city, sought out this little cabin left vacant by the death of an old slave, and with Claire commenced that life to which she had convinced herself she was committed by fate and by principle. It was an extreme of resolution to meet an extreme of disaster. Ameliorations of her lot were intolerable even in thought. She had made her destitution complete by renouncing even friends, relations, social amenities, with her humble neighbors.

Thus she *had* lived her retaliation against fate — there was no doubt about that now — thoroughly, effectively, and death was upon her. But Claire? The handkerchief could not hide the convulsive movement of her bosom as she recognized now the short range of heroic vision.

The figure of her pale, cheerful, brave, toiling granddaughter came before her with the unearthly vividness of those visions which in stormy nights bring women their dead. The agony she had felt in abandoning her children to the isolation and ugliness of the tomb resuscitated poignantly at the abandonment of this her last child to life.

What tomb could be lonelier or uglier than this little cabin would be to Claire when she, the grandmother, was dead?

Would the patriotic death of the girl's father, would the martyrdom of her mother, would a proud disdain of law quibbles, would the renunciation of friends and the defiance of enemies, alleviate her affliction then, or solace her in her youthful, unaided life-struggle, in those conditions for which ancestral glories, refinements, and luxuries had but poorly equipped her? Could, in fact, their enemies have prepared an extremity of suffering beyond that to which Claire was predestined by her own grandmother?

The sun went down on the little back street earlier than elsewhere on account of the huge old square house blocking up the west. The windows and doors unclosed as its rays withdrew, and the hidden community finished the day's task in the publicity of the front steps, until twilight released them to indulge in the relaxation of neighborly gossip — all except the corner cottage, which maintained its distrustful reserve even through the gentle, winning shades of evening.

When others went in front to greet each other with the commonplaces of human interdependence, Claire and her grandmother went back into the contracted area between the house and kitchen, and expended their tendernesses on the mendicant groups of potted plants that formed their garden. The old lady walked this evening from shrub to shrub, laying her gentle, withered hands with maternal expertness amid the green leaves, straightening distorted branches, and searching out diseased spots. Her own heart felt bruised and sore from suppressed emotion, and craved the faint fragrance, which, it seemed to her, her plants had never yielded so willingly or so abundantly. Did they understand all, and sympathize with her? The tears came into her eyes again, but Claire had gone to take the embroidery home, so there was no need to hide them.

The brilliant sunset sky burned overhead in deep ingulfing masses, reaching clown to the pointed roof of the cottage — the despised roof whose shelter she had sought as the deepest insult she could inflict upon the world. The old, worn, menial house! it also looked kindly, protectingly, at her, as if it also had penetrated her secret — the last secret of her life. An old, old sentiment thrilled in her heart as she looked through her tears at it for the first time as at a home. "Ah, mon Dieu," she thought, "everything seems to know and feel for me, just as it used to know and feel when I carried other secrets in my breast!" The youthful, timid faltering came over her once more, the virgin shudder before unknown mysteries, the same old girlish need of help and encouragement. But she overcame the expression of her face as she heard the key turn in the lock of the little back gate behind the cistern. Claire entered boisterously, followed by Betsy with a bundle. She tossed off her hat with its ugly veil of blue barége.

"Oh, bonne maman! Such a delicious walk! If I only had embroidery to take home every evening! And the old 'Varon' could not have been more amiable. Ah, it's so good to go out on the street!"

She stretched her arms over her head, tightening the faded waist around her swelling breast as she looked up in the brilliant sunset sky above.

"Mon Dieu! but it's all beautiful. I wish I could walk up there in all that pink and blue and gold; walk deeper and deeper in it, until it came up all around and over me!"

She drew a long, quivering breath.

"Do you smell the night jasmine, bonne maman? I do not know how it is with you, but it is as if it came thousands and thousands of miles just to me and no one else, and it makes me feel faint with its sweetness."

She threw her arms around her grandmother and embraced her impulsively.

"You see, it is so good to go on the street, bonne maman. It makes one feel so gay, so fresh, so strong. Ah, you ought to go sometimes with me, just to see all the people. How many people there must be in the world! And I know only three — you, Betsie, and old Varon. But I am glad they are there all the same, even if I do not know them."

A loud, coarse, passionate waltz seemed to fall in rhythmic links over the glass-protected brick wall. She released her grandmother and danced round and round, as if caught in its melodious wheels, until it left her panting and glowing.

"When I hear music like that, bonne maman, it is as if my blood would come out of my veins and dance right there before me. Sometimes in the night I hear it; I think at first I'm dreaming, but then I wake and listen to it until I stop my ears and hold myself still, for, oh, bonne maman! I want so much to get up and follow it, out, out, wherever it is, until I come to the place where it begins fresh and sweet and clear from the piano, and then dance, dance, dance, until I cannot dance one step more!"

The words fell in unguarded fervor, and her eyes began to burn with feverish brightness. Betsy plucked at her dress.

"Mamzelle!"

"Sometimes I wonder whether it is in the music or in me —"

"Mamzelle! Mamzelle!"

"Whether it is in me alone or in everybody —"

"Mamzelle Claire, just one word!"

"Decidedly that Betsie is very badly raised," remarked bonne maman, in an undertone.

"When I smell the night jasmine I feel it a little, and when I look up in the sky like a while ago; but it's never so strong as when I hear music. Oh, bonne maman, can't you give me something to make me stop feeling this way — to make that music let me alone?"

"Mamzelle!" — the negro excitedly placed her hand on Claire's arm to enforce attention.

"If Aza could see that!" The old lady turned away in disgust.

"Mamzelle! I can't stand by and see you dancing and singing to that music you hear over there, and hear you talk about getting up in the night and following it." The old black woman's voice trembled, and her fingers tightened convulsively over the slim white arm. "I don't tell the madam, 'cause it's no use bothering her; but, mamzelle, as sure as God hears me now, them niggers over there don't play no music excepting for devils to dance by, and that piano don't talk nothing fittin' a young white lady to listen to."

"Eh? What do you mean?"

"Mamzelle —"

"Does that hurt the music who plays it? Do you think I want to dance to it, to listen to it?" She pushed Betsy's hand off, with her fingers grown clammy; her cheeks were crimson, and her lips blushed at the strange maturity of expression so new to them.

"Did I say I was going to get up at night and follow it? Did I say I was going on the street every evening? Did I say I would rush up to the people to feel them clasp my hands only once? I only" — and her voice came in a sob — "I only said I wanted to."

The music came now lower and sweeter. She stopped her ears. "There! that is what I must do — eh? Why doesn't *it* stop talking to me?"

"But, mamzelle, they is —"

"It doesn't cost anything," she interrupted, furiously — "it doesn't cost anything to listen to music, to know people. I don't have to work for it, like bread and meat; and, grand Dieu, how much better it is!"

Two tears rolled from her hot eyes; she paused in startled awe and carried her hands up to them.

"Claire! Claire Blanche! you had better come in, child."

"Yes, bonne maman,"

Outside, in the street, the steps filled up with white-sacqued women. The men tilted their chairs back against the trees and the walls of their houses and smoked their cigarettes. The children — and this street could have supplied a city with children — raced from corner to corner to dance out the sample tunes of passing organ grinders. The conversation flowed in an easy murmuring tide from group to group, soared over every now and then by a dominant cry in pursuit of some refractory fugitive.

"You Var — iste!"

"A — na— to — le!"

"Ga cette Marie là bas!"

"Jo — seph — ine!"

"Josephine, to maman 'peler toi!"

"'Polite! tu veux pas finir?"

The lamplighter threaded his way among the chairs, scoring off a dim record of his passage up among the green leaves of the trees. As the darkness settled over the bushy tops of the orange hedge, blotting the vague outlines of the screened house, prodigal fragments of merriment seemed to be thrown in scornful carelessness down the street — dance music with its impetuous accelerations, overtures of song and chorus, breaking off in loud laughter and the tread of dancing feet.

"They are gay over there this evening."

"When one is like that —"

The women united their heads for female comment; but the men, their cigarettes spangling the gloom, listened in silence, casting secret, wistful glances in the direction of the occult merrymaking.

"They won't sleep much over there to-night," said one, pointing to the corner cottage.

"As much as any Saturday night," was answered, with a shrug.

It was long before day when Betsy, with minute particularity, closed the little gate behind her, and started out with her stick in her hand and her sack over her shoulder. She belonged to that division of humanity who seek their daily food in the daily refuse of others. She was a ragpicker — a gleaner in the nocturnal fields of a great city. Her harvests were not beautiful nor savory; but compensations in the shape of freedom from competition, weather influences, and a stable market are not to be despised, particularly by one for whom the darkness has no terrors, the loneliness no trepidations. She had contracted a stoop in her shoulders from so much bending over barrels and buckets and tubs, and peering through dim light into the slimy bottoms of muddy gutters, so that her face seldom met the glance of the passing world, in whose litter it was ordained she should seek her food; but when she did

45

look up, there was seen no reflection of corruption or filth in her small clear black eyes; no grovelling purposes conceived in grovelling pursuits. Although dressed in a picked-up, motley livery, thrown off from the shoulders, per- haps, of vice, sin, or crime, the audible thought which fell mechanically from her lips as she plied her trade carried the conviction that her harlequinade was one of costume only. The old creature's twilight meanderings had taught her much of life, and while she knew little of the gifts of civilization, she had not many of its banes to find out, having had more experience with vice than with virtue, which with purity and goodness dwelt a long way back in her memory, or a long way forward in Biblical promise.

The repertoire of her monologues was not large or varied; wherever they ended, they generally began with an early morning like this, "nigh on to three years ago," when, going forth to pick rags, she found a mistress, and in lieu of daily bread gained daily bondage. She was turning over the contents of a very destitute box indeed that morning when a gate behind her suddenly opened, and a young white girl appeared.

"A young white girl in this here quadroon faubourg! My Lord! what does this mean?" her cultivated suspicions prompted her to exclaim.

But the young girl, frankly, in the confidence of innocent childhood, said, with a polite propitiating smile, in stiff, unpractised English:

"I hear you every morning; I attended for you this morning; I want that you direct me the way of the market."

"You git up this time o' day to ask me the way to the market?"

"Yes, for my grandmother yet sleeps. I wish to go there before she wakes herself."

"Honey, 'ain't you got nobody to go for you?"

"No, nobody now, for —"

"And what could a nigger do?" muttered Betsy, in self-extenuation — "more inspecially a Baptist, a fresh-water Baptist and a cold-water Baptist, and a hanger-on of the Cross?"

It was the chance that links together husband and wife, that determines the fall of a dynasty, or directs the feet of the outcast to a loving home.

Circumstances never permitted the childish appeal for assistance to cease, and an unselfish, tender heart never permitted it to meet with disappoint- ment. It was three years now since that morning, but the sun, measuring their horizon hour by hour, had never shown on a moment of distrust in ei- ther to their simple confidence, or of disloyalty to the pious obligation of serving, by fair means or foul, the proud old lady glorying in her lofty ideas of self-support.

"I can see the end," Betsy told herself, fishing around in a pestiferous heap, "but I can't see after the end. The old madam's a-failing; I seen she was a- failing the first day I laid eyes on her; and the young mamzelle is a-growing- and a-ripening and beginning to notice things woman-like. The old madam, she don't suspicion nothing, nor the young mamzelle neither. The end's a-coming, and it's bound to come. The laughing and the singing and the working all day and half the night ain't a-going to put it off, neither; and it's a crucifying world, anyhow."

The old lady that morning was also trying to look beyond the end, and was seeing Claire growing up instead of remaining forever a child — growing up in spite of tragedy, starvation, imprisonment, into beauty, gayety, joyousness; craving sympathy, companionship, mental food; throwing out woman tendrils in all directions; cut off by short-sighted precautions from friends, from relations, even from certification of her own identity; alone, literally alone, but for the homely friend picked up out of the street. She had sent Claire to church, for the first time in her life, by herself that morning in order to carry out the one project that had come to her in her agony. She called Betsy to the side of her rocking-chair.

"Betsie, you approach me."

Her English, like most of her youthful possessions, was hers yet only by an effort of memory. She spoke very slowly, reconnoitring for equivalents for her agitated French thoughts.

"Betsie, it must we all die."

"Lord! old miss."

"Betsie, it must you die, it must me die, but more maybe me than you."

"Yes, ma'am."

"Betsie, when it comes we die, we look for friends — hein?"

"I reckon so, old miss."

"Betsie, when it comes I die, me, I look for friends, what see I? Mademoiselle Claire and you. You and Claire, nobody more — eh, Betsie?"

"Yes, ma'am."

"Betsie, all this time I have been fool; but I be fool no more. I not work for myself; no, Claire, she work for me; you, you work for me; but me, I not work for myself. Oh! I think so, I work for myself, but no. Now, I know, me. My eyes, they have been shut, but now they see everything."

There were tears of mortification in the proud old eyes, whose first coquettish scintillations lay so deep buried under the grief-drifts of a lifetime.

"Since a long time I work not. Claire Blanche, she make my 'broderie' for me."

"Please, old miss, don't you go and get mad with the mamzelle for that!"

"Me, I do nothing more; for why? I die. Since two years I die. I do not know it before; but I know it now, well, well. Betsie, you come close, close." The negress could not sit; standing, her face was too high up. She knelt down by the chair.

"Betsie, I very sick; I die to-day or to-morrow."

"Not so bad as that, old miss."

"To-day, to-morrow, or soon. I know not when, but soon."

"Can't you take something, old miss?"

"No, Betsie. I do not need medicaments; it is death what I need. Die, Betsie, that is something terrible; no, not for the agonizing, but for the others. It lasts long sometimes — hein, Betsie?"

"God knows, ma'am."

"Betsie, when it comes I die, you stand here, so, close; Claire, she stand there" — pointing to the next room. "You here, she there; then she not see."

Her voice, obedient to the strong will, was clear, but at times a weakening tone from the heart marred its firmness, and turned the command into a petition.

"I understand, old miss."

"Betsie, in my life I have seen much die. It did me nothing. For why? I was happy. I have hold the hand; I have made the prayer. But I had much family still. Betsie, if it comes I die, like you and me we have seen some die — Betsie, ma bonne femme Betsie, you will not let ma petite Claire see. Betsie, swear me that. My good God! Betsie, you think she ever laugh like last night when she see me, her bonne maman, die? Betsie, swear me that."

"I swear you that on the Bible, old miss."

"Betsie, you will say her nothing — nothing. God, He will tell her — oh, He will tell her in time. You say I strong; you say I well — hein, Betsie?"

"Yes, ma'am."

"That is all — that is all for the moment."

"There's something else, old miss, you've done forgot," began the negro woman, still on her knees, her short, thick eyelashes crystallized with tears, a surpassing pleading in her voice. "Old miss, ain't you gwine to send for none of your folks — none of your friends? Old miss, you heerd that child out there last night just a-yearning for some folks and friends. Old miss, let me go out and find 'em for you. I will search this town through from end to end, but I'll find 'em for you, old miss. For God's sake, old miss, don't leave that child here with only one poor old nigger for her friend! Old miss" — putting her eager lips close to the bleached, withered ear — "old miss, they is all out there; the earth is full of friends, old miss. Just let me go for 'em."

The bonne maman reached out her hand and laid it on Betsy's head - handkerchief. "You have reason, Betsie — you have more reason than me. You are one good woman, and I ask the good God to bless you. For me and for my grandchild. I do not know to talk it, Betsie, but" — she drew the black face to her and pressed her lips on the forehead — "that is what I would say, Betsie."

"Old miss, you will send for your folks?"

"Yes, Betsie, to-morrow. Betsie," she called again, as the woman was leaving the room, "you will tell Mademoiselle Claire nothing — nothing; it will come to her soon enough — eh?"

"'Fore God in heaven I promise you that, old miss."

But she was never strong enough to send the summons; the angel had delayed too long on the road with his warning.

The first kisses of the spring sun bring out the orange blossoms, and the first movements of the spring breeze loosen them with gentle frolickings from their stems, to carry the sweet fragrant betrayal of their wantonness round to all the open windows of the city. The children, with their quick divinations, have the news of the blossoming betimes, and they muster in full force on the banquettes under the trees, intrepidly braving for the nonce the insulting volleys of their ambushed foes. Before the dust of the street could pollute the flowers in their abasement, before the sun had time to wither their unsheltered freshness, deft little black, brown, and yellow fingers had heaped them in high-drawn skirts, old hats, scraps of pottery, rag, or paper, to garner them, not on their favorite steps, but in a cache selected for temporary use. For on the silent green doors they loved Death had affixed his standard, and the long black crape floating with majestic solemnity in the sweet air frightened them away. The little cabin, always so dark, so quiet, so unobtrusive, thrilled the early openers of the windows about with the unexpected sign of its stigmata. Sleep had lulled them all into unconscious unhelpfulness, and daylight wakened them to accusing repentance.

"La pauvre vieille madame là-yè, morte pendant la nuit."

"Ah, miséricorde!"

"Si je l'avais su."

"Et moi."

It was Sunday, the church bells were calling them all to mass (all except one — one who they remembered had always gone to the earliest mass), slipping along the street masked in veils. It is an old-fashioned Creole city, with a pompous funereal etiquette, where no dispensation is sought or given for the visit commanded by the crape scarf. Death himself had unlatched the reserved green doors, and was host to-day. And where Death receives, the house is free to all the "blanchisseuse en fin," the "coiffeuse," the "garde malade," the little hunchback who kept the "rabais," the passers-by to and from mass, the market-woman with her basket, the paper-boy with his papers — all entered the little chamber, if but for a moment, to say a little prayer, or bow in respect to the conqueror and the conquered. The old aristocrat lay in her coffin in the bare, unfurnished room, where she had lived with her poverty, her pride, and her griefs, looking up through her mutilations of age and infirmity, through her wrinkles, discolorations, and the stony glaze of death, with the patient resignation of a marble statue looking up through the turbidities of a sluggish stream, while the eyes she had so carefully shunned in life gazed their fill of her.

The hour of noon approached, the siesta hour of the neighborhood.

A large, heavy-limbed woman dressed with showy elegance moved slowly down the street, and stopped for a moment before the door, while her eyes with languid curiosity measured the length and texture of the black scarf. Past middle age, but not past the luxuriant maturity of her prime, she held her head insolently back, challenging and defying observation, proclaiming and glorying in a pampered self-consciousness. From under the black lace of her veil jewels glistened on the soft, barbaric brown skin. Pleasure seemed to have sensualized features and form into dangerous alluring harmony, and panoplied her mind against thought. Her sleepy, large eyes rested on the door while she paused, hesitating between the instinctive craving of morbid curiosity and half-dormant reminiscences of recent gratifications; then, without glancing at the paper fluttering from the door, she entered the room. She bent over the coffin with its emaciated, pitiful human contents, and her eyes dilated with the fascination.

"White!" she whispered, in surprise, with a contemptuous smile on her voluptuous lips. What exquisite flattery to her own rich, exuberant, sumptuous flesh! What triumph for the fierce, bold blood thrilling and leaping in her veins! She raised herself with complacent comeliness, and looked again before leaving.

"Mais! I never noticed it before. It is very strange. Mais grand Dieu!" she screamed, in reckless self-abandonment. "It is she! I know it is she!" She remembered the paper at the door, and tore it off and read it. "I tell you," she screamed again to the impassive watcher, Betsy — "I tell you it is she! Mamzelle Nénaine? Mamzelle Nénaine?" she interrogated, in an agonized whisper, throwing herself on her knees by the coffin. "Is it you? Oh! is it you?" She looked around fiercely and wildly. "But what does it all mean? What can it all mean? Can't you answer me?" she demanded, in English, of Betsy. "Are you a fool? How did this lady come here? Who did it? I want to know who dared do it?"

Betsy had risen respectfully. She was trying, with God's help and the old lady's cold, silent presence, to see now beyond the end. In conformity with her ideas of responsibility to the dead and to the living, she had put off her rags and dirt, and — the last sacrifice of her unselfish heart — had put on a new black dress, white neckerchief, and "tignon" — her own grave-clothes, bought with cold and starvation, and guarded religiously through years of vagabondage for her final apparelling.

"Who are you? What are you doing here?" demanded the imperious visitor.

"Me, ma'am? I am the madam's servant."

"You lie! You know you lie! The madam never owned a servant like you."

"I never said the madam owned me; I said I was her servant; she hired me."

It looked as if the visitor could find no adequate expression for the passion that raged in her. She shook her fist at the bare cold walls, she stamped on the rough, uncovered floor, she caught sight of the jewels on her arms, and hurled the massive bracelets away from her, she tore open her dress to ease her swelling throat, and her bosom panted violently under crushed garnitures of soft white lace. She fell down by the coffin again, and, bursting into tears, hid her face in the darned, worn, white "blouse volante" shroud, moaning, with long, wailing cries, "Mamzelle Nénaine! Mamzelle Nénaine!"

"Where are her friends?"

"Please, ma'am, she 'ain't got no friends, excepting the apothecary gentleman at the corner. He was mighty good and kind; he come when I went for him, and he stayed all night."

"But, my God! where are her relations?"

"I 'ain't never heerd of any relations besides the mamzelle — Mamzelle Claire."

"Mademoiselle Claire! Claire Blanche? Monsieur Edgar's baby?"

She was silent again, as if unable to comprehend it.

"And God allowed this! How long have they been living here — here in this cabin?"

"I don't know, ma'am; it's nigh on to three years since I've been with them, and they've been here all that time."

The stranger looked up to heaven with a muttered blasphemous adjuration.

Betsy had been gazing with her keen eyes as if into a murky depth; then a cloud seemed to have passed away from the sun, for the room was a little lighter. "I see you now," she said, in a hoarse whisper. "I didn't see you before, the room was so dark." Throwing away all effort at self-restraint, raising her whisper into a command: "Clear out from this room! How dare you show your face here! Clear out, I tell you, before—"

"Ha!" exclaimed the woman. The exclamation had a dangerous intonation, a menace of one fearless and unscrupulous.

"Go out of that door, I tell you!" Betsy increased her distinctness and determination. "Don't you dare look at the face of my madam! Don't you dare touch her again!"

"Your madam! Your madam!"

The stranger cursed her with a French imprecation. "Don't you dare call her your madam! She was my madam! I was her Aza! I belonged to her. I was given to her before I was a day old. I slept by the side of her bed; she carried me around in her little arms like a doll; she raised me like her child; she was my godmother; she set me free. I loved her, I worshipped her. O God, how I worshipped her! Mamzelle Nénaine, you know it is true! Mamzelle Nénaine, if you could speak to Aza once more! Just one word! — just one word!"

A torrent of tears choked her voice. Betsy recoiled in horror.

"Your madam! Your — My God in heaven! And she lay a-dying here, and the mamzelle a-starving, and you her servant, what belonged to her, in that house over there! You! a-scandalizing, a-rioting, a-frolicking, a-flaunting yourself in carriages, you and your gals, right past this house! a-carrying on your devilment right out there, and your mistress a-slaving and a-starving! You! You nigger!" The old woman's crooked back straightened until she could look the quadroon straight in the eye.

51

"You — you are not that —"

"Yes, I am! Yes, I am that same dirty, stinking old rag-picker what did scrubbing for you. Not for me, mind you! but to buy medicine for the poor old madam there; a-lowering myself for her, a-dying and starving and freezing, while you was throwing away in the streets the money you stole out of the pockets of them white men!"

"Hush! Oh, for God's sake, don't talk so loud!"

"And last night, when the end come — when the end come, I tell you — with the piano music a-pounding up the street, and the hollering and the laughing, and the poor mamzelle —"

"Mademoiselle Claire Blanche?" repeated the quadroon, vaguely.

Betsy misunderstood her meaning.

"The last thing before the madam there died, when your music and your devilment was going on the loudest, I told her — I told her I would look after the mamzelle the same as if I were her boughten slave; and I'm going to do it. And I tell you, nigger, standing there before me in all your brazenness and finery and sinfulness, before you so much as speak to that child, before you so much as touch the tip end of her gown, you will have to trample the life out of me under your feet."

The inspired figure of the black woman came nearer and nearer, advancing between Aza and the coffin, pointing to the door. The quadroon tried to glare back her speechless rage; but the arraignment was too crushing, the action too full of meaning. She dropped her eyes in shame.

Ashamed before whom? — a common rag-picker from the streets! How dared she steal the language and sentiments of the dead one in the coffin, and talk to her like a mistress? — her, the insubordinate, irreprovable one! With a characteristic gesture she threw her head back again; but in Betsy's fine, determined face, in the holy passion of her voice, in her firm, commanding eye, she recognized, not the stolen or borrowed principles of a white lady, but the innate virtue of all good women. She measured herself not with her dead mistress, but with Betsy, and for the first time in her wild, daring, passionate life felt the humiliation of repentance. Following the direction of the imperious black finger she left the room.

The day wore on to the hour before the funeral. Visits had ceased, and the silence of prayer was in the room about the old lady. Betsy, sitting at the head of the coffin, fanning unweariedly, heard in the other room, where Claire was, the sound of footsteps, the murmuring of voices, and her name called with a moaning cry; or she fancied she heard it, for the solemnity and oppression of death had benumbed her faculties, and she felt uncertain of everything. At last, to end the dream-like confusion, she went to see, and left the old lady, for the first time that day, as much alone as if she were already in her grave.

The children — a hushed, awed band crouching on the steps outside around a white tissue-paper bundle, had been peeping, and waiting long for this opportunity. It came now, to paralyze them with faintness and fear. At first they could make no impression on the green door with their trembling fingers, all holding their breath, and working at it at once. Then it slowly yielded, opening to them the darkened chamber within. They all stood up to follow, as they had promised one another, but when the door swung to again they were still in their places outside. All but one — the bundle-bearer, an appalled, scrawny, ragged, wild little creature with black, unkempt head and yellow skin, naked arms, shivering, bare legs, and feet clinging to the floor; with white teeth clinched, and fear-distended eyes looking anywhere but at that undefined object in the centre of the room. It took an eternity to cross the space to it, and yet the eternity ended too soon, it ended too soon. A barrier stopped her. Involuntarily she looked down. The locked teeth prevented the scream, but in the tense grip of her fingers the white tissue-paper gave way, and for the second time that day the orange-blossoms fell, but this time to break with eloquent fragrance the damp stillness of death, enshrouding the rigid form in their loveliness, and crowning with a virgin anadem the earth-worn face looking heavenward through its last human experience — of love, not hate. The door slammed behind the fleeing messenger, still grasping her fragments of paper, and the children sped away again to their distant corner of observation.

Betsy was not mistaken; the bedchamber was filled with people — ladies and gentlemen whispering and moving around, calling Claire by name, laying caressing hands on her head and shoulders. The girl only crouched lower by the side of the bed, and pressed her closed eyes tighter against the pillow taken from under bonne maman's head, and moaned, "Ah, Betsie! Betsie!"

Betsy looked around in amazement.

"If you please to walk into the next room —" she began; but seeing that they persisted in trying to arouse Claire, she pushed through them, and placing herself in front of the girl, said, querulously, "Let the mamzelle alone; she's not harming any one; what do you want to bother her for?"

She could not understand their explanations at first, being dull and dazed with fatigue and excitement.

But when she did the joy in her heart weakened her. She bent over and steadied her trembling hand on Claire's head. "Child, they is all your kin; done found you out. Honey, they wants to know you. Honey, they wants to love you."

But the head only went deeper into the pillow.

"You must excuse her," she said, looking around, anxious to excuse the offence. "You must really excuse her; she don't know, herself, what she's doing. She 'ain't lifted her head from that pillow sence last night."

After a pause of decorous silence, the ladies and gentlemen, as they will do at funerals, recommenced their whispering. It was excusable this time, the first gathering of a family which had been separated by the whirlwind of revolution a decade ago. There was much to talk over and a long roll of the dead

53

to call; but chiefly there was to recount to one another, each version charac-
ter-tinged, their utter dismay at the intelligence brought them by Aza that
day. How like a fiery cross she had carried the tale around from one household to the other, and had rallied them once again around the old standard of
family pride and family love. With what passionate eloquence had she told
them of the death of bonne maman — of bonne maman whom they had supposed living at ease in France! Dead! here! a wretched, forsaken exile in their
own city. Dead! in the very reach of their hand, in the sound of their voice.
Dead! without a friend! she, whom living, not so very long ago after all, they
had surrounded, a crowd of eager, obsequious courtiers. They spoke of the
old plantation days, with its magnificent, luxurious, thoughtless hospitality;
of the ancient, aristocratic distinction of a name which had been a knightly
pledge in two countries; and they looked at the little room with its inexorable
revelations. In the exaltation of quickening emotion they forgot to whisper.
Vying in their efforts to atone for the present, they brought from their
memory such glorious tributes that the old lady in her pine coffin appeared
clad in garments bright enough then and there for a bodily ascension to
heaven. Pride and reserve were sacrificed, painful secrets hinted at in this
holy revival that all might be said, now that it was too late for anything to be
done; until it became evident, as evident as the misery surrounding them,
that in their own persons or the persons of dead parents they were bonded
by unpaid dues of fealty and obligation to their deceased kinswoman, or, failing her, to the shrinking, cowering, fair-haired girl kneeling by the bed.

A quadroon woman in the corner, dressed in the old servile costume, listened in bitter weeping. At the grating sound of wheels outside she arose and
crossed the room. Calling them by name, Master this and Mistress that, she
pointed to Betsy, and in hurried, broken tones related the simple facts of her
devoted service to those who owned her only by virtue of their dependence,
who could pay her only with their thanks. In a wild, penitent way she was
adding more, but Betsy, listening to one and to the other, tears running unheeded down her cheeks onto her white handkerchief, raised her voice also,
and, after several attempts, succeeded in saying, "And the apothecary gentleman at the corner, he was mighty good and kind; he come when I went for
him, and he stayed all night."

The sincere tones and voices, in which ever and anon came a chord like
bonne maman's, penetrated, in spite of the pillow, to Claire's ears, and won
her to listen. Such glorious, tender homage to her whom she bitterly supposed unknown, uncared-for, abandoned even by God, raised her head as if
by enchantment. She arose in an excitement of love and gratitude, showing
all her people her sad, emaciated beauty, her outworn, out -grown, wretched
clothing, and when they all rushed forward impulsively to embrace her, she
clung to them as indeed to the successors of bonne maman.

A pauper's funeral had been ordered by the kind apothecary, but the family and friends summoned by Aza formed a cortege that filled the little street,

and the service in the mortuary chapel where Aza directed the hearse to stop was such as only the wealthiest could command. At the end of the procession walked — where had Aza found them all so quickly? — a retinue of old slaves, the last, highest local affirmation of family worth; among them, one of them, in costume, race, condition, was Aza herself, bearing the conventional black and white bead memorial "Priez pour moi."

It was late in the night, when the deserted streets promised security from recognition, that she hastened through them and entered, secretly, the little back gate-w-ay of the triangular fence in her slavish dress, worn for the last time. The piano had already commenced its dances.

Madrilène; or, The Festival of the Dead

NOTHING was silent about the old cemetery but the dead themselves — nothing respectable, all the noises and confusions that had harassed them in life were here to harrow the atmosphere above their rest in death; all the mould and ugliness of an undergrowth population, which their living feet had avoided, lay thick and fetid all round about the walls ramparted with tombs that enclosed them now.

The city had grown densely around the cemetery, but the houses had backed up or sidled up, as it were, not caring to face their grim neighbor. Those which by necessity did face it had the aspect of houses accustomed to look at worse things in life than death — houses that had not enjoyed the sad privilege of falling from a higher estate or disappointing hopeful prospects, but which had been preordained from the beginning to degradation and ostracism.

A broad space had been left in front by the city ancestors for some beautiful boulevard or funeral parade-ground, but it had become an unsightly waste, a "common" for street children, a lounging place for social refuse, a medium for back-door convivialities and intrigues, a dumping -ground for unmagazinable traffic, and the lower end of it the landing -wharf for a schooner fleet, which discharged daily cargoes of lumber, brick, and charcoal onto the frazzled grass, and daily crews of negroes, "dagos," and roughs into the ill-favored coffee-houses at the corners.

Up in the air the thin fine spars of the vessels could be seen coming in from the distance along the invisible canal, gliding into and out of occultation, past trees and houses and open garden spots, and past the cemetery. And sometimes they seemed sailing or being cordelled straight through the cemetery; and then, by a fancy, the masts and spars looked as if they might be anchored there with their vessels, and the marble crosses, spires, and angels, and effigies as if they might be moving, gliding along in the air, sailing on through and above the noisome foulness of the place, with its unwholesome effluviae of corrupting morals, carrying their freight over an invisible canal to some pure, quiet, serene, distant basin. It was a closed cemetery lifetimes ago; burial in it had become an inheritance, or a privilege of society partnership, the funerals dwindling away into a steady, slow monotony, calculable to a fractional certainty. On Sundays and holidays, with strange, inexplicable regularity, the sociétaire, funerals, with music and banners and regalia and unlimited carriages, conducted by drivers of unlimited thirst, to the great pecuniary profit of the coffee-houses. Once a month, or perhaps not quite so often, there was a last pompous effort of some of the old elite, well worth looking at, if only for the ecclesiastical demonstration and the flowers and the sedate affectations of the Sunday tippling drivers. Oftenest, however, so fortunes change, it was the hearse and single carriage affair, with a fragmentary procession on foot, the furtive, almost surreptitious, admittance of the poverty as well as death stricken heir or heiress to the ancestral sepulchre. And even these were interesting, particularly in a crisis of quiet in the neighborhood, or on rainy days, for the poor seem always to be buried on rainy days, as the society members on holidays.

Perhaps it was this guarantee of daily pleasure food which made the houses in the locality attractive as residences. Sure it is that the necessity of living in that one spot became the tyrannous necessity of a vice to those who once adopted it. When vacancies sometimes occurred in the shambling tenements through rent failure of tenant or patience failure of landlord, the billet seldom remained long over the threshold. If it were not a place for the industrious, it nevertheless required a certain amount of industry to live up to the daily advantages of idleness; and the countenances of the people thereabouts, if they did not show the fatness of good living, showed neither the inert vacuity of the pleasure-starved.

It was the last day of October, in its beautiful morning, with but the gentlest suggestions of autumn radiating through the atmosphere. The long, lingering summer had faded away like the febrile dream of an over-luxurious night which leaves the mind tranquil but alert, the body enervated but pleased. The fine weather for "la Toussaint" has passed into proverb.

La Toussaint, the Festival of the Dead, is the fete *par excellence* of the city. It is a day encrystallized by time and sentiment with poetic superstitions and custom; the one day upon which the cemeteries resurrect out of the things they are, and become the things they should be: radiant sanctuaries, exhaling beauty, purity, and fragrance; when the dead — the impotent, despised dead — lie enchased in their tombs like saints in their shrines, to be propitiated with flowers and importuned with prayers. It is the one day in the city during which the glittering supremacy of wealth is nullified; when not he who lives finely, but he who is buried finely is envied; when the good families of the past are compared with the parvenus of the present; when old romances and histories enjoy an annual blossoming out of the names on the mortuary tablets.

"Oh yes, they are *grand' chose* now, but show me where their dead are buried." The most ordinary servant felt herself in a position to make that remark, and gossiping tongues, whose usual vocation was to spread reports of shameful neglect of the living, on this day busied themselves about the more shameful neglect of the dead — if such cases ever occurred. And those waifs and strays who begin life in the maternity ward and end it on the dissecting-table of the hospital, and those vague asylum humanities who date from nothing recordable but a parent's death or desertion, and even the criminals

57

who have suicided from the moral life of their kind — at no other time do they feel their deprived condition as on this day. And some — the cunning ones — go so far as to affect graves they do not possess, and sally forth on the morning of All-Saints with the emblems of remembrances and regrets they have never known, "just like other Christians," as the local comparison is.

Coming at a season when strangers yet shun the place, there is no festival that calls out as it does the full muster of the populace — a populace of un-fermented original types, strong and full with the salient untempered flavors of race ingredients, a *vin brut* of humanity.

And if the festival could rouse a whole city to intensity of excitement, what must it produce in the neighborhood of a cemetery, and a cemetery the old-est, most aristocratic, and most important of the city? And if November first were such a day, what must the last of October be, when, from local appear-ances, the whole world seemed to have been caught procrastinating, and had but a few fleeting hours to prepare their tombs for the morrow's judgment? Such hurry! Such maddening confusion!

In the cemetery itself the most extraordinary "house-cleaning" was in pro-cess, such whitewashing of stucco, scrubbing of marble, reddening of brick pavements, cutting of grass, trimming of shrubbery, spreading of clean white sand over walks, and laying parterres off in fanciful designs with little shells, and such transplanting of blooming bushes of marguerites, roses, and bor-ders of violets into sterile beds! And the voices ordering, protesting, wran-gling, hurrying, scolding, directing! One would think they never had had more than a day to prepare in.

Outside, on the banquette was the usual market scene of everything that could be required in today's confusion for to-morrow's ornament: hillocks of sand and shells, flowers in pots, or torn up by the roots, or loose in baskets, or wired around stiff forms — marguerites, dahlias (white, yellow, and pur-ple), and amaranths, dropping over with their bulky, fleshy, rich redness; carefully guarded trays of plaster angels, Madonnas, infant Jesuses, Saviours, and saints, all fashioned in Italian likenesses and clothed with Italian gor-geousness. And all the length of the wall, hung on nails, wreaths, crosses, hearts, anchors, fabricated of curled glazed paper, black or white, or black and white mixed, or of flowers; white roses with black leaves, or black roses with white leaves, or of dried immortelles (purple, black, white), all tied with shining satin ribbon, gayly fluttering in the breeze, carrying their legends in gold and silver printing. And there were not wanting, also, these for the mil-lionaire griefs, so to speak — handsome, elaborate, bead memorials, jingling and showy, carrying their succinctly pictured desolation in a medallion in the centre: a tomb, a weeping-willow, and a weeping figure, addressed in letters around the rim to all the different mortuary members of the human family, with all manner of passionate invocations from the bereavable human heart.

And wherever one could edge herself in, sat old negro women in *tignons*, before waiters of *pralines,* molasses and cocoa-nut candy, or pans of *pain patate*, or skillets of dough-nuts frying over lighted furnaces; keeping the flies and the gamins off with long whisks of split palmetto, while they nodded their heavy sleepy heads. All the venders crying their wares at once, in the deteriorated traditions or personal perversions of half a score of dialects, with a vociferousness and persistence that proclaimed the transient nature of the opportunity.

The coffee-houses at the corner kept up their usual steady holiday business, realcoholizing their patrons and turning them out to doze through the time between drams on the convenient bench under the awning, or to digest in one long gluttonous sleep on the grass their one long gluttonous drink, or only slightly exhilarated to drift as far as the planked crossing, where a hilarious crowd was gathering around a quadroon lad, who held the only novel feature of the day — a monkey in leash.

The long, lean, lanky animal climbed and sprang unceasingly at the end of its tether, collecting an unfailing toll of screams and fright from the passersby, responding with human eagerness to the prompt applause of its malice. "Loulou," whispered a little negro to the quadroon, "look!" — he pointed to a figure just turning in from the corner — "Madrilène!"

The girl's height enabled her to carry her long, flat basket easily above the heads of the people who streamed over the plank walk with her on their way to the cemetery. The stiff funereal glazed paper wreaths piled in her basket stood out in ghastly becomingness above a face which, though young, seemed created to be overshadowed by the emblems of death: a thin, scraped profile skin sallow to blackness, hollow eyes, brooding brows, a mouth held rigid and expressionless by determination, and eyes fixed in studied abstraction. As she came closer to view, her costume seemed not less appropriate to her burden than her face: her worn shoes, faded stuff skirt, shrunken sacque, and the ragged bandanna kerchief tied not around her head, but under her chin.

She arrived opposite the ill-behaved group of 'men and boys.

"File!" whispered Loulou to the monkey in his arms.

But the wily animal mistook the aim, or substituted another one. He jumped not to Madrilène's basket, but to the head of an unsuspecting child walking in front of her, and there poised himself, arching his serpentine tail around his bald, ashen-gray face, peering over at the child, and grinning at the terrified screams that fell upon the air.

Madrilène's expression changed to one of pure rage. She threw her basket to the ground, and, as quickly as the animal himself could have done so, she caught the monkey around the neck, throttling him as she dragged him off.

"Stop, stop, Madrilène! Curse you! stop!" screamed the quadroon boy, running to the rescue of his pet. "Stop! You are choking him to death!"

She flung the monkey to the ground to seize the boy's head by the short, black, curly hair. She slapped him vigorously. "Dare! dare!" she said, "dare frighten white children again!"

The monkey — his simulated distress had been but another evidence of his versatile talents — bounded nimbly from the ground, amid the loud admiring laughter of the crowd.

The boy, who had lain resistless enough in Madrilène's grasp, recovered himself as soon as released. Construing the laughter behind him as mockery to himself, he furiously sought to recover his lost prestige. Shaking his fist at the back of the girl, he shouted after her:

"Mulatresse! nigger! nigger! 'coon! 'coon!" (a localism of irritating significance to the colored), adding other insolences of his quick and ready invention; and the insolences of his class are the unrepeatable of language.

The crowd paid no attention. It was only the usual street quarrel to them, pursued with the characteristic violence of the colored. The girl walked away unheedingly. She paused at the corner, hesitating between two courses, and then slowly, as if yielding to temptation, turned to the right towards the iron cross that rose above the gate of the cemetery.

Almost unnoticed in the voluble excitement around it, a funeral was driving up.

A hush spread over the banquette, pantomime paused, and instantaneously a hedge of spectators was formed on each side of the entrance, from which, with that never-sated curiosity of the living about the dead, eager heads craned forward to look.

Madrilène waited, watching the slow backing up of the hearse until, struck by a thought, she turned her head towards the cemetery gate, glancing into it. "Where was the sexton. Monsieur Sacerdote?"

Pushing her way out of the throng, she ran quickly across the cleared space into the enclosure and down a path. It had been designed for a brave, fine cemetery — a fit repository for the mortal remains of aristocracy and wealth, with handsome monuments, broad avenues, gentle vistas, and pleasing perspectives. There were some costly family mausoleums in it and palatial society sepulchres — huge mortuary hotels; but death had been too indiscriminate and too busy; and periodic epidemics in the past had annulled all plans and calculations. It showed now the confused *plenum* of a caravansary into which tired, pilgrims had been driven by stress of weather or nightfall, glad to huddle themselves together pell-mell, in any position, confident only of their fatigue and slumber. Whichever way a coffin could be placed upon the earth, there had arisen a tomb' over it; and vaults had been arched upon vaults, rising higher and higher, stretching their burial capacity in the only direction left them.

In the early days the sexton could not be too young, strong, and vigorous for his work. Now it was a mere somnolent porter's task to sit inside the lodge day after day, waiting for an order to open a tomb here, or a certificate that time, by making a vacancy, authorized a new lease there. And Monsieur Sacerdote — Fan tome Sacerdote, as the people pronounced the "Vendôme" of his name — octogenarian, and decrepit to the verge of vital tenuity, did not find his physical functions taxed by his office.

It was not an easy labyrinth for the feet to unravel. Life itself had not more vicissitudes than the gnarled paths, with their obsolete grave mounds for stumbling-blocks, and their fair openings dammed unexpectedly into aimless culs-de-sac. But Madrilène ran through them swiftly and easily, without pause or breath, looking sharply from side to side, impatiently waving away arresting voices and gestures, venturing from time to time a whispered call: "Monsieur Sacerdote! Monsieur Sacerdote!" She arrived fruitlessly, at the corner where a scrubby cypress-tree had managed to rear itself to some maturity of funereal foliage, and where the 'tiers of rented mural sepulchres ("ovens," they are called) rise against the terminal wall. She ran her eye along the old worn slabs, with their tottering balustrades and crumbling bases, pulled by the sinking ground into queer distortions, like a paralytic's grin. From the half-submerged bottom to the grass-covered top one, there was not a gap in the drear solidity.

"Monsieur Sacerdote!" she called, louder.

There was only the gay chattering of the people cleaning their tombs to be heard, and only their moving forms to be seen. The girl turned into another path, and after a few steps almost fell over the one she sought.

"As I thought — asleep!" she muttered.

One could hardly have been more so inside the crumbling brick coffin-shaped structure on which the old man lay, in face of the tomb he had just opened. His hat had fallen off, and his long white hair lay spread out like some curious lichen growing in the masonry. The warm sun gleamed on the scant silver threads and shone on the round, small, red, semi -bald head, and on the face sinking into formlessness almost as though corruption and not decrepitude were the cause. He held a piece of bread in his withered hand, and the flies buzzed over him and over the contents of an open tin bucket indiscriminately; and the lizards took his figure in as a matter of course in their frolics after the flies.

"He looks like a runaway corpse," thought the girl. "Monsieur Sacerdote!" she called, loudly, to him in French — "Monsieur Sacerdote!" She shook him by the shoulder. "Awake! awake! The funeral is at the gate!"

The old man's head rolled over into another position, and the toothless gums resumed their suspended movements of mastication. The shaking had an effect, but deafness protected his ear. She put her lips close to it, and sinking her voice to a piercing distinctness, repeated:

"Wake! Get up! The funeral is at the gate. The funeral! the funeral!"

"What is it, Marie Madeleine?"

He closed his eyes again after one feeble opening of them.

"The funeral! They are looking for you! Run! Run to meet them!"

61

"Eh, Marie Madeleine?" He was the only one who ever called her by her name, instead of by the vulgar contraction of it, and he kept repeating it over vaguely, as if it were a part of the degustation of the bread in his mouth.

She got him to a sitting posture and then pulled him to his feet, talking, repeating, gesticulating, coaxing the senile incomprehension out of his eyes. He finally started, as she bade him, down a certain path, trotting, with short, stiff, rheumatic steps.

"He will be caught some day, and then, yes, he will lose his place, and he will be sent to the Little Sisters of the Poor. Monsieur Sacerdote with the beggars at the Little Sisters of the Poor!"

In desperate hurry she began to clear away some of the disorder — hiding the tin bucket, gathering up the scattered tools, sweeping the debris of masonry together. She put her head close to the opening and peered through the gloom into the interior of the tomb. Undefinable accumulations rounded the sides and filled the corners. The far end was hidden in darkness, but there was a twilight path down the swept centre.

"He has done, indeed, everything. All is ready. He was only tired."

She worked over the mortar on the board and piled the bricks nearer to hand.

Never could guests arrive more inopportunely than a funeral at the cemetery at such an hour. The procession was long in coming. The pallbearers carried their difficult load slowly through the hard extremities of narrow spaces and sudden angles, made still harder by standing buckets of whitewash, pavements slippery with soapsuds, and unremoved heaps of trash. All the bustling workers had to jump into attitudes of respect— the women, simulating prayers with their lips, while secretly tugging at their skirts; the men gingerly taking off their hats with their soiled fingers; the street urchins hurried away from their momentary jobs, around by-paths, into advantageous positions whence they could make grimaces and signs at the tormented-looking acolytes.

Marie Madeleine stepped back as the priest appeared, and put herself in a corner where she could see, but not be seen. Her figure was so frail and slight it looked like a shadow thrown where she stood; her face like a relievo ornament cut into the marble against which it leaned. The dazzling white surface, illumined by the full rays of the sun, made distinct the ordinarily insignificant minutiae of her features, revealing some of the mysteries of character and age which make up expression — the softness under the chin; the deep indenture of the upper lip; the sharp claw scratches on the lower; straight, outstanding eyelashes, an irregularity in the line of the nose; the unfleshed cheek-bone; the thin, bruised rather than dark-looking skin; the opaque, dry, burned-out eye-sockets; the eyes black and disturbed, not with hidden conflicts and rebellions, but carrying, like godless worlds, their unshaped contents in chaos. She had pushed her kerchief from her head; short rumpled strands of ill-kept black hair fell over her forehead and behind her ears.

"Her first evening here! All clean and beautiful and bright! She comes to her tomb like a bride to her home, and to-morrow it will be all flowers and ornaments and burning candles, like a celebration in her honor. Her family will come year after year to lay flowers under her name. Her friends will pass by her tomb every All-Saints and talk about her. And her family will die, one after the other, and they will all come in there and lie with her; and little children, far, far away in the future — children of her family — will be brought here, all to be buried together, all to rise together."

Self-abandoned, self-unconscious, she followed her thoughts, undisturbed by the muttered functions of the priest and the sharp outbreak of grief that followed the placing of the coffin in the vault, and the long, whining sobs that accompanied the tap-tapping of the bricks by Monsieur Sacerdote's trowel. She watched the barrier rise higher and higher, past the coffin, past the flowers on top, past the black vacant space, to the one little crack left; past that, past the breath of life, past life itself! Immured in one long dormitory, with dust of skeletons, flowers, wood...But Madrilène took not this view of it.

"It is like getting at night into a bed where one's father and mother have slept. One should sleep well in that bed."

Madrilène's bed was a pallet on the floor of Madame Laïs's room.

"One should have none but beautiful dreams there, and no thoughts to chase one awake all through the night. And the walls about such a bed would not show faces to grimace at one. The night would protect one there from the day — those horrible days that come back and come back to remembrance, like dishonest duns collecting their bills over and over again. It is a fine thing where parents leave such a bed as that for their children — regular parents."

Very few of what are called regular parents live about a cemetery. Ties and relationships assume a voluntary and transient character in that careless neighborhood, life flowing by choice through crooked rather than straight channels. Madrilène had never lived in any other neighborhood.

"And the dead will have their festival to-morrow, and she will be among them, fresh from earth. It will be a birthday to her. To-night at twelve o'clock she will come out of her new tomb with them, and they will walk down these paths, visiting one another, and talking and laughing." (A common superstition.) "They will hurry away at daylight, but not far away. They will be above us there in the air, watching, listening, seeing everything, knowing everything. They see who come to their tombs and who stay away; who remember, who forget, and who are ashamed, and who deny them. They will see the little orphans around the table at the gate, 'chinking, chinking' the money in their plates. They will see who give to the orphans and who do not. The parents of the orphans themselves will see it. But the orphans cannot see their parents. Oh no! Those who can remember them can see what they knew; but those who have not known, who do not remember, they look into the faces of the passers-by, and say, 'Was she like that lady? Was he like that gentleman?' The white orphans pick out white ladies and gentlemen for their parents. God leaves the photographs perhaps in the hearts of the children. But sometimes the children don't like the photographs, and then — even the colored ones pick out white ladies and gentlemen for their parents."

Her thoughts were leading her up to that empyrean to which human thoughts can rise from lowest depths, seeking, it may be, their heavenly source, or it may be only seeking their earthly lackings.

The funeral procession went away again, the grave became deserted, and the busy day seemed about going, too. The sinking sun began to cast oblique rays over the tombs; the breeze blew the white sails stealthily along the canal outside; the noises were ebbing; the throng dispersing. Almost — almost — there was quiet in and about the cemetery. The preliminary warning of the bell for shutting the gate rang, but the girl heard it not. As the rich and the happy do, she luxuriously let the moments pass unheeded.

Monsieur Sacerdote commenced his rounds with his long stick to make sure that no evil-intentioners nor stragglers were shut in, striking the tombs briskly to herald his approach.

"Ah, mon Dieu!" she exclaimed, as the stick found her out. "It would be good to stay here this way all the time. Monsieur Sacerdote," she said to him, stretching out her hand to stop his staff, "how good it would be to stay here this way all the time! Never to go back — never to go back! To lie here among the clean white tombs until judgment-day!" This had been in her mind all her life. When she was a little child, half naked, all dirty from the streets, she had begged to be left in the cemetery, "With the dead, with the good dead, with the white dead;" and as she said then, she as childishly said now: "Maybe I might die, and you might slip me into one of these tombs here — who would know? And then on resurrection-day — it would be a good thing for resurrection-day to come on All-Saints, wouldn't it, Monsieur Sacerdote? — on resurrection-day I would rise with the others. We resurrect white, do we not, Monsieur Sacerdote? I would be found out otherwise. All white — white limbs, white faces, white wings, white clothes. Not yellow — not black corpses rising with their white bands." She closed her eyes and shuddered. "Oh, the fearful sight! And if I arose with the white, would they turn me out, do you think?"

The old man raised his dim eyes to her face, and began to move his nerveless lips to answer, when a violent blow aimed from behind missed the girl, and rang on the tomb beside her; the torrent of abuse that followed was surer. "Devil! Dog! Vileness! Wretch! Filth! Detestable animal of the earth! Mulatresse! Negress!"

The assailant, a quadroon woman, came into view, making ineffectual attempts to repeat the blow. Her passion supplied words too fast for utterance, the threats and abuse choked her breath and overloaded her lips. She would hold on to one word and repeat it mechanically, until the phrase would come bursting out, carrying a spray of white foam with it.

"You think you can beat Loulou! You think you can beat him in the streets before everybody! I will beat you! I will show you! Filth of the last gutter in the city! You shall feel the weight of this hand, I tell you! You beat my child for white children! White ... Let me get hold of you! Let me put hands on you! I will fix you! I will teach you! I will strip you! I will kill you! You..."

She seemed to be afraid of saying nothing; no term repugned her, and no impurity seemed too impure to apply to the girl, who contented herself with avoiding blows, pressing her lips tightly together, while Monsieur Sacerdote, looking bewildered, alternated his "Marie Madeleines!" with "I command you! I command you!" to the virago.

She was a large woman, well formed, and had all the points which go to make the beauty of her type. Her cheeks glowed with the only blushes vouchsafed them— the heat of passion; the blood seemed almost to start the dark thick skin, and back of her heavy black eyes it glistened like red coals of fire. A white scum settled around her lips — large, full, pampered, pulpy lips — with their inevitable subtle suggestions of immodesties. There appeared to be no lengths to which the tide of passion might not carry her.

"May I ask the price of these?"

The interruption came from a man, the unperceived spectator of the scene, and the concealed observer of the girl from the moment she awoke Monsieur Sacerdote. He pointed with his stick to the basket of paper wreaths.

The quadroon woman instantly included him in her discourse, giving the girl no space to answer in.

"A miserable creature, sir, who is always forsaking her own race to run after the whites. And she has the temper of a demon, sir. She beat my son, beat him almost to death, out there in the street! A little child — ah, but I shall make her pay for it!" Then, controlling her passion, she glided miracu- lously into the obsequious civility of her class to the whites, and sought to please, by voice and demeanor, and a deft flattery of prejudice. "She should stay in her class, sir; me, I stay in my class. If God made us quadroons, we should be quadroons. She tries to pass herself off for white,"

The girl almost opened her lips to speak.

"When quadroons try to pass themselves off for white, it is for no good purpose, sir, as you know."

"I will buy a half-dozen of these, but you must come and put them on the tombs for me, yourself." The man turned and walked away. Madrilène waited in her same attitude.

"Go— go follow the gentleman! Don't you see he wants to buy some of your wreaths? Go, but remember — to-night!" The woman added this in a muttered whisper, half closing her enraged eyes.

Madrilène, after a moment's hesitation, picked up her basket and walked after the stranger. He was reading over the names on a tomb when she caught up with him.

"These, sir, are not fit for you; they are for the colored cemetery and the very poor." Her voice was low. It sounded like a voice seldom used. "I was on my way to the colored cemetery. I only stopped in here a moment."

"I shall buy some of these, all the same."

"If you would permit me, sir, I could make you some flower wreaths to-night - real flowers."

"But I would like to put them on the tombs to-day."

"Show me the tombs, sir, and I will have them decorated by daylight to-morrow. Or tell me the names — I know every tomb here."

"I will show them to you." He pointed out one or two, and then walked on rapidly through one path after the other.

"Are these all, sir?"

He started out of his absorption. "Ah, yes, yes!" and then, one would have said almost at random, he pointed out three or four other tombs.

"You can pay me to-morrow, after you see them," she said, in answer to a gesture he made towards his purse.

And then the delayed evening bell rang imperatively, ordering all out of the cemetery before the closing of the gate. It was full early, as some discontented grumblers did not fail to remark on their way to the exit.

"That old sexton is so blind, he thinks it is sundown at mid-day."

"He is too old to see, he is too old to hear — in fact, he is too old to be alive any longer."

"You noticed he was not there for the funeral to-day?"

"Somebody ought to report him."

Madrilène passed out into the street. The stranger paused by the sexton, who stood holding the gate in his hand.

"Who is this girl?" he asked, abruptly.

Monsieur Sacerdote looked at the questioner; he was neither young nor handsome, nor "that kind of a man."

"Marie Madeleine, but those people call her Madrilène."

"Who are those people?"

The old man shrugged his shoulders.

"Do you think that woman will carry out her threats?"

Another shrug of the shoulders.

"Where does she live?"

"Those people keep *chambres garnies* somewhere on --- Street."

The stranger seemed to understand the indefinite reference. He looked at the sexton a moment, as if to gauge the advisability of further questions, and then he, too, walked away through the ugly wasted boulevard.

Marie Madeleine resumed her deferred itineracy, turning the corner at which she had before hesitated, and walking down the street to the cemetery set apart for the burial of the colored.

It was more neglected, and if possible more outraged by *entourage*, than the other place. There was no sidewalk, the dilapidated walls patched up to irregular heights, for the accommodation of vaults inside, threatened to fall and burst asunder at any time. On the high, level places a miniature forest grew — weeds, grass, and chance seedlings of trees, and vines that drooped almost to the ground outside.

As she had done the length of the other cemetery, Madrilène touched the walls as she walked along with her out-stretched fingers: "Dead in there! dead in there! And who were you? and who were you? All dead! all dead!"

It was only thought, and in words not her own. Her own words, from the common store of language about her, could not have expressed her thoughts; or perhaps the thoughts as well as the words were foreign to her; perhaps the thoughts were transplanted with the words from the books read aloud to Monsieur Sacerdote in surreptitious hours, in that stolen acquirement which neither Madame Laïs nor her family suspected. Reading! They would as soon have provided her with a looking-glass.

There were the same scenes around this cemetery as the other one. The same or rather a greater throng, and greater hilarity. Nature was the same — sun, atmosphere, verdure, houses — all the same. But the faces of the people, they were different; passed over, as it were, with a color for a travesty; with an ochreous wash. Yellow, yellow, brown, black — almost all yellow. Differences of feature and expression, height and figure, were all lost in the one monotonous hue — the hue of a race creeping down, or is it a race creeping up the scale? A *patois* race.

Madrilène hastened through it as if flying from pursuit. But who can distance thoughts? And she had been fury-driven since she could think. And such thoughts — such strange thoughts! Did she think the thoughts herself, or did God, who sends so much into the hearts and minds of young girls — even to the most abject — send them to her? How could she ascertain? Could she have questioned Madame Laïs, or Palmyre — the virago mother of Loulou— or Antoinette, or Philomène, or Athalie, or any of Madame Laïs's other daughters? Or any of the yellow men who came through the back gate to visit them? Or any of the white men who rented rooms from Madame Laïs?

She might have had ample opportunity to ask these last, if, like Antoinette, Philomène, Palmyre, and Athalie, she had chosen to serve them — carry them their coffee of mornings, attend to their chambers, wash and mend their clothing for them. There could not be found more amiable servitors than the four daughters of Madame Laïs, whatever their back-yard character might be, and so they never lacked pocket-money, fine dresses, and jewelry.

But Madrilène would never serve the lodgers. At first she had to endure suffering to maintain her obstinate refusal. That was a little over a year ago, when people began to call her *cette jeune fille*. She would not have been clothed in such rags now had she yielded to Madame Laïs. Selling these wreaths on commission once a year was not a lucrative profession, and the rest of her time and service was due Madame Laïs for her food and clothing.

She entered the colored cemetery, and went down the broad central walk, Midway before her a black iron arch held a black iron cross high up against the evening sky. The tall, narrow tombs on each side arose close together, almost touching. Were they really different from the tombs in the other cemetery, or did they only appear so to the morbid eye? They were not all black, nor all white, either, but mixed, like the people they enclosed, with interfusions, trimmings, and fleckings of one color upon the other, unconsciously sinister. And the nomenclature on the tablets! Such a different reading from the tablets in the other cemetery! Names, fictitious, assumed, composed, or stolen; some of them sounding sweet in the mouth, like the anonymes of poets and poetesses; some of them that might have answered at the roll-call of Charlemagne; some of them petting diminutives, like the names of birds and lapdogs; some of them catching the eye with their antique integrity, like bits of jewelry in pawn-shop windows. But all of them one-sided names. For the black that had tinged so many fair complexions, muddied the depths of so many clear eyes, and alloyed the expression of so many noble profiles, the black that had diverted the course of so many names and destinies — all that was nameless and unrecorded, barred out, like the pure black people themselves from this cemetery.

Marie Madeleine sold her wreaths the length of the walk. The night promised so fair that over the society tombs draperies were being hung, in readiness for the morrow, the funeral trappings of a by-gone regality — black velvet palls, spotted with white tear-drops; old -fashion black hangings for the outside of houses, with profuse applications of skulls and cross-bones; and hearse and coffin ornaments borrowed from the undertaker.

When she had sold her store out, she waded through the tall grass of a side path until she came to an isolated tier of vaults. As she had expected from the lateness of the hour, no one was there. Each one of all the square tablets in the rows carried its memorial — all except one. "Rosémond Delaunay" was the name it bore. Delaunay was the family name of Madame Laïs.

From under the paper at the bottom of her basket the girl took a bead medallion — the conventional tomb, weeping-willow, and weeping figure. It bore the inscription, "À ma Mere." She held it for a moment in her hand. It seemed to weigh heavy, pulling her arm down, while she looked before her into vacancy. Returning to herself, by force of will, she hung the tribute on the nail fixed for that purpose in the tablet. The crumbling mortar loosed its hold, nail and medallion fell to the ground.

"Pas ramassez li! li tombe par terre! Bon Dié la oule!" (Do not pick it up! It fell to the earth! Good God wished it!)

Before looking, Marie Madeleine recognized the voice of old Zizi Mouton, the occult terror of Madame Laïs's life, reputed to be one of the "old people" who know everything. She was seated on the ground, her feet in the dry ditch; an old, decrepit black negress; her face a bundle of wrinkles tied up in a head-kerchief; the bright little black bead eyes seeming to draw the whole physiognomy in to some interior fastening. She pushed out her long stick, and held the medallion to the earth. "Pas ramassez li, mo dit toi! Pas ramassez li!"

The girl did what Madame Laïs would have been afraid even to think. She pushed the stick aside, picked up her wreath and the nail, saying, in Creole: "Let me alone, Zizi!"

"Hé, Madrilène! Vie Zizi a raison! Bon Die a raison!" (Old Zizi is right! Good God is right!)

Like all voudoos, old Zizi professed to be the oracle of God. Madrilène hammered the nail back into its place with a piece of brick, and hung the wreath up again, and stood hiding her face in her hands.

The passers-by thought she was weeping or praying, as many others were doing around her, for these tombs, at this season, move the heart almost beyond control.

The Strange gentleman who had ordered the flowers from her in the other cemetery, always walking behind her, always observing her, might have wished, as he stood there out of reach of her eye, to hide his face also, as the girl did, the thoughts that would intrude on a gentleman, not to say a moralist, like him in this cemetery being perhaps more comfortably entertained in solitude and silence, behind folded hands.

After Marie Madeleine had walked well away, old Zizi prized herself up with hand and stick from the ground, tore the wreath from the nail, and beat the nail again out of its place, muttering, "Ah, Laïs! coquine!"

When the old woman had left, the stranger approached and studied the inscription on the tomb and the inscription on the bead memorial; and then, still in pursuit of an object or an idea, walked out of the cemetery into the street, retracing his steps towards the other graveyard.

Darkness had fallen after the short twilight. Those of the "marchands" and "marchandes" who had obtained advantageous positions against the wall were preparing to hold them by camping on the spot all night. Others were slowly bundling up their wares for a reluctant departure. The coffee-houses had gathered in and were holding their noisy clients about them. Aboard the schooners in the basin, lighted fires began to show, flaming against the bottoms and sides of overhanging caldrons, casting magic circles of red brightness around lounging groups of swarthy men. Through the gloom the evil night humanity that haunt such spots could be seen beginning their quest for adventures and victims, and old Zizi Mouton, hobbling on her stick, was dropping, or pretending to drop, those voudoo charms which, picked up this night around the cemetery walls, were peculiarly potent for good or for evil.

As he had accosted the sexton, the stranger accosted the old negress, and with the same inquiry, "Who is this girl Madrilène?"

He had passed the girl on the street. She was leaning against a high board fence, her basket on her head, unobservant to blindness from inward preoccupation.

The voudoo did not need to be questioned twice. "Madrilène, eh? And Madame Lai's!" She put her finger on her lip, and motioned the gentleman to follow her.

There was one person to whom Marie Madeleine could lay bare her mind — Monsieur Sacerdote. Those who dwell in the serene atmosphere of prosperity and happiness know not the findings of sympathy, love, and devotion that lie in the murky depths of poverty and misfortune. But the tie that bound Marie Madeleine to Monsieur Sacerdote was hardly the human confederacy known as friendship. If one called it a religion, one would more fitly describe it. Was it not a thing of the soul with her? An aspiration, an inspiration, the semblance of a hope, the invisibility of a faith? Where did she look for him when she sought him in her mind? At her level? On a platform of earthly elevation? Or above her in those unattainable heights in which one must be born?

He was above her; born above her. Oh, there was no doubt about that! The most audacious, the most impudent, the most infuriated, the most drunken, the lightest of the light-colored, whatever they might say, in their secret hearts, she knew, never disputed that the white are born above the black.

Was not God white to them? The Saviour white? The Virgin white? The saints, martyrs, angels, all white? The people they read of in books, were they not all white? And the people they saw on the stage? Did the whites want to change their whiteness for blackness? Did the blacks want to change their blackness for whiteness? However much they might despise old Fantome Sacerdote for his wretchedness, however much they shunned him with superstitious terror, he was what they could never be, and he was of the color of those whom they worshipped. The deduction was very simple and easy to Marie Madeleine. When she looked at him she saw the originals of the pictures that hang in churches; when she listened to him she heard them, and when she talked to him it was almost as if she were praying; only the prayers to God, once learned, were always the same. What she told Monsieur Sacerdote were the ever-new accumulations, the constant drippings day by day from the invisible into an opening mind. Into the busy mind of a waif and stray about fifteen, however, thoughts do not drip, but flood in storming torrents, particularly about the time of All-Saints.

The place where Monsieur Sacerdote passed his nights might have been blamed as being more insalubrious than where he passed his days. A high, close fence hid the interior from the curious eye, and a heavily bolted gate protected it from intrusion. The tall fence was responsible for some of the misery it hid, for the sun had a chance of entering that way at least. The

dampness trickled down the sides of these high brick walls into the little enclosure as into a well, and from the street the green moss could be seen flour-
ishing on the peaked roof of the low house, and planks had to be used to
bridge the mud from the door-step to the gate.

The superstition was not against the sexton's office — experience all over
the city refuted that. It was against the man, about whose uncanny personality the stories were never allowed to die out. He was even used as a reproach
to the hovel that sheltered him, a hovel whose wretchedness and poor appearance should have rendered it below reproach; and he was used not only
as a reproach, but a missile of insult against Marie Madeleine, not only by
Loulou in the street, but by Madame Laïs at home, and by the malicious everywhere. What she suffered from her refusal to serve the lodgers was even
less than what she suffered from her persistence in serving the sexton.

Arrived at the gate with her empty basket, she did not attempt to make
herself heard. That would have been a noisy process. She leaned, as usual,
against the fence and waited. If Monsieur Sacerdote wished to let her in, he
would come after a while and open the gate for her. If he did not, she would
go on home. Is God required to answer all prayers?

If he wished to see her, the taper floating in its glass of oil would soon be
creeping along the plank walk to the gate. The rusty bolt would resist, and
the rusty key would squeak, but, with her weight added to the outside, the
gate would finally open, and the old man would say, "My child, come in." Fancy if God should speak out and call her "my child!"

And then he would give her a book to read aloud to him — a book that for
age could have been her grandparent, and she would read aloud to him in
that beautiful reading he had taught her. No one suspected — Madame Laïs
least of all — that she could read. Because Madame Laïs would never let her
go to school, she thought that she would never learn to read. She had learned
her alphabet from the tombstones, helping Monsieur Sacerdote in his work,
during the first days of their friendship. In the cemetery the sexton would tell
her about the people in the tombs, but in his little house he would tell her
about the people in books. When she would go home at night, her head
would be filled with what she had read and what he had told her, and so she
could stand Madame Laïs — her tempers, her language, her atmosphere —
her whole world, in fact. And while Madame Laïs lay in her bed, and Madrilène lay on the floor, as in old times slaves lay in the sleeping chambers of
their mistresses, her head would be lifted far, far above her surroundings by
the ideas the books gave her. And when Madame Laïs would call her and
wake her and treat her as, let us hope, few mistresses treated their slaves, it
was still an affair of the body, and not of that soaring, inflated mind. It was
those evenings when she did not read aloud to Monsieur Sacerdote that the
walls grimaced at her, and the days came back to torment her, and the close
ladened atmosphere of the room suffocated her, and life took on terrific features. She would look far, far back in her memory for some help, but there

was none. She would look far, far ahead in the future, and still there was none. Madame Laïs behind and Madame Laïs before her, and all about her the Africanized wall of Madame Laïs's children and grandchildren. Better for her, fatherless, nameless, to be lying in the tomb with the husbandless Rosémond Delaunay than live with these husbandless, fatherless nieces and sisters of Rosémond Delaunay.

What desperations, what agonizing impotencies, did she not feel at these moments! She was so ignorant, so brutalized, so blind!

No, evidently Monsieur Sacerdote was not going to let her in this evening. She must go home. The nine o'clock bell was ringing. He never let her in after nine o'clock.

Arrived at her street, she selected among the row of ill-kept, ugly-looking back doors that faced the cemetery the one that belonged to her home. As she was about to put her hand on the latch, it was lifted from the inside, and old Zizi Mouton, bending herself more double than ever, slipped out as noiselessly as a black cat, and nimbly ran down the banquette, in the opposite direction from Marie Madeleine. "She is preparing some of her devilment," thought the girl. "She does not imagine that I have seen her."

There was loud talking inside — Palmyre's voice. Madrilène waited with her hand on the latch, listening.

Zizi Mouton, after her more than voluminous revelations, had conducted the stranger to the front door of the same house. It was as pompous as its obverse was contemptible. The placard "Chambres Garnies" swung from the gallery at the end of a long wire, just over the heads of the banquette pedestrians. Here and there on the block other placards swung and fluttered — an ominous sign for the neighborhood. The appearance of the first of such placards is the appearance of a first taint spot in the value of property in a locality — a symptom of corruption, and the forerunner of depreciation.

Chambres garnies mean different things to different people, or shall we say, different minds. A furtive visit to an involved landlord or landlady by a hesitating, heavily veiled woman; a high rent offered and guaranteed by the confidential communication and signature of some well-known name; a new light thrown on some hitherto immaculate character, or an old one rekindled from a smouldering scandal; the hesitation on the part of the property-holder between putting an insult out-of-doors or putting it into the pocket — *chambres garnies* mean this to some. To others they represent only a comfortable system of lodging where landlady and servant are harmoniously one; where references are not required, and supervision is carefully abstained from; where freedom of movement and secrecy are guaranteed. To strangers they are attractive as repositories of romance, magazines of tropical poetry, studies of picturesque domesticities, a curious half-world, legitimized on the one side by prejudice, on the other by sympathy.

A ring of the *chambres garnies'* bell fetches, after a long interval, a black boy or girl, scrubbing brush in hand, thin, poorly clad, miserable-looking, as a negro must be who serves his or her own color: has it been said that *chambres garnies* are always exquisitely clean?

A stranger would ask for Madame Brown or Madame Smith, but a townsman asks for Madame Laïs, or maybe Laïs. He then remains standing during another long interval, glancing around him.

The hall and staircase are perfectly bare, except for the foot-fall-stilling drugget. The chambers, however, unless occupied, always stand open, advertising of their handsome interiors — the velvet carpets and damask curtains, the great bedstead with lace-trimmed dressings, the *armoire à miroir*; the lavabo, with its fine porcelains and linens; the biscuit statuettes and vases of paper flowers on the mantel. Interiors of a vague, undefined, differentiating luxury, inexplicable, or it may be simply unexplicable....

A scraping rather than a rustling is heard in the upper regions — a scraping from skirts sharpened as well as stiffened by unstinted starch. They scrape down the steps slowly, for Madame Laïs is stout, and finally come to stillness and quietude before the expectant stranger. And he sees, if it is spring, summer, autumn, or winter, a long, loose, white "Gabrielle," with elaborate trimmings of ruffles and lace, that show the yellow neck and arms underneath, a yellow face, thickly dusted with white powder, and hair smoothed into a topknot with French heliotrope pomade, and a soft, fat face, whose values, not at first appreciable, begin to make themselves felt as beauty by force of certain underlying suggestions. But what the stranger sees is infinitesimal in comparison with what Madame Laïs sees. Her eyes have been trained to see as other eyes have been trained to shoot, and men, not boards, have been from time immemorial their target. What Madame Laïs sees in a stranger decides in an instant whether she has a vacant room, the price of it, the price of laundry and personal services — serving coffee in bed mornings, attendance when ill, etc. A great many apply for rooms to find them always filled. Some never apply without finding the best one vacant and at the disposition of monsieur.

If he likes the *modus vivendi,* it is very comfortable for the stranger after he is once taken in by this or another Madame Laïs. He rarely ever seeks other lodgings, and he will travel willingly year after year from one house to the other with his *chambres garnies'* hostess, who does not attach herself generally to buildings. He has his coffee punctually in the morning, and his mending and laundry without a remission. If he falls ill, he is nursed; and it is safe to say no one in New Orleans can nurse like Madame Laïs — the tenderness of a mother, the devotion of a slave, the delicacy of a wife, the unflinching patience of a hospital Sister, all combined! One never thinks of blushing before a Madame Lai's, or apologizing. One has absolutely no self-consciousness with her. One can be or do what one pleases before her with surety. There is no shocking her. That makes, in short, the merit of her class, putting them as lodging-house keepers beyond competition and rivalry. And she is comely, too, and young; or at least her daughters are, or her granddaughters, or her nieces. She sometimes nurses the stranger through life to a good old age; and when he dies, if he leaves anything — but he rarely leaves anything. If he does, however, soon after the mortuary certificate there is generally a little testament produced, written very recently — produced by Madame Laïs herself — a testament unknown of the expectant nieces and nephews. When they read this testament they thank God, perhaps, that there are no other documents produced — only witnesses. When these last are forthcoming, it is a nine-days' talk in the scandal world, if the matter gets into court. And the disinherited nieces go to sewing or piano playing for a living; that is, if the family is of the city. If they live outside or in foreign parts, they are generally saved the pain of knowing anything beyond the fact of death — unless they are contentious and sceptical. And the handsomely furnished chambers are always getting more handsomely furnished, and the petticoats are always getting stiffer, and the "Gabrielles" more elaborately trimmed, and the *chambres garnies'* granddaughters and nieces wear more and more jewelry, and drift, more and more of them, into salaried positions under the government. What Monsieur Sacerdote saw with his dull vision, Madame Laïs could not fail to see: that this stranger who applied to her at nightfall for lodgings was not "that kind of a man:" a grave, sedate, middle-aged scholar, but with eyes, for the matter of that, that gathered as much in a glance as Madame Laïs's. They were not, however, the eyes through which occupants of *chambres garnies* look at life, and his voice was not propitious.

Her rooms were all full — unalterably, irrevocably full; not even a vacancy on the highest gallery, not even the bare closet he persisted in demanding.

Madame Laï's regretted it very much in her voluble, frank, amicable way, telling of houses all around her where chambers were vacant; not two doors off was a white lady, one of the best old Creole families, who took boarders.

"Where is that loud talking?" questioned the stranger, inappropriately.

"Those young girls amusing themselves in the yard," she answered, shrugging her large shoulders.

He listened with ill-concealed interest.

Madame Laïs opened the door to facilitate his departure, but sprang back in dismay from the exposed threshold.

"Ah, misère! Ah, grand Dieu! Do not let them touch me! Kick them away, monsieur! For the love of God, kick them away with your foot!" She ran backward into the hall as far as the staircase, pointing with both hands to the spot where lay scattered a dozen or more minute paper parcels. "Ah! what is going to happen to me now? It is that old voudoo! It is that old Zizi Mouton! My God, why does she not let me alone? Kick them away, monsieur — kick them away!"

At that instant a scream sounded through the long passage-way — a call. The woman turned and ran in the direction from whence it came, the man after her.

Madrilène, outside the gate, listened to Palmyre's voice rising louder and louder.

"No one shall lay hands on my child! I will kill any one who lays hands on my child! My child is as good as any one!"

They always use extreme threats, the colored. Madrilène had heard her rage in the same way against Loulou himself; had she not, in fact, taken a hatchet to him more than once? The best way was to leave her alone, to take no notice of her; let her talk herself out until exhausted, when she would throw herself down anywhere upon the ground, upon the floor, and snore until daylight. Madrilène heard the others answering her, laughing at her. She knew, if they did that, Palmyre would keep it up all night; Madame Laïs herself could do nothing with her in that mood.

"My child is as good as any one! No one shall touch my child! I will cut any one open who touches my child!"

The men and women inside laughed again.

They were exciting Palmyre. Fools! Did they want her carried off by the police to the calaboose, as she had been not so very long ago? Madame Laïs had to pay enough money for that temper.

"I will show you! I will show you! I will break every bone in her body! The moment she comes in you will see! Oh, I'll pay her!"

The girl outside felt a thrill of terror. Would Palmyre dare, would she dare touch her? Even Madame Laïs had never dared that but once — the day, so long ago, when she had fled into the cemetery for refuge, the first clay she had ever seen Monsieur Sacerdote; the day she had begged him to leave her with the good dead, the white dead. Would Palmyre dare touch her? Would the others let her — that crowd of disorderly men and women laughing and jeering in the yard? And the cemetery was lock-fast now, and no Monsieur Sacerdote at hand!

"I will strip her naked! I will stamp her! I will make her howl!"

She could run back, she could call, she could beat on the gate, and make herself heard of Monsieur Sacerdote! But — but pass those drinking shops again? Pass all those roistering men? Go again through that dark alleyway? She was afraid. Born and raised in the streets, she was afraid of them at night; afraid of them at the very age when other colored girls frequent them. No, she was not afraid of Palmyre when she thought of the streets. Palmyre? Palmyre was afraid of her. They all were afraid of her, even Madame Laïs.

"I dare her to come in! I dare her to open that gate! I dare her like..."

The girl shrank back involuntarily. Did Palmyre suspect she was out there?

But this street was no place to stop in; this gate was known; any moment something might happen to a woman all alone at this gate, and no policeman anywhere, except, perhaps, drinking in the coffee-houses.

"Low scum of the gutters! Let me lay my hands on her! She will wish she was dead!"

A crowd of noisy men were coming along now, singing. They would think she was there purposely. Oh, she was afraid of men! Afraid of them? None of Madame Laïs's family were afraid of men. Afraid of ghosts and voudoos? yes; but men, no. And Madrilène was afraid of men, but not ghosts nor voudoos. The men were getting nearer and nearer, singing like firemen: firemen were the worst kind, or the men that follow firemen. In daylight her heart would jump and start if one looked at her. What was she afraid of? What could they do to her? She did not know; only she was afraid, afraid.

"Oh, I will make her dance!"

They laughed inside at Palmyre's wit!

The men were passing now. They had seen her. They were all around her. She flattened herself against the gate. One pinched her arm, one pinched her cheek, one — Oh, better Palmyre! She pressed the latch; the gate fell open with her weight; she was inside!

"Ha! There she is! Ha!"

"Palmyre, do not dare touch me!" she cried.

"Dare? Dare?! Oh, better the men outside than these blows, these scratches, this tearing of hair.

"Do not dare! do not dare!" she kept calling. She was still at the gate; she could still gain the street. She was almost outside.

"I will strip you first!"

Her sacque was torn with one jerk from her body. Palmyre had her safe enough now inside. Could the others not in the darkness see the blows descending upon her? Could they not hear them through the cursing and swearing that accompanied them? Did they not know that Palmyre carried a knife in her bosom — she carried her bosom naked enough for them to see it. Madrilène sprang from under the heavy arms of Palmyre to the steps, to the gallery above. Oh, if the lattice were only away, she could spring into the street below!

"I will catch you! I will cut you open!"

"Help! help!"

The naked fleshy mass crowding her, the blows, the darkness, the epithets, the hot puffing breath, the odor. "Help! help!" She felt the knife. It was cutting — cutting! "Help! help!" She knew not herself what her lips were screaming. It was a crucificial cry, an alarm not from herself, but from something within her driven to voice by extremity of pain and humiliation. "Help! help! Negroes are murdering a white girl in here! Help! help!"

It was a cry to awaken the dead in the cemetery over there, to raise and arm a mob, to paralyze the fist over her, to paralyze her own lips — an unheard-of, an unknown, an uncodified cry, an unrepeatable one! She heard the air carrying it out high over the street, shrill, quavering, forking a sudden, jagged course like lightning, rebounding from high walls, echoing in hollow alleyways, leaving behind it one dark, still, stark, void moment of suspense— and armistice.

Then hearing, clotted with the answers, the sound of voices, the tramp of running feet, opening of doors, banging of windows. "Hold on! We are coming! we are coming! Hold on!" Far off in whispers, near at hand in shouts. "We are coming! we are coming!"

She had fallen. It was dark before her eyes when they came, but she saw them: heads, heads, heads, row behind row — dishevelled coffee-house heads, glossy parlor heads, "dago" heads tied in handkerchiefs, firemen heads under helmets, the heads of the men who had pinched her cheek and arm, and women's heads, with open, screaming mouths. She had summoned a race to her rescue; they had come! How the floor trembled when Palmyre was flung upon it!

Away off, Madame Laïs's head; behind her, the head of the stranger who had ordered flowers from Madeleine in the cemetery; behind him, old Zizi Mouton's head; behind, behind, the head of Monsieur Sacerdote. And the dead were coming, too, from the cemetery — the good dead, the white dead. Far up above the ceiling she saw lights and flying bodies — all white! all white! White faces and white gowns, with paper wreaths of her own manufacture, dressed for the morrow's festival. They had come at her cry; they, too! they, too!

What noise — what confusion down below! In the room, on the gallery, in the yard, on the street. What cursing! What threats, threats, threats! Voices, leaping higher and higher in the effort to be heard, reaching her, and dragging her down to earth again.

"Is she killed?" "Hold the woman!" "Fling her to us!" "Tie her hands!" "Drag her out!" "Secure the knife!" "Police! Police!" "No police! No police!" "Fling her to us!" "A doctor!" "The coroner!"

All quiet and beautiful around her, up there by the ceiling. So sweet! so soft! But she was pulled down like a balloon to where the loud tongues of Palmyre's sisters had rallied for ready disculpation.

"Madrilène didn't do anything!" "Madrilène didn't slap Loulou!" "That she-devil Palmyre!" "I wish to God she was dead!" "I told her so!" "I held her back!" "And I!" "And I!" "And I!" "Loulou is rotten!" "Loulou rides over us all!" "Tell the truth, Madrilène!" "Tell the God's truth!" "See, she can't talk!" "She's fainted!" "She's dead!" "Palmyre cut her!" "Palmyre has no business carrying a knife!" "I tried to take it away!" "And I!" "And I!" "She's not the first girl Palmyre has cut!" "And she's won't be the last, I tell you!" "Here's the police!" "Here's the doctor!" "Lift her up, so he can get at her!"

It was the stranger who lifted her up. Some one — old Zizi Mouton — threw an apron over her shoulders.

A groan of rage fell from the crowd at the sight of the beaten girl's face. Tempers became uglier, more menacing; the shrill voices of Palmyre's sisters more pressing, more anxious.

"She's only pale!" "She's not white!" "No, sir, she's not white!" "She's a nigger!" "She's no more white than me!" "She's told a lie!" "Before God, she's not white!" "We are all niggers!" "It's only a quarrel between niggers!" "Niggers will fight!" "No, sir! Palmyre wouldn't touch a white person! Palmyre's no fool!" "Madrilène's our cousin!" "She is Madame Laïs's niece!" They all called their mother Madame Laïs; it is one of the arrangements of their class. "Madrilène knows she is the daughter of Rosémond Delaunay!" "She is buried in the colored cemetery!" "I can show you her tomb!" "Everybody knows it!" "Ask anybody!" "Ask Madame Laïs!" "Ask Madrilène herself!" And the chorus recommenced: "Tell the truth, Madrilène!" "Tell the God's truth!"

She struggled to find the ground with her feet, to put away the crowd, to say one word. They would all go away then. All — those around her, those up there. They thought she was white — white like themselves. Would the quadroon-faced come when they went away? The white garments with quadroon faces and hands?

"I — I — I am — I am not — I only — called — the knife!"

If she could only push the words between her lips! But they burst on her tongue like bubbles. She felt them, the words, in her hands; if she could only shove them where all would see them! But they weighed down her arms like the bead chaplet in the cemetery. If Palmyre only had not been so strong!

Her head fell over on the stranger's shoulder and her eyes closed, and she began again to ascend, far, far above them all, where the white forms were still waiting for her as if she, too, were white. But still the voices from earth reached her 4nd held her stationary. If some one would only cut the voices, and let her rise— rise never to come back again!

"She wanted to talk!" "See how well she looks!" "She's only weak!" "She's been bleeding!" "Hush! She hasn't been cut at all!" "She fell over a hatchet!" "He, Madrilène, how do you feel, chère?" "Madrilène, did you get the dinner I saved for you in the kitchen?" "I tried to help you, didn't I, chère?" "See, she hears me!" "Madrilène, you remember, don't you, Toinette tried to help you?" "Yes, she nodded her head." "I never did have any use for Palmyra!" "Palmyre's temper's too quick." "I love Madrilène like my sister." "Madrilène always loved me." "Who-o-o! look at all the police!" The words caused a scramble. "Here, let me go!" "Let me get away, quick!" "For God's sake, don't take me!" "I had nothing to do with it!" "I wasn't even in the yard!" "I never laid eyes on Palmyra and Madrilène all this day!" "I swear to you I have bean dressing the tomb of my grandmother!" "I came in with the crowd!" "Madrilène knows nobody was here but her and Palmyre!" "Madrilène could talk well enough if she wanted to!" "There's nothing the matter with her!" "Palmyre barely touched her!" "Take Palmyre; she was the only one!" "Take Madrilène!" "Madrilène commenced it!" "Madrilène had no right to beat Palmyre's child!" "He was doing nothing to her!" "Madrilène drew the knife first!" "I saw her do it!" "I swear I saw her do it!" "Palmyre was only funning!" "Palmyre only did it to frighten her!" "She's not hurt!" "She's only making out!" "Madame La — ïs!" "Oh, Madame La — ïs, they're taking me!" "Madame La — ïs!" "Where's Madame Laïs?" "She was here a moment ago!" "She ran back to hide!" "She ran back to lock up!" "That's right, Palmyra, you fight!" "Don't go with them!" "They've no right to take you!" "You let me alone!" "Take your hands off me!" "I won't go with you!" "Go to the devil!" "I won't go to jail!" "I wo — n't go to jail!" "Madame Laïs, oh, Madame Laïs, they are taking me to jail!" The women could be heard far down the street, drawing a procession after them.

The police tried to question the girl. She could not answer. They questioned the stranger. He gave them his name and address; he had heard threats, suspected rascality, etc. They questioned Monsieur Sacerdote, hallooing to make him hear.

"They have found Madame Laïs! They are arresting her!"

"Oh!"

"She won't come. They are dragging her along."

"Oh!"

"What does this mean? What are you doing here? What are all these people doing in my yard?"

Madame Laïs held her head thrown back, just as during the war, when she was a little girl, she remembered seeing her mistress, old Madame ---, throw her head back when invading soldiers entered her house, and she talked to the white people about her and the police not as if they were soldiers, but negroes.

"I order you to quit these premises on the instant? Where is the girl? What is the matter with her? What does she mean by screaming in that manner? Here, give her to me. Let me attend to her."

She put forward her hands to take Madrilène from the stranger; he put them aside, and felt that they were wet with perspiration and colder than Madrilène's. Her lips were trembling, too, in spite of her efforts, and her face — quadroons do not get white, they blacken for pallors — black spots settled around Madame Laïs's mouth, under her eyes, on her cheeks. In her assurance she was white; in her fear she was all negro.

"What are you doing here? What have you to do with that girl? What is this man doing here?" she demanded of the police. "It is an intrigue; it is —"

Old Zizi Mouton, crouching out of sight behind the stranger, plucked his sleeve, and whispered, "Send her to the calaboose with the others."

Madame Lai's shook the policeman's hand off her arm. It was an arm that had become accustomed to light handling. For a moment she looked the enraged quadroon, like her daughter Palmyre.

"Do not dare touch me! I will complain to the Governor! I will complain to the Mayor! I will see the chief of police! I will have you discharged! I will sue for damages!"

"Have her arrested. Send her to the calaboose," whispered Zizi Mouton.

"I have money! I have friends who will protect me! General —, Collector —, Major —, Colonel —, Dr. —, Judge —, Senator —, Mr. —."

The police themselves fell back at her resources of money and influence. The women in the mob laughed.

"Oh, the old rascals!" "Oh, that Laïs!" "Eh, mon Dieu! let me go home after that!" "You heard the names, heirs?" "Lord! Lord! Lord!" "Send her to the calaboose." Zizi Mouton plucked the stranger's arm as well as his sleeve.

"I dare you to arrest me! I dare you!" But even in the prospect of success, assurance deserted the quadroon, and fear, the ugly, gibbering African fear, took possession of her. "Sir," she pleaded to the stranger, "you were with me at the time. You know I was not here. For God's sake, don't let them arrest me. It will ruin me. The property of the boarders lies unprotected in my rooms. My house has never been visited before by the police. I will furnish bond. I — Take Palmyre! Punish her! Take the girl. Do what you please with her. Take her! take her!" Her mind was in a panic. God only knew what she feared.

The crowd made suggestions. "She is afraid they will search her house!" "She is afraid her boarders will be coming in!" "They are gentlemen who do not like to get their names in the papers!" "There might be sensations!" "It will be all up with her then!"

"What are you afraid of? Do you think I am going to run away?" continued Madame Laïs. That must have been it, for the police hemmed her in, and held her arms, and looked in her face, and the stranger made no sign of intervention in her favor.

"You want my name? Here it is."

Ah, she had a choice of names. She had only to put her hand out and take from the community. Who could contradict or deny were they graven all over her, as they were over the tombstones in the colored cemetery? But, in extremity though she was, she was discreet. She gave a name *de circonstance*. She would save the others for the great emergency.

"What is the name of the girl?"

"The name of the girl? Let her give her own name. She can talk."

She was slowly coming to assurance again.

"Make her give the name or send her to the calaboose." Zizi Mouton jostled and shook the stranger's arm,

"Everybody knows her name — Madrilene, or Marie Madeleine, if you will."

"Marie Madeleine what?"

"Marie Madeleine — nothing," shrugging her shoulders. They must understand that, these men.

"White or colored?"

A routine question — mere formality, police etiquette. But that scream! What made the girl scream that? She had often enough been asked the question, for the girl was light-colored, and Laïs had answered it glibly. She had been asked about one or two of her own children. What made Madrilène scream that? What made her scream it? Who put it in her head? What was that stranger doing there? Could he be — And old Fantome Sacerdote? Fantome Sacerdote, he knew her of old — knew her as well as the Collectors and Senators and other official military and civil dignitaries. And the time was passing. Her house must be silent, dark, discreet by midnight.

"White or colored?" the officer of police repeated, pencil and note-book in hand.

Who was that stranger? . . . White? Oh no! Say Madrilène was white! before that crowd! There was Madrilène herself. "Col —"

Whence came that lean, crooked, bent, black figure on the floor in front of her? a little bent black figure with brilliant snake eyes, and a raised stick of curling, twisting, coiling vines like snakes.

Had the room only been dark that Madame Laïs could not have seen it! But they were still fetching in lamps, candles — lights from everywhere. She opened her mouth again to answer, and she inflated her breast; her tongue was dry — a bone — and her breast too heavy to move. She lifted her head again and again. Always that voudoo stick raised before her eyes; always those voudoo eyes fastened on her face. Why, a glance from them blighted! Spells flew around them like candle bugs; she was sending them in swarms now over her: Laïs!

White powders and black powders, babies' bones and snake eggs, and those hideous hobgoblins of chicken feathers that come in pillows and mattresses, rooster combs and crossed keys, the herbs and grasses, the signs and symbols that haunt the day; and the black June nights, the flame of spirits, the coiled serpent, the writhing dance of naked black forms, the orgiac round circling in and out of shadows and light, the casting away of clothes of decency, the "tam tam" of the gourd drums, and the monotonous chant — Laïs saw them all in the floor before her, and the omnipotence of the "Evil One," and the omniscience of the "old people," and the patient vindictiveness of old Zizi Mouton, setting, setting, hatching vengeance year after year, and blackness and fear rolling over and ingulfing her. She felt her eyes grow haggard, her limbs shake. "My God! My God!" She beat the air with her nerveless hands.

But the devil, the god of Zizi Mouton, he was the Stronger god. Laïs felt that; she knew that; now, here. The god of the negro against the God of the white man! — voudooed! voudooed! voudooed!

And the burden in the stranger's arms — it rose stiff and stark before her. Was that death in the long, thin, white face? Ah, *she* got *white* when she paled; they could all see that. Were those staring eyes gazing into eternity? At God, or at her, Laïs? Was that tall, thin, pale white woman Madrilène, her servant, her drudge. "Was it *rigor mortis* that held that bruised arm extended, pointing, pointing at her, Laïs, those staring eyes looking at her, those opened falling lips? Had Palmyre been voudooed, too, to commit murder? Had Zizi Mouton brought the gallows, too, to Laïs — the gallows and hell, burning, flaming hell?

"Colored? No, no! White! White, I tell you! Do you hear me? White! Take that woman away! Take her away! Voudoo! Snakecharmer! African!"

Zizi flung Madrilene's black and white bead memorial on the floor before the quadroon.

"No, no! Take her away! She is not the daughter of Rosamond Delaunay! My God! my God!" She fell her length, with hysterical wailing.

"Eh, Laïs, coquine! Ta pé payé, chère!'" (Ah, Laïs, rascal! I have paid you up!)

In the long-worked-for moment of triumph, Zizi Mouton renounced her supernatural pretensions in favor of enjoyment of human revenge.

"The 'coon gets ahead of the nigger when she is young, but the nigger lives long, and gets even with the 'coon at last. Didn't I tell you the truth, monsieur?" To the stranger. "I was there when the gentleman died. I knew she was his child. But I waited — I waited! Ah, Laïs, coquine, you took my man — hein? Ta pé payé, chère!"

"White! White!" Oh, the other cry was nothing to this! That one filled a street, this one the world! White! It joined past to future. It lifted a being from one race to another. But it fell like the weakest sigh, this cry from the lips of Madrilène. This time she did not rise in her unconsciousness; she sank down, down, through sightlessness, dumbness, deafness, to nullity.

"Get her to a bed quick!"

"Not in there!" Zizi Mouton arrested them at the door of Madame Laïs's room. "In the fine front room! In the fine front bed! Madame Laïs knows why. White young ladies do not sleep in the bed of negroes." The old voudoo led them to the bed herself; she undid the girl's garments, flinging the head-kerchief aside. "Eh, Laïs! White young ladies do not wear tignons like negroes! He, monsieur! I knew — I knew all the time, but I waited. Send for the doctor; he will know, he will remember. Ask Fantome Sacerdote; he will remember; he buried him. Rosémond Delaunay, ha! Who said that? Madame Laïs!" Sucking the words like sugar between her toothless gums. "Ah, Laïs, coquine, ta pé payé, chère!"

The Christmas Story of a Little Church

IT was a little ugly brick church, and it had been built out of a little ugly brick house — a cheap, made-over concern. There was hardly a new brick, a new nail, or a hodful of new mortar in it. What could possibly be made use of had been left standing. Of what had been torn down, the bricks were cleaned, the mortar pulverized and sifted, and the nails extracted from the joists and beams: such a spirit of economy reigned in the erection that even the broken pieces of slate from the roof were trimmed and put in a pile by themselves, to use, instead of breaking up a new one, to fill up a corner or end a row.

The little dago girl from the end of the block was the indefatigable observer of it all, as if she wanted to learn the process, and apply it herself, too, one of these days to the changing of a house of the devil into a house of the good God. For that it was a house of the devil no one in the length and breadth of the town had much doubt — one of those consular buildings of a great potentate who never fails to provide a representative in every town. The village must be very small and insignificant indeed, and blessed, where there are not more than one of these official residents, and the villagers not enterprising, or *progressive*, as the word goes.

The neighbors had complained of the house, the servants had gossiped about it; the very garbage man, looking as if he himself had been fished out of the garbage of humanity for the office, grumbled that he had to add its leavings to the reeking contents of his cart, and when he could, neglected it, thus insuring a further malodor to the precincts; for, as he reasonably explained to any one who would listen to him, as if corroborating also a questionable fact about himself, half-drunk as usual, on account of his profession, "I is a man, if I does drive a dirt-cart."

As everything was used in the building which could be used, and very little carried away, and as the former building had been bought at a great bargain, having, it seems, depreciated the value of the land upon which it stood and the tone of the surrounding neighborhood, the conclusion was inevitable to the little girl that God was not investing much money in the affair, perhaps because He had not much to invest. It was a financial condition which Marianna understood better than any other, for the oyster and orange trade slackened at times to a degree where there seemed to be no cohesion left, and dago life almost hung on one cent more or one banana less to the price, and the street could hardly contain the amount of Sicilian *patois* expended to obtain either, when the little Marianna with her nursling was forced to wander abroad for the ordinary peace and comfort necessary to the human mind, dago or otherwise. It was in this way she saw so much of the building of the church, and found out that money was as scarce in heaven as on earth.

"When will it begin to be a church?" she questioned herself. The foundations were laid down and the walls went up, but in no manner different from an ordinary dwelling or shop, and nowise more churchly. It was evidently to be a sudden transformation. Afraid of missing the critical moment, she was at her post, a door-step opposite, in rain or shine, as regularly as the bricklayers were at theirs, persistently looking: thanks to the baby's constitution, she could do it. If it had been any other baby it would have died long ago, of croup, or colic, or such great broad teeth, or ennui, or over-dieting on bananas; but fortunately there had been no mistake — a regular dago baby had been sent to the dago family; one with black hair and black eyes, and an orange skin that grew out of dirt into cleanliness like an orange, and demanded (not that it would have got it for the demand) no expenditure in the way of washing.

"How did the workmen know God wanted a church built?" "Who paid them?" "Who gave them orders?" "Were the workmen who built churches different from the workmen who built dago houses, for instance?" "Did they feel they were building a church?" "If they didn't build it well, what happened to them?" Marianna's mind was constantly occupied with such interrogatories. It was a *Sicilian* mind, and had not been subjected to the tamperings of education or religion, although public schools offered the one in every district of the city, and churches in every parish begged to distribute the other.

Suddenly one day the cross was put upon it, a gray painted wooden cross; and then the building became a church as quick as a flash of lightning. One moment before it might have been taken for a warehouse or a tall stable; but now there could be no mistake. The cross said it all, and said it well. It was the crown of thorns which changes the face of a simple sufferer into the face of a Saviour. It was the door-plate which tells who lives within, and the child sanctified the edifice in her mind accordingly, and, ugly or little, saw not its proportions nor defects henceforth.

As for the church itself, if it had not been a church it must have felt shamed, humiliated, degraded. Not only made of second-hand material, but completed in such niggardly fashion that with the exception of the dago cabin, the Chinese laundry, and the locksmith's shop, it was the meanest house on the block. The boarding house opposite was a palace in comparison, the freedmen's drinking saloon at the corner more imposing; as for the drinking saloons for the fashionables, on the fashionable street, the papering of one of them alone would have paid for the church and the ground underneath, not to mention the mirrors, pictures, marbles, and cellars.

In fact, the little church could look nowhere from the elevation of its cross and not find indeed that, judging from appearances, God was the very poorest person in all that neighborhood. There were club-houses around the corner the initiation fee of which alone was a minister's salary, and beyond the club-houses the grand bric-a-brac shops, the milliners' shops, where the body is clothed and beautified at such a price that the merest trifles on the counter are doubled in value to pay for the grandeur of being sold there; and still, beyond all this the cross could penetrate and see other expenditures and displays: it is better to imitate the ignorance of the little girl, and not enumerate them. What would become of little girls in a great city if God did not frustrate the devil by limiting their comprehension? for the prince of darkness holds no intercourse with fools.

But the cross did see it all, and the little church, if any knowledge of its pre-existence survived in its brick and timber, must have thrilled with joy to think that the cross did stand on top of it at last — stood up there to watch and to see, aye, and be seen too, a sign as well as a symbol of regeneration.

If the church could feel this, and the very wooden cross on top, what must the parson have felt! He was small too, so small that he certainly could not have carried his heart, not one day's work of it, around inside his cassock. He was insignificant looking, and as pale as a whitewashed house which the owners cannot afford to paint. He looked somehow second-hand too, something thrown away from a different use and picked up cheap, a made-over sinner. To judge from his appearance, he also was small recommendation of his employer. Any of the handsome, well dressed gentlemen in the boarding house opposite would have made more creditable ministers; or any of the clerks in the bar-rooms, for bar rooms are more particular about their ministrants than churches are. Three-fourths of the men who thronged the bar-rooms were better equipped physically even when they came home at night, some of them stumbling against the electric-light poles. As for the clerks in the other shops, they were better dressed and better cared for than the Reverend Herbert Sting, or they would not have been employed there. Even his name was about the poorest and least attractive in all the catalogue of human appellations, as well as the most inappropriate, he having wandered far away from any inheritance of those qualities which made it a complimentary ancestral title. When people had objected to his size, figure, color of his hair, expression of his face, accent, nose, eyes, clothes, and walk, they filed one more protest against the whole business and connection by, if they were women, condemning the incongruous name of Sting. But he did not recognize this in the least. He was as unconscious of the objections against his name as the little Marianna was of the objections against her neighborhood. He pursued his way as indomitably as if he had been called St. Paul or St, Augustine, or the British peerage rifled to celebrate his aristocracy.

We all know, though the little girl did not, whence the money and directions came for the new church building. The primal source, if divine, was a little mixed. The congregation of the parish, through its official mind, the vestry, had gradually found out that their church was simply doing a breaking business; that while the new theatre, started on a venture next door, was paying dividends on its investment, while new and varied shops multiplied and throve all around, while each establishment could pay and did pay for its scores of clerks, its light, full wear and tear, and patronage on the increase, their venerable granite edifice had to confess to a precarious income and a diminishing membership, not in a month fetching as many to a sermon as went in one evening to the ballet, not in a year taking in all its alms-basins as much as went into the till of the least patronized saloon of them all in a month. They could not, do what the financiering vestry would, make the two ends meet — the debt and credit ends — without a break in the middle to sprout out in another cancerous debt. And so the fact was no longer to be disguised that the old church, which had risen out of the early virtues, was slowly sinking under the later vices of the city — sinking as surely as at one time it was believed all stone buildings would sink and disappear in the marshy soil of the place. They reduced and reduced the salary of the minister until living within it was a feat of prestidigitation; they lowered and lowered the gas bill until service became an effort of memory; as for fires, the zeal of devotion was all the guarantee the blood could obtain against rheumatism, neuralgia, and catarrh; and then, when these measures had also reduced the congregation and certified the financial failure, they determined to sell the church and transport the proceeds of the whole establishment into a more progressive, enterprising district, to plant their cross where souls would not only come to be saved, but pay for it. As for the vicious souls round about who had neglected their opportunities and obligations, they were to be left quietly behind in the evacuation, to make what terms they could with the enemy.

After a little advertisement and judicious puffing the old church was sold — all sold, with the ground it stood upon; its outfit and its infit too, though this was not mentioned in the deed of transfer. Its consecration, its dedication, the pious will of the old gentleman who had bequeathed the lots to the parish, its memories and associations, its spirits of dead ministers who had read and preached from its pulpit, with the spirits of dead congregations who had sat under them in the pews; the graces strengthened by confirmation, the hungers stilled by the Lord's Supper, the marriage troths plighted at the altar, the baptismal vows taken at the font, and the cold dark place in front where the dead rested one moment more in church, amid life, to hear once more the promise of resurrection, ere they went their way to the tomb to await its fulfilment — all sold, with the roofing and flooring and guttering, the glass and slate and gas fixtures.

"Sold out of house and home on account of failure in business," the Saviour like any one else.

Walking around the banquette which had once encircled the church, day after day, night after night — for the spot had a fascination for him — the Reverend Herbert had strange thoughts and fancies, particularly at night, the unreal thoughts and fancies that spring from unknown seed in the virgin soil of a young mind.

Did not the stars hanging so low over the low fiat city, threatening to fall with their weight and brightness into it — did not the stars miss the tall square steeple which thrust itself up among them, and made of them jewels to ornament its weather-beaten head? And the moon, shedding its benefaction of light over all buildings alike, good and bad, humble and rich, did it, in the monotonous expanse of roofs and chimneys, look for the peaks and gables which it must have been a delight to gild and beautify? The sun, rising damp and red from the marsh, had always sent its first rays over them, and its last also, as like a great fire-ball it sank hot and dry into the river. The atmosphere, once ploughed by the vigorous bell, had closed in over the space now, and rippled with many sounds and noises, but none which could have rejoiced it like the brazen clang which seemed to dissipate the clouds of rainy Sundays and dominate the violent thunder.

The little minister could always see the church, however, a ghastly, airy structure, hovering over the old foundations in purified resurrection, and he loved to think he could see, though he knew he could not, the figure of the ancient proprietor, wandering around his alienated domain incognito like some deposed, ill-treated heir, without rancor, but in all love and forgiveness looking after those interests connected with his property, those entailed possessions which could not be sold or bartered without his consent: a little singing beggar-girl, a gambling newsboy, a desperate woman, or an unprincipled man — the outcast, the cripple, the inebriate. Wherever he imagined this white clad, barefooted visitor going, there went Herbert. He bent over what he saw Him bend over, he touched what he saw Him touch, he spoke what he heard Him utter. He accompanied Him into places where none but He and the police could go with impunity, and he ministered with Him at times when no police could have been paid to remain. He never faltered in thought or deed. In truth, if all the wickedness in the world had been stored for deposit in Herbert's heart, he could not have known more about it, been less shocked at it, and if he himself had invented all loathsome diseases of the soul and body, he could not have more readily applied the antidote or suggested the alleviation.

Indeed, in the delirium of agony sufferers would sometimes take him, the accessory, for his principal, and so hail and bless him, notwithstanding the contradiction of his threadbare clothes and homely features.

As he saw the old church pulled down, the idea came to Herbert that another one must be built in the place of it. The idea came not only to him, but to all those who could not afford to ride in the cars to the desirably progressive locality selected by the vestry for the new church; to all those who had attached themselves like cats to the old locality, for romantic reasons, over which they, like cats, have no control; to all the constitutional kickers against authority, civil or religious; to all lukewarm enemies or lukewarm friends of the empirical vestry; to the Sunday school children who felt perhaps, and were, more aggressive than all. The idea came to a sufficient variety and number to warrant co-operation in an effort, and the effort was sufficiently vigorous to bring from an idea into being the identical little church of this story.

It is almost as much labor to destroy as to build a church. They could not shoot it down with cannon, they could not burn it down in the good old way. The carpenters did the best they could, poor men, with their peaceable instruments and peaceable hearts, reversing the natural order of their profession, travelling down from the topmost spire of the steeple, prizing out posts, chiselling out bricks, brick by brick, down to the foundation. The first tap of the hammer sounded to poor Herbert like a slap on a dead giant's face.

It was all so solid, so massive, the plan was so perfect, the materials so good, the workmanship so honest! If it had only been a prosperous church it might have lasted ages. Nothing would totter, nothing would fall, nothing would even shake itself loose; it was a unanimous position of resisting protest, passive stability: "I can be destroyed, but I cannot surrender."

At last it was all taken down, and the dismembered parts buried, contractors only knew where, second-hand stuff from churches fetching no higher price than from any other edifice. The space was cleared and swept, and with bright new material a grand circus was erected in it, a show and a wonder to the banquette idlers. The ring was described in what had been the body of the church, the trapezes hung from the ceiling, the orchestra sat in the old altar. Through the doors on the side, where surpliced boys and ministers used to march singing, the horses pranced and clowns tumbled and velocipede girls whirled. A grand novelty circus, so it was, a magnificent circus, and patronized by such numbers that managers and performers were not only paid, but munificently paid, and were making a happy fortune out of it. So much so that if the church people had only had the wit to do themselves that which they had sold out for others to do, they would have been able to construct a grand cathedral in the new fashion locality, and paid people well for attending it.

The circus was octagonal, with arched sides, and under every arch were places of attractive resort of all kinds, and so attractive that at night frightened inhabitants screamed, whistled, rattled in vain for policemen, until some volunteer would hasten thither and fish the officer of justice out of one of the octagonal rooms, as surely as a boy in spring-time fishes larvae out of a wasp's nest.

The minister thought many a time what a miraculous draught St. Peter would make again if he could but cast his net over the whilom place of worship!

When the little dago girl had nothing more to look at, when walls, roof, floor, and cross were in place, pews carried in, shavings and blocks carried out, workmen dismissed, she naturally concluded that the church was completed and ready for the abode of Him to whom it belonged. She knew no more of the inside workings of a church than of the inside workings of a clock, and Herbert was very little wiser than the child, for it was his first church. The quantity of springs and machinery necessary was indeed enough to surprise and confuse a tyro. The ladies came in, whence neither he nor any one else could tell; they swarmed about the church like insects about sugar; only they possessed what insects lack, organization. By authority of what tradition, by order of what transmissions or laying on of hands, in what version of the Testament, Old or New, they read their title and commission, or whether they had any authority, divine or human, for it at all, whether the whole legislation was not an unwarranted act of assumption, Herbert did not question or investigate the matter. He quietly submitted, and with his church bowed under the guild to whose mysterious care the parish had by occult power been confided. The guild was composed of chapters, and the chapters were so numerous that every active worker was fractionally represented in them, to look after some fractional division of the church, the service, and the minister. It takes a very large church to woman all its chapters, and provide meeting-places for them. Judge how the little church was taxed for both, when they all came together — condensed, as it were — on special occasions: Building, Altar, Vestment, Choir, Library, Sunday-school, Industrial School, Mission, Visiting chapters, with presidents, vice-presidents, secretaries, treasurers, and members. They atoned for the smallness of their number by the multitude of their opinions; they represented not a volume, but a library of dissenting sentiments worthy the greatest church in the land. There were just about days enough in the week to contain the meetings, and none left over for pacification, except Sunday, which grew in importance as a kind of "Truce of God," without which church business would have been an unfinished story. For instance, whoever crossed Mrs. Bunnyfeather in the Altar Chapter, crossed the secretary of the Choir, the president of the Visiting, the treasurer of the Sunday-school, and the vice-president of the Library chapters, and broke a quorum in all the other chapters. And when Mrs. Goodenough (which is a name the constitution should forbid) was made to weep by unkind remarks over the laundrying of the Reverend Herbert's one vestment — a shrunken, narrow, transparent surplice — parliamentary rules were suspended by acclamation until the sensitive lady was soothed and the remarker rebuked, for it was an early Monday morning, and never a meeting could have been held during the week. After he had learned by practice and discipline to steer clear of organizations, the young minister found that he could not walk from portal to pulpit without tripping against individual solicitude. The motherly ones were always there to tender advice, the sisterly ones to ask it; and poor as he was pecuniarily, and thin and miserable to look at, there was not a mother among them who did not accuse some other mother of trying to catch him for a daughter, and not a sister whose heart did not occasionally beat with ill-feeling against some other sister on account of him.

But though to the pastor they all appeared to be pulling in as many different directions as there were names in the chapters, the general tendency was
forward, and the new little church was jerked and pulled and tugged along
through October, November, and into December without more than one seri-
ous stalling a week, and a jar a day. If they had not been women, and the man
a Herbert, it would have jolted into some big rut and stayed there forever, a
wreck on time, and never have reached December at all, not to speak of
Christmas Eve.

The little Marianna had changed her position. She had crossed over the
street, and now sat with the baby in her arms in a corner of the stone steps.
Sheltered from the rain, there was little cold to dread; the bright blue sky
overhead was as Sicilian as her own hair and features. She silently watched
the entrances and exits of the young priest, as she called him, the assembling
and disbanding of the various yet unvaried committees, theorizing, perhaps,
on the passers-by, who seemed to be arbitrarily separated in kind and degree by the different hours of the day, and walked along in their different
costumes on their different avocations, as if fulfilling some predestined fate
rather than individual volition. The passersby must have theorized about
her. Immovably constant, she was to them as fixed in her place as if she had
been built there with the church, or sculptured and set up for ornament. A
pretty ornament, and not inappropriate, for she had the proper turn of the
neck, the proper droop of the shoulders, the sweet, modest, soft eyes, and the
proper clasp of the arms around an infant which God has given to her nation
that sculptors might have a model, that painters might paint, and mankind
know the portrait of the Madonna.

The young priest sat almost as immovably indoors when the church business was all transacted, the chapters all gone, and he and the good Lord were
in the way of no one except Mrs. Bunnyfeather, who worried over his conduct, thinking it altogether inexplicable, if not improper, not to mention Ro-
manistic, necessitating a new chapter — Ministerial Conduct.

One evening in December, at the time when the sinking sun made rain-
bows through the western windows, and his thoughts travelled easiest the
heavenward journey, a woman rushed up the aisle of the church to the altar,
a pale, wild-eyed woman, holding a bundle in her arms.

"Will you christen her, sir? — will you christen her? For God's sake christen her, to save her soul!" She held the bundle towards him, and began to
untie, unwind, untwist it, with fingers all disobedient and astray as to their
proper vocations, and so slow that her feet began to give way, and she would
have fallen on her hopelessly entangled bundle if the minister had not caught
it with one hand, while with the other he eased her to the ground.

"I'm only dizzy, sir — I'm only dizzy and weak. I've just been discharged
from the Charity Hospital."

She lay back against the steps of the altar and closed her eyes. Shade after
shade of gray and blue pallor palled over her thin, pinched features. Her long

limbs lay as stiff and straight under her calico gown, as they had lain under the sheets of her cot at the hospital. And as she vibrated back and forth in and out of unconsciousness her cheek sank wearily against the step, as if it were a soft pillow, or turned away from it, repulsed by the coldness of the timber. She did not attempt to rise nor to look at him, but talked along dreamily, almost deliriously.

"The Sisters would have christened her, but I wouldn't let them. They would have put her in one of their asylums. The Sisters would have christened her and put her in an asylum. The Sisters —"

She became conscious of the repetitions of her tongue, and by a struggle raised herself to a sitting posture and relieved her thoughts.

There is no telling how old a sick woman is. As she lay on the ground she looked weazened and shrivelled; yet her way of hiding her face in her arm, and her petulant opposition, were very childish.

"There's no need for her to be damned too, is there, sir?"

The face that looked out from the shawl was as old as the mother's, and so red and wrinkled, and with such an unpromising outlook for the soul, that the minister felt he could assume the responsibility of a decided negative.

"They said she was a fine child; Tm sure she's very pretty; don't you think so, sir?"

There was a huge stone font, which the guild had begged from a pious stone-cutter. It was as large as a child's bath-tub, and not unlike one in shape — a font in which babies by the half-dozen could have been immersed. And there was a small pitcher of water which the kind old colored sexton daily placed in a corner of the choir for the minister's refreshment. As careless of the ritual as the Saviour had been before him in all his ceremonies, ignoring the printed requirements of his prayer-book, and trespassing against ecclesiastical etiquette in almost every word and gesture, Herbert administered the rite, humbly praying on his own behalf, at the end of it, that the good Lord would stand by him on the last day, when his bishop, before which dignitary ministers like Herbert are the worms of the earth, should find out the full irregularity of the proceeding.

"What is her name?" he asked, not in the formal conventional tone, for he did not venture to bring the dignity of the Church into the transaction; it was only a matter of a fortnight-old soul, between the Lord and himself.

The woman had risen. He saw now that she was really young, and had been pretty.

"Oh, sir," with a twist of her head, "do you think Daisy would be too good for her? Daisy is such a beautiful name! I read about a Daisy once in a novel."

Decidedly she was very young. He christened her Daisy, and cast about for some saint with whom he might take a liberty. He remembered his mother, a saint, though not in the calendar; her name was Elizabeth; so he made up "Daisy Elizabeth," and for what an informal baptism was worth the little child in his arms lay indebted.

"I can carry her now, sir; I was only a little weak. I should have left the hospital yesterday, my time was up; but the Sisters wouldn't let me. It was raining, so they made me stay one day longer."

She was standing right in a rainbow, looking through the colors younger and younger, prettier and prettier; the church was already beginning to get dark in the corners.

"The Sisters were very kind; they would have put her — But I was an asylum girl myself, sir."

Oh, the mother-lack and the father-lack in that plaintive confession! It sounded through the little church like a wail from all the sun-bonneted, uniformed little girls foredoomed to heart misery in asylums. She turned, and with uncertain feet, unaccustomed to her light weight, went out of the church.

It was a fiction of his imagination, and he knew it; but if the good Lord had been there, He would have followed her, would have taken the young woman under the arm and conveyed her to a sure, comfortable retreat, just as Herbert thought he saw Him do, just as Herbert did himself.

There were questions to be asked, information statistically useful to be obtained. As a clergyman he was empowered to satisfy his curiosity; but he had none. Why should he surmise sixteen instead of knowing it? why steadfastly overlook her marriage finger? — who she was? — what she was? — a little woman with a child — a new mother in the world with a pathetic body staggering from the ordeal, and a heart most carefully, most femininely concealed.

She walked rapidly, trying to look businesslike, trying to deceive people. But the white women they met looked their comments; the black ones uttered theirs coarsely with laughter, glad to find a flattering equality of vice; and the men — she shrank and winced at every one that passed, clinging more and more helplessly to the arm that supported her.

The sun, as usual, had saved cityfuls of warmth and brightness for Christmas week, and was up bright and early Christmas Eve, eager to commence the donation. In the gardens the bushes had still a reserve stock of flowers all ready to blossom out when the sun gave the signal. May must have effected a change with December; for if ever a bright, joyous, exhilarating, bouncing May rushed in rosy and laughing, among the months of the year with exaggerations of warmth, show, glitter, sunshine, and blue sky, that month, or week of it, came on the 24th of December to a certain city, and fell all in a heap around a certain church. And the largesses of nature were imitated, if not surpassed, by the people. All the poor had to do was to name their menu for Christmas dinner, and they got it, and the older, the poorer, the uglier, the more disreputable, the more certainty of getting it. Christmas-trees sprouted in every asylum, and if ever orphans had occasion to forget the loss of parents they had it that night. Sunday-schools, yielding and consenting, finally embraced foolishness, and spent money hoarded for foreign missions on cakes, candy, and lemonade for the heathen at home. Santa Claus was expected ubiquitously in all the hospitals in the city at once, and anticipation thwarted anodynes in the children's wards. The generous gave until they almost destroyed all prospects for future giving; the mean and stingy gave; even the rich and fashionable gave. The commercial exchanges all gave, and the clubs almost got a majority in favor of the annual motion for a grand newsboys' dinner. The butchers sent complimentary roasts, the grocers cordials, the confectioners bonbons, to their customers. From the city went oysters, oranges, and good wishes to the country; the country responded also with eggs and monstrous turkey-gobblers. There may have been some unfortunates who did not receive, but there were none who did not yield to the season, climate, and the prodigality of their natures by giving. If there were any babies born on Christmas Eve — and there must be some, for it is said they are born half-minutely all over the world — and if they had any recollection whatever of the blessed kingdom they had left, they must have stifled their sharp birth-cry of disappointment, pain, and regret, for this spot of earth was so full of goodwill, so bright, so redolent of flowers and peace, that they could not have been otherwise than glad to come here.

"But," thought Herbert, walking his beat from the old church to the new, "the reachings of money are limited. There are other wants that need other currency. Empty hearts may be hung like empty stockings on Christmas-trees this night which no Santa Claus is coming to fill — the mother who sits by an empty cradle, the husband who stretches out his arms in the dead of night for his absent wife, and the wife swathing her bleeding heart in widow's weeds. The old pensioners, looking around vainly in their eleemosynary shelter for comrade, kith and kin, to pass the feast-night, chide death for tarrying. The old maid, my cousin Ruth, who sits in a grudging home sewing for another's children, who mock at her loneliness and lovelessness, sees, alas! the vision of her own children that might have been! And the old bachelor sitting in his club window, drinking whiskey-and-water to keep up his spirits and frighten away the ghosts of the past, the realities of the present, his sordidness, meanness, selfishness, what exorcism does he exercise against them? An asylum boy or a sick child in the hospital is happier on Christmas Eve than he!"

Night had fallen as low as it could over the broad brilliant street. The tall electric light poles held the darkness aloof like a canopy over a saturnalia. The deep, narrow shops from under their beetling galleries gleamed out Golconda splendors. In the show-windows jewels and. precious metals, brocades and laces, pictures, porcelains, fans, feathers, and crystals, were displayed as mere advertisements of the greater beauties within. Violets, roses, and jasmines mingled their fragrance on the flower corner, and almost beautified— so sweet and fresh they were — the withered, faded faces of their venders, the flower girls of half a century ago. The banquettes held their usual kirmess of nations: white, black, yellow, in rags, in silks, in velvets, old,

93

young, middle-aged, handsome and hideous, and a babel of tongues that taxed the versatility of the noisy itinerant peddlers with their new stock of wares, impudence, and wit for Christmas Eve.

Christmas was setting in in earnest, the tropical, maddening, typical Christmas of the place; Christmas that comes but once a year, to make good the long, dull, hot days of summer; to defy the chill, pleasureless days of old age; to remind young and old of the shortness of life and the sweetness of it. The horn -blowing had commenced, too — all sorts of horns, blown by all sorts of lips: great horns, borne on the shoulders of tall men, bestridden by manikins, and blown by a united effort; little horns tooted by street ragamuffins, impudently blown in the faces or maliciously blown in the ears of the dignified and unwary; horns by scores, by fifties, by hundreds, matching the lights by their multitude, involving ears as well as eyes in their confusion; joyous, melancholy, melodious, and discordant horns; horns that produced tunes, and horns that were barren of all but noise; exciting, fretting, whipping up the blood, kindling it like tinder, sending it off in screams and explosions like the firecrackers that danced on the streets under the horses' feet. And the subtle nocturnal influences; the excitation of money spending, the delicious consciousness of losing self-control, the extravagances, the unrestricted expressions, the hilarity, the equalities, the friction of humanity, the grotesque banquette procession, where out of strange faces gleamed eyes bright with incipient contagion of vicious blood: it was Christmas with a latent symptom of orgy in it!

Herbert looked not above for the aerial spires of the old church, nor about for the Vision which usually guided his steps; it was not His hour yet. He hastened on and around the corner, and reached his own little church. His hand was on the door to close it. "Should every house be open and hospitable on this His birth-night and not His own sanctuary? Who am I, that I should selfishly be His only guest?" He propped it wide open, as if for service, and entered the gray gloom inside. The electric light over the way threw a mild radiance up the aisle to the steps of the chancel, garnished for the morrow's feast.

The labors of all the committees of ladies had ended, and so, he hoped, had their wranglings over the decorations. The wranglings were not to be charged to their discredit, for the excitement of the day was upon them, and the vexing contrast between the poverty of their own and the wealth of other churches. Their hearts (foolish women's hearts) hankered after possibilities beyond attainment, their spirits grieved over the acute disappointment of what could not be, and their tongues became partisans and disseminators of discontent. If the motto had been "Discord and Ill-will," instead of the contrary, it would have been far more appropriate to the state of mind which pervaded the discussions as to where it should be hung.

He had a lamp in the choir and books for evenings when he felt inclined to pursue the vast science of theology, of which he was so lamentably ignorant.

He waited to-night, however, until his eyes had become accustomed to the quieting obscurity and his ears delivered of the noisy abandonment of the street sounds in the church.

It was not to be denied that the preparations were meagre, hardly less so than those on the original night in the stable. Nothing but greens and mosses from the swamp, to be got at the small expense of hiring a cart to haul them in. They garlanded the rails and table and desk and the huge font, which resembled, indeed, a veritable manger. The dimly transparent windows, three on each side, piercing the thick walls, looked with their pendent wreaths like marble tablets with funereal cypress memorials to the dead. The effect would not have been festal were it not for the star. It shone over the altar on a shield of green — the donation and triumph of Mrs. Goodenough, the humiliation of Mrs. Bunnyfeather. A beautiful star (frosted with some glistening powder), a white, radiant, diamond star, a gleaming spirit star, a silvery effigy of the joyous living ones in the heavens outside, shining on its green shield as if from the cavernous mouth of some subterranean mystery. For it did shine and gleam and glisten in the dark damp church for all the world as its celestial prototype shone and gleamed and glistened in the East above the trackless desert to the astonished eyes of watching shepherds. Whether helped thereto by unseen celestial sources or by some reflected, refracted contribution from outside electricity, or whether it burned with an effulgence cleverly contrived by Mrs. Goodenough, it was the star's own secret where the illuminating power came from; and the eloquence, too, with which it spoke to the little minister, speaking as it spoke nineteen centuries ago, driving him to his knees as it drove the shepherds to their feet, forcing him to bow his head and hide his face in the moist, odoriferous leaves of the chancel rail — that was the star's secret, too.

> "Out of the night.
> Into the light,
> Star of Bethlehem, lead!"

A band of negro singers paused on the steps outside, trying their voices together before starting on their Saturday night round, stringing their improvised rhymes to suit the occasion, carelessly hitting or missing the sense to satisfy sound, the accordion playing an interminable pulsating accompaniment.

> "Out of the soil,
> Out of the toil.
> Star of Bethlehem, lead!"

They walked away, the weird, thrilling falsetto, a ventriloquial voicing of a distant woman's plaint, griped the heart like a spasm. Fainter and fainter they sang, keeping step down the street, trailing the tune after them long after the words were swallowed up in the blare of horns, the fusillade of fire-crackers, and the indistinct murmur of tumult that surged and rolled like a near tempest.

"Let us stand in here, Harry; I can tell you better. There's such a din out there. It's a church — a little church."

A woman led the way in, more at home, as women are, in churches. She caught the man by the hand and drew him up the aisle, in the path of light, out of danger of overhearing or being seen from the street.

"It's a church, but God knows we mean no harm or disrespect." She had the soft accent of English that has grown alongside of French. She barely came up to his shoulder — not that she was so small, but he was so tall. He had length, breadth, and strength in him for two men.

"Well, what is it, Janey?"

His low voice was rich and sweet with love and premature concession. He must have taken both her hands in his while he said it.

"No, no, Harry; don't touch me. I —"

Now that the time was come, she did not know how to begin it. Should she begin it at all? How sweet not to! To go on and on in uncertainty, but in love; to vacillate another fortnight, and then another, to temporize!

"Is it about to-morrow, Janey?"

"Yes, Harry." She was more resolute than her voice. "I want to tell you I can't; indeed I can't. You must give me back my word; I cannot keep my promise."

"Janey! Janey! are you in earnest?"

"It's no use, Harry; I've tried and tried. I thought I would be able to do my duty to both; but it's no use. I made up my mind to-day, and Christmas is as good a time as any. When I saw everybody to-day so pleasant and happy — ah, me!" She stopped a moment. "It's been before me for some time. To go away from the children now is simply to give them over to the bad; the only chance for them to be better is for me to stay with them. I've waited and waited with hope and courage; I'm at the end of both; and I thought that Louisa one day would make an effort; but she has less thought, less industry, than ever. I thought that father would. The boys, I mean — the boys are getting worse and worse. Never a day but I expect to be called home by some dreadful messenger, ever since Johnnie was run over by the dummy. They curse; they smoke; they run the streets from morning till night; they will not go to school; they will not do anything but hang around the corner groceries and theatres. It will be drinking next, I suppose; and gambling and pistols and knives, if not the gallows at the end!"

"Why, Janey, Janey, little woman!"

"No, Harry. The time has come for me to do something about it. I fear I have not done my duty. It rises before me at night, when I go to bed, that it might all have been different. Instead of working out, I should have worked at home. My thoughts go too much to you; they should all go to them. How can I think of leaving them forever! Who would feed them? Who would look after them? What would become of them? What would become of my peace of mind?"

"Bring them all with you, Janey! bring them all with you!"

"No, Harry; you know I cannot; I will not do that. Besides, there's father. There's only one thing to do. I must give up trying to do two things. God has settled my life for me. He has put those children in my charge, and father. And, Harry, you must find some one else to be your wife, some one who can bring more to you than I — more heart, more time, more youth, more beauty, less disgrace and shame. If it had been different! Harry, it is harder on me than on you! Harry, Harry, you should help me out!"

She would not let him touch her, but all the time her hands were holding fast to his arms, to his hands, travelling over the front of his coat.

He did not help her out at all, listening to her speech in dull, dazed silence.

"Instead of getting married to-morrow as I promised, we must part; and — and it is better I should never see you again." Through the incoherence of mind and thought there was a driving determination in her mind which urged her on with desperate recklessness of the pain in her heart and the pain in his. "May God keep and bless you, Harry! and may some other woman love you as I do, and be to you what I cannot!" She raised herself on tiptoe, and put her hands up to his face, her fingers sinking in his soft bushy beard. She pulled him down to her, seeking his lips in the dark with her lips, and kissed him once, twice.

"Janey! Janey! If you throw me off, you throw me to the devil!"

"Harry! Harry!" she screamed; "don't, don't say that!"

She put her arms out again towards him; he was gone. "Harry!" She ran out of the church after him, down the steps, up the street; he was nowhere to be seen. She crossed from one side street to the other, looking for the tall, straight, burly figure. She heard a step behind her, and paused; it sounded familiar; she had to press her hands down over her beating heart.

"My pretty one!"

She struck at the proffered hand and leering, unknown face. "If Harry were only there to protect her!"

In her flight from insult she instinctively abandoned her search, and breathless, trembling, flew homeward.

Harry had only turned aside in the vestibule, avoiding her in the dark as she ran after him. He came back into the church, and sat on a bench.

He knew so little about women, though he knew and loved one.

He bent his head down on his crossed arms, swaying his body from side to side under the mastery of passion which took the form of ungovernable rage, and swept all his reticence away.

"Curse it all! — all! — her father, her family — throw me off! — like a dog! — pretend to love me! Lies! lies! lies! I'll make her repent! I'll —"

A light touch fell on his shoulder. It was not Janey, although it was a figure not any larger, a voice fully as soft and tender.

"Harry," said the minister — he knew no other name to call him by — "I heard it all, and —"

"I don't care who heard it! I don't care if the whole city heard it, from Carrollton to the Barracks!"

"Hush! you have forgotten she told you this was a church."

"I'll leave it. What did she bring me here for? I'll get out of it. I'll go on the street."

"Will you go after her?"

"I go after her? I speak to her? May God — I'll cut her on the street! I never want to lay eyes on her again! I'll disgrace her! I'll drink, I'll—"

He could think of nothing more certain to hurt her than injury to himself.

"I'll go to the devil! Oh, she'll regret it! She'll repent it!"

"Why should she do it?"

"Why! why! I know why. They've bedeviled her and pestered her at home till she's 'most crazy. They've worked her till she's got no heart, body, nor soul left. They've dragged her down and down till her pride is gone, and she's ashamed even of me. Some of the brats have done something — the devil himself isn't up to more rascality than they — or her old daddy has gone on another spree, been locked up, or kept her up all night abusing her. Her wages are used up, and this Christmas Eve, when all the world is a-pleasuring and frolicking, she must go home and sew till daylight to buy bread and meat for them. It's — it's —" His temper rose with a sudden bound. "Is't a hell, this world? — the whole world?"

The pews shook under the stroke of his clinched fist.

"You love her, then?" Herbert alone knew whether it were a question or a logical conclusion in his own mind.

"Love her? I swear to you, sir, as God Almighty hears me, I never loved any woman on earth but her, and she knows it. I never shall love any other woman. I ain't given to talking about it. I couldn't even tell her. There's no one knows it or understands it but myself. If I were to think of it, sir, I wouldn't work another lick. She isn't pretty, and she doesn't look young any more, and she's worked to a shadow; but God knows, if I was on my death-bed, and life would be given me to marry the prettiest girl in the world and not her, I'd turn my face to the wall and die. I want her! I want her!"

His face went again into his arms.

"And to think she could throw me off like a dog! I might just as well go and jump into the river. It's the end of it all. It is not the look that is in her, sir." He was up again and talking. "It is the look about her. It's the pale face and the sad eyes; it's the poor, thin, tired little body I want to ease. It's her little slim feet I want to hold tight and still in my one hand. It's her little mite of hands I want to give a holiday to." He could feel her little hands passing over his face, her fingers in his beard; the tears gushed in his eyes. "I wish I was dead and buried and out of it all."

"It would be different," he continued, after a silence — the minister was so motionless at his side it was the same as talking to himself — "It would be different if I thought she was going to be happy, or comfortable, or anything like; but my mules — I drive a float, sir — have a better time than her. From morning till night she's going on not enough fodder to keep a bird, and not as much ease and peace as a penitentiary convict. Her father's a sot, that's all. They used to be very respectable and high-minded before he took to drinking. He worked in a cotton-press. There seems to be no end to his sinking now; it would be a God's mercy if he would drown in a gutter, or be knocked over by some of his drunken gang. I wonder she don't take to drink, too! If I were a woman with as little chance as her I would. But no, she'll work and work and kill herself — and that will be the end of it all. They've been at her again; they've had a scene; I could see she'd been crying. She doesn't know what to do, so she flings me over, the only friend she's got in God's wide world. And that ain't going to make it easier, as she thinks. It will kill her. Mule nature couldn't stand it, let alone woman nature.

"I'd fixed it all. We were to go off somewhere to-morrow and get married without any one knowing it. I was afraid they'd get at her — the children. I've told her over and over again I'd take care of the children like — like children of my own," He stammered, for the comparison with him had ceased to be conventional. "Good for nothing as the children are, she loves 'em as if she were their mother, and his own wife wasn't as patient with him as she is with that whiskey barrel of a father of hers. I 'ain't got any use for him, and she can't help seeing it; that's what hurts her. She ought to have had the best and proudest father in this city, that's a fact; and God ought to have done better by her.

"Great Scott! to go around all day Christmas with the feeling in my heart that Janey was my legally married wife! My sweet, sad, tired, dainty bit of a Janey! And no one know it — not a soul — until evening came and time to go home. 'Janey, my wife, come home!' Paradise would have been a fool to this earth then; and if any man would have dared say it wasn't a merry Christmas, I'd have knocked him down. Yes, sir, I would. It's all ready and waiting for her — my little shanty. I haven't slept in my room since she promised me; I was afraid of soiling or mussing something. I've slept out in the stables with the mules. I own two teams, sir; six of the finest mules in the city, and have paid for them too, every cent. I'll never sleep in that room again. I'll eat and drink and sleep with the mules the rest of my life; and this is the last bit of paper that will ever carry the name of Harry Farren to marry any woman!"

He pulled the license out of his pocket, and would have torn it, but Herbert took it out of his hand.

> "Out of the sin,
> Out of the din,
> Babe of Bethlehem, lead!"

99

The singers, passing again, had increased their following. A battalion's tread resounded on the pavement. The rhymes taken up from the front were repeated down the line, falling off with the squeaking mimicry of gamins' voices, out of hearing and jurisdiction of the accordion.

"... You want to go to the devil this night? The devil, no doubt, will give you opportunities enough," began the minister.

> "Out of the dust,
> Out of the lust,
> Babe of Bethlehem, lead!"

A shout hailed the locally and timely successful hit of the couplet, and the contribution of a stentorian basso was sung with continued and deafening satisfaction.

Harry, nevertheless, could hear what the minister said, faint and low as the tones were. If it had been of a Sunday or daylight, and from pulpit to congregation, he might have recognized it as a sermon; the disguise now, by time and circumstances, was so complete that at the end of it he stepped into the street unconscious that he had been quietly and obediently listening to one.

However deficient in morality, even according to the naturally lenient statement of their eldest sister, the little Wiggenses were not to any perceptible degree wanting in intelligence where their own interests were concerned. They did not expect Santa Claus, like the sun, to smile on the just and unjust alike; indeed, their own past Christmas-treeless experience gave the lie to such an expectation, but they did hope this year to manage, or, as they put it, "get ahead of him." As he only came once a year and stayed but a short while, they determined to test their strength and his perspicacity by a short, sharp trial of goodness. With handsome munificence, they cancelled from their minds all remembrance or even knowledge of past naughtinesses, calculating that by conduct superlatively exemplary for one night and day they would refute for once, if not for all, the calumny of the neighbors, who persisted that the "Wiggenses didn't know what good was," and render themselves worthy candidates for those largesses which they understood fell only to the obedient and pious. Their devices to this end were varied and endless.

Johnnie — called "Tipple" — whose foot had been amputated by the dummy, that special rewarder of bad boys, took the initiative. He begged, entreated, commanded, that he should be tied in bed, tied with a borrowed clothes-line, and so restrained from hopping around on the floor on his one foot, to the killing amusement of his sister and six brothers, and the exasperation of the unfortunate young practitioner who attended him — an individual who had far more charity than brains. Johnnie also requested and instructed them to put a head on him at the first indication of gab on his part to the old stick-inthe-mud doctor, and called them all to witness that they might depose when the time came that since that morning he had not loosened the bandages to see, himself, how the stump was getting on, or to show them, though he assured them they might beg him on their knees to do it. And the brothers and sisters were not to be outdone, though it went hard with them, for every day the doctor's visit was funnier in virtue of new original impromptu variations. Instead of hiding behind doors to squeak and scratch and whisper "Rats!" when the young man made his appearance, asking him, when he went, about his "ma," requesting a loan of five dollars, or a cigar for a light, pinning fragments of newspaper to his coat-tails, and calling "Extra!" behind him down the street, or by opposition show and variety dancing behind his back frustrate his attempts to gain Johnnie's attention — instead of this daily performance, which, as noted, was never more delightful, they wished the doctor "good-morning" with such decorous politeness of tone and manner, and were so successful in their hypocrisy generally, that the poor young fellow, having the infection of the day upon him, went directly from the house to a fruit-stand, and bought all the oranges, apples, and bananas he could not afford, ordering them to be delivered in sure secrecy and mystery the next morning, that Santa Claus, the scape-goat of other people's generosity, should get the merit of it. And more recklessly still, he opened a credit, on what assets he alone knew, and bought a crutch, which was also to be delivered anonymously to Johnnie. He was a country lad, and had not quite learned city ways yet.

Time never fell so heavy on the hands of the Wiggenses before; they found good days much harder to fill than naughty ones; in fact, there was no comparison between the ease of finding occupation for the one and for the other. The *short* and merry life of the wicked is not merely a figurative expression.

Janey's little cupboard of a room was always securely locked against them, but their own apartment offered as fair a field for reform as for depredation. They swept and dusted it, not once, but a score of times, until the borrowed broom was recalled and a renewal of the loan peremptorily refused. They washed their faces and combed their hair for months in advance. They tied and retied Johnnie in his bed, each one separately, according to some new Individual idea of comfort and security, in such high good-humor all the time, laughing and shouting with such boisterous hilarity, that they made themselves, if possible, more annoying than ever to the neighborhood, until, long as the day was, it began undeniably to draw to a close. Louisa, the eldest of this set of Wiggenses (Janey belonged to a long -forgotten first wife), had bethought herself at the last moment of washing her frock. It was done standing, and going at the dirty spots singly all around the skirt; and now, being energetic in any undertaking, the basin being handy, with water and soap, she had just completed the same satisfactory task for her hair. She stood in the centre of the room shaking her long, dripping red locks over the floor, forgetting her object in fascination of the elegant variegated pattern which, with a little care, she could design all over the dusty surface. They had had an idea of scrubbing the floor at one time, but now rejoiced over the abandonment of it.

"Make it go round and round like shells, sis," suggested Bobbie, in envious admiration.

"No. I tell you, diamonds, diamonds is the prettiest. It's too dry; go get some more water on it."

"Pshaw! now it's too wet."

"You ought to hire yourself out for a waterin' can, sis."

"Or a whitewash brush."

"A yellow-wash brush you mean." Johnnie always was the wittiest of all.

"It must feel funny to have all that stuff on your head."

"Suppose a horse had his tail tied on his head?"

"Let's cut it off, sis — eh? Just to see how you look without it."

"Geewhillikins! I could laugh till I bust. Janey she thinks I'm smoking cigar stumps round by the Academy, just 'cause she told me particular not to."

Bobbie swaggered up and down, smoking an imaginative cigar stump, his hands under an imaginary coat-tail.

"I reckon she's traipsing round now, looking for me everywhere." Louisa swung and switched her hair superciliously. "She seems to think I can't never stay at home."

"She'll just keel over when she sees me a-lyin' here all tied up," said Johnnie, pulling himself together to make his bonds tighter, glancing down at the immaculate bandages over his ankle.

"Tell us how it felt when it was a-coming off, Johnnie."

"Oh, tell us once more."

"It felt a —" prompted Louisa.

"Pshaw! don't be mean."

"It felt a —" continued Louisa.

"You hush up; you don't know. Was you there, now? Say, was you there?" And Johnnie felt obliged to save his anecdote by telling it again for the thousandth time since the accident. The rest clustered around the bed not to lose the least part of word or expression.

"It felt a scrinchin'" — twisting his hands as if wringing something off — "and a scranchin'" — twisting his face now — "and a scroonchin', and a — hell!" with that side-splitting wink of his left eye at them.

"I 'ain't done nuffin all day." Baby, the youngest, four years old, who usually did the gutter business, had patiently waited to enter his claim.

When Janey did come home and opened the door in her habitual despairing way, they must, unless they were altogether insatiable, have been satisfied with her surprise. At the moment, they were hopping over the floor to show the delighted Johnnie how he would have to walk in future; each one holding the shoe off the naked upheld foot.

"Hurrah, Janey! Here we are!"

"Every single one of us, Janey."

"We haven't been out all day, Janey."

"And we've been being good, Janey."

"Look at me, Janey!"

"Look — look at Johnnie, Janey!"

"Don't you see, Janey?"

"I tied him, Janey."

"So did I!"

"And me, too!"

"But I told 'em to do it. Didn't I? Didn't I, now?" screamed Johnnie, over them all.

"I 'ain't done nuffin all day long, Janey," claimed the baby again, looking so unnatural with his clean face that it is no wonder Janey kissed him over and over again for a dear little fellow.

"See, we are going to hang 'em up, Janey," showing the shoes.

"Santa Claus has got to give us something this time, sure!"

"We 'ain't got stockings, but shoes will do."

"And we are going right to bed, so as Santa Claus can come as soon as he likes."

"And right to sleep."

"Here's Tipple's shoe. He 'ain't got but one. Had to let the old car mash off the tother one."

"In course! in course!" Tipple would be sarcastic. "It was my fault. I ought to have took off my hat, and made a low bow to the dummy, and axed the cars please to stop till I took off my shoe, or tell 'em to call round again, or to come in summer when I was barefooted."

"I hope Santa Claus will bring me a red parasol," and Louisa sidled and arched as she imagined the fortunate possessors of these luxuries to do in their promenades through the streets.

They were indeed that evening as good and affectionate children as were to be found anywhere among all the miraculously good and affectionate children of Christmas Eve. They kept their word about going to bed, and what was more surprising, about going to sleep, leaving Janey to novel evening hours, undisturbed by care or anxiety about them, and scoring a point in their own favor which no Santa Claus could by any possibility ignore.

Janey lighted her lamp and got out her sewing that she might think, for one process with her had become inseparable from the other. She had been a precocious adept in both, and since Louisa's age had been hemming, running, stitching, basting, and button-holing year after year, or year on year, first in one, then in another, dressmaker's room, carrying her thought around with her needle-book, adding chapter to chapter, period to period, from childhood to womanhood, finishing up one job of thinking to open another, as if she were paid by the day for it also.

Going through heavy stuffs for the winter, light ones for spring, thin for summer, light for autumn; as the months slipped by, she only knew the seasons, in the close room, by the dry-goods she sewed. Going into mourning and out of mourning, changing, twisting, turning, fashioning old garments to look like new, and new ones to appear more than their price, receiving constantly new orders about placing the whalebones, ribbons, buttons, laces, hooks and eyes, cutting out one year this way, another year that, draping and undraping, life had outwardly become one long monotonous servitude to change. If she had had imagination, she would have said that she was not a woman — her woman charms drying up unused upon her — but some devil's imp or gnome, one of a vast league, in some stolen woman's body, sent from some devil's little hell of fashion on a special mission of corruption against womankind; to aid, abet, encourage, assert, and produce dissension between the mind and body; to tempt into perils of debt and perils of morality; to delude with beauty and reward with ugliness; to uncover in pretending to cover; to disclose in pretending to hide; to draw the laces tighter and tighter, cut the bodice lower and lower, the sleeve higher and higher, the skirts narrower and narrower; to push a suggestion to a suspicion, a suspicion to a conviction of impropriety; to efface standards; to inure to exposure; to push flesh and blood forward into ever greater evidence, and the soul backward into ever greater discredit.

But such were not Janey's thoughts, although a morbid companion at the work-table gave utterance to similar ones. Her thoughts wandered in other directions. They were off and away at the first stitch for beautiful gardens, or for sandy shores rippled by the waters of a blue lake, under golden skies, listening to sweet music, locating the pearly streets of heaven. Or they spent millions of money in schemes of charity, or went on missions to unfortunates; or, coming home, they cleaned, repaired, and beautified the poverty and disgrace-stricken domicile; they educated Louisa into a respectable young woman; they made the boys sober, honest, industrious laborers; keeping Dick from gambling, Bobbie from smoking, and Tippie from catching on behind the cars; they sent the baby to a free Kindergarten, and reformed — God help her! — her old rascally father, bringing him from the grog-shop to sit at home of evenings, refining from his face the blotches and marks that incrusted the features, and hid them from what they were in her childish recollections of him. There was to be a table with a lamp on it; around it they all were to sit, she with her sewing, the others with newspapers and books. She could see the very pattern of the table-cover. God help her again, and all women who toil on through life after *ignis fatuus* hope, to be led into disappointment and a bog!

At the end of all the planning, cleaning, reforming, at some distant point in a long vista, her thoughts, and her needle too (for it was distinctly officious in the process), would marry her to Harry. And then the repose, the caresses, the leaning on a strong arm, the reclining against a strong breast! And now, God bless those thoughts which come to lonely women, and give them a taste of the love they are never to know, and provide them with the mate, family, and home which their nature craves, but their destiny denies!

She had much to think about to-night, but her needle threaded only stitches together. She was to start anew in life to-morrow; she had taken the first step already; but her feet were already tired and apathetic. The children all slept in their little beds, quiet and safe. Perhaps if she had had to hunt them up, as usual, to scold and punish them, if they had been unkind, impudent, ungrateful, as usual! She shed tears over the bitter thoughts that had come to her that day about them, the bitter feelings which had lashed her on to her own immolation. The revulsion which their change of conduct had caused in the judgment of the poor young physician was as nothing to that which the young Wiggenses caused in the heart of their sister, simply by coming in early and going to bed quietly.

Hark! how happy the people were outside! She threw down her work, opened the window, and leaned out. Tramping by, with bundles under their arms, men and women talked and laughed loudly, full of Christmas plans and presents. The market stores were all ablaze with light. She could hear fireworks all over the city; an occasional rocket burst in her horizon, throwing new constellations over the thickly-starred heavens. She knew they came from the aristocratic mansions up-town, sent up by servants hidden in flower-gardens to amuse the silk and lace clad ladies in the galleries. Bands of music crossed each other at street-angles; great fire-crackers like pistols were shot off like minute-guns over a victory, startling and frightening her every time. What joy and merriment there could be in the world, and what sorrow and heaviness of heart! Why was it that only the latter portion had come to her? The children thought it was their naughtiness had prevented Santa Claus coming to them; what would they say to-morrow when their goodness would be found unrewarded?

> "Out of the chase,
> Out of the race,
> Man of Bethlehem, lead!"

How the voices hurt! the quivering, drear, negro voices, changing every melody into a dirge, funereal in mind as in skin.

> "Out of the tears.
> Out of the fears,
> Man of Bethlehem, lead!"

How often at night they had passed through her dreams, these street minstrels, waking her with tears in her eyes, and she had loved them for their musical gratuity, and gone to sleep again singing the tune over to herself! God may have afflicted them, but He had given them the expression and alleviation of music.

"Eleven o'clock! They would have passed this evening together, Harry and she, the last evening of their separate lives, hand in hand, and — No; when they were together, it was not all endearment and embrace; that was only in

105

her thoughts. Why should she think that which had never happened, never could happen? Why now did she feel his lips upon hers?" She hid her face in her hands and stifled a moan on her lips. Why should her heart involuntarily moan?

What carousing was going on at the corner, in the groggery where her father was? They had better be at home, these men. Where were their women? Leaning out of windows, watching, sleepless, unhappy? Those fire-crackers, how could the police permit them? Murder could be done by pistols under cover of their noise. Harry had looked forward to to-morrow — her great, burly, high-tempered Harry! He was dull about some things, but she loved him all the better for it. "God knows I thought it was my duty!" She said the words aloud, and started at the sound of talking to herself. A black cloud had been gathering over her for a week; perhaps she was not well, perhaps she had worked too hard, and, and — if she had waited! Would Harry go to the devil as he said? Wasn't it always a woman's fault when a man went to the devil? She had meant to save her little brothers — from what? What immediate danger threatened them? Harry had no sister, no family to look after him — Harry, who had given her only the constant love-tokens of an unswerving devotion. Her heart was getting beyond her control; bounding, leaping, demanding, crying, craving — Harry! Harry! no brother, no sister, no father — only Harry, her promised husband! She was so weak and tired, so helpless against this sudden heart fury. "Would he go straight home — ah me! — and sit in the dark thinking hard things of me; or would he go to a saloon too, and make an all night of it?" She had once taken his pistol from him, and made him promise never to wear it again. Would he love again and get married? There were few women who would not be glad of him for a husband, and she had thrown him off — for what? To think that her life would go on the better without him! And the children, why should he not have helped to train them, her husband, their brother — without him no future, no —

That was a pistol this time! again, again, and again! Screams, oaths, a rushing crowd; a cry of murder! "Harry! Harry!" She rushed from the room to the street. She would pierce the crowd; she would tear her way through; if he were there she would drag him out; if he were shot, it was she had disarmed him. There were assassins and drunkards at that corner.

"Janey, Janey, what is the matter? Where are you going? Janey!"

Harry's arms held her; Harry's voice was in her ears. He had waited, as he promised tire parson — waited until midnight, his last vigil on the little box steps in front of her house. The bells were just going to ring now.

"Janey! little woman! little wife!"

For she clung to him so,' she cried so over him, she kissed his face, his eyes, his beard, his hands — his hard, heavy, mule-driving hands.

"Harry, Harry, Harry, darling!"

That was the way she always called him to herself, but it was the first time he had ever heard her.

"Harry, I'm all wrong; Harry, I can't — I can't live without you."

What a maddening jubilation! what a peal the bells were ringing about them! as if all true, happy, reunited lovers in the world were pulling at the ropes' ends.

Herbert remained alone in the church to the meditations, for which eighteen centuries have furnished the soil, and which, even in a Christmas story, perhaps cannot with discretion be revealed. Whether he wandered up and down the narrow aisles, or whether he stood in the dark, with his head against the walls, staring blankly before him, or whether he sat in a pew, his face in his hands, or looking up at the cheap radiant star over the altar; whether he fell on his knees before the altar, murmuring inarticulate words of prayer, or shedding tears on the green leaves, or cried "Avaunt!" to lurking Satans, or shut his lips to keep back the rising tumult in his heart, it was intended for none but the eye of Him whom the star typified.

Oh, the sadness that comes on Christmas Eve! All the noise and merriment is but to neutralize it. Never does time appear to move so fast, and good resolutions so slow; never does childhood appear so beautiful, or so remote; never does innocence appear more heavenly, or more impossible; never do longings for the dead and gone so wring and torture the heart: never does the hard reality of the present so clash with the anticipations of what it was to be — as when, hour after hour, Christmas Eve passes, and, hour after hour, Christmas approaches. Herbert struggled to make the present one yield some mitigations of future ones; some recollection which would stand out in Christmas Eves to come, and challenge the black spectre of despondency that glides in midnight hours to whisper in the ear of the conscientious, "Thou hast failed." And if any prayer addressed at such a moment might be recorded by profane hands, it was the prayer that rose from his heart to that effect.

And he felt that the answer would come to him, not in the church, but out there in the multitude, surging and rolling out noise, leaving now and then a rocket here, a voice there, cast up solitary and shrill on the air.

Out there were hands to be clasped, hearts to be raised; out there sympathy, companionship, love; out there a whole population for a desolate, loving heart. Out there, where the barefooted vision walked, were sisters and brothers at this moment waiting for them both — sisters and brothers in spite of religious, political, financial, racial separations.

> "Out of the tomb,
> Out of the gloom,
> Christ of Bethlehem, lead!"

The accordion was tired and tripping, the voices thin and irregular; both were on their last round.

> "Up, up above,
> To Heaven and Love,
> Christ of Bethlehem, lead!"

107

The words ran together and stopped suddenly, as if butting against a wall; the tune had been lost in the various transmigration of voices. "Would it be safe to leave the door open now?" Had He no more use for His little church tonight? If He should come and find it closed against Him?

Herbert did not shut it as he went out. The dago family hung around their shop like bunches of their own tropical fruits, gorgeous in their bright clothes, which nature must have furnished and renewed from year to year, like foliage, so harmonious and unconventional were they; Maria with her dress open, perhaps, a trifle too much over the thick yellow skin, for nature is not prudish; but there was a long lock of black hair to fall across it, just where baby hands could clutch and play with it. Every year there was a new bloom, so to speak, around the door; a new baby to toy with the hair and lie on the breast, to be weaned afterwards by Marianna, and then turned out with the rest into the whole street for nursery. They slept on the stem as their fruit did, for all the street knew to the contrary, the latest retirers and the earliest risers never hitting on the moment when their banquette was empty or their house full. They were doing a rushing business this evening, uniting all the forces of the family — Salvatore, Maria, Marianna, down to the last lisping tongue— for English in which to negotiate it.

The great thoroughfare still held its throng, but the brilliant shops looked rifled and empty; the tired clerks leaned, pale and haggard, over their disordered counters; the flower-women were gone, the street booths were being covered up, buying and selling were over, yet still the moving procession filled the banquettes and blocked the corners. The theatres were discharging their audiences, the great octagonal circus giving forth as if it had hidden inside some inexhaustible source of human beings. The easy swinging doors of the saloons swallowed some in as they passed; some went in to the grand entrances of the social clubs; the cars carried loads of them away; skimming off by degrees the more respectable element, and all the women. The harmless period of jollity was passing; the horns became instruments of disturbance and annoyance; the fire-crackers were too loud, and left behind them the reekings of gunpowder; evil-looking men in shabby garments prowled about their lairs in obscure side streets and dark alleyways.

Almost midnight! Almost Christmas morning!

Once! Four, five, six times! — too quick for counting — well-known sharp reports fell upon the air; pistol-shots, no fire-crackers; the imitation sound, after all, was imperfect. A rush of men out of a side street, with the fear of murder and the witness-box behind them, gave the clew to the curious.

"Killed?"

"How many?"

"Not dead yet?"

"Who did it?"

The galloping horses of the ambulance went by; policemen lead through the crowd three suddenly sobered, pale-faced men, one with a pistol still in his hand. The ambulance returned slowly, and a cab passed with men in it trying to hold erect an inert body; then the bells, which had been waiting a year for this moment, pealed out with all their might and brazenness; the big bells calling up the little bells, the church bells summoning the fire bells, and all together rousing every bell in every factory, market, and depot, till there was not an idle or a stationary bell in the city. Peace, good-will, peace and good-will on earth, on earth as in heaven.

The great, vague, dim ships and steamboats on the river, wakened like sleeping monsters from their mist and inertness, gave voice, tardily taking up the cry with their hoarse steam-whistles, bellowing an inarticulate and beast-like accompaniment to the sweet human rejoicings of the bells. And all who had breath or horns or fireworks left expended them royally during the first five minutes of the great Birth-morn.

Herbert obeyed the bell that called to midnight mass in the cathedral, down a narrow street, overhung with iron lace-work of balconies, following the file of worshippers contributed from every house door. The bronze equestrian statue in the square gleamed like silver through a coating of dew; the sharp electric light pierced the hidden places of the roses and jasmines, whose perfume freighted the air into heaviness. Through the open doors of the cathedral the lights of the altar were seen, over an undistinguishable mass of heads; the steps in the possession of a mob, pushing and elbowing for entrance; negro faces under head -kerchiefs, white faces under laces, still flushed from the dance, lips still wet with champagne; the greasy jacket of the boot-black rubbing against a dress-coat, the calico sacque of the "marchande" brushing aside a silk cloak from bare shoulders. The cross, gaunt, old uniformed Suisse burrowed in the crowd, rebuking the loud-mouthed, tapping with his staff the irreverent, collaring small boys, and cuffing them all the way out to the street. The sleepy, indifferent priest mumbles the prayers to the sleepy, indifferent saints niched in the darkness above. The motley congregation arrested their conversation to make the sign of the cross, or dropped momentarily on one knee; until the familiar voice of the favorite opera singer sang the "Cantique de Noël." "Noël! Noël!"

A hush fell on them all. Even the Virgin, in her gaudy incarnation of paint and gilt, must be impressed. Even the most thoughtless, the wildest, the wickedest, must pause for that one moment of singing.

"What do men and women like those feel and think in such a pause?"

Herbert looked at a group, staying their laughing and jesting and undue familiarities of hand and tongue. The hymn was ending, one last note thrilling the air, the current of people already setting towards the street again.

"Where is your baby?" Herbert recognized one of the young women by an inspiration tlirough her blazonry of silk and jewels — the asylum girl.

Her face paled at his question as it did that afternoon on the chancel steps, showing on each cheek a spot of rouge in startling relief.

"My baby?"

She tried to say it derisively, tried to make her pretty eyes flash at him, tried to throw off his hand, tried to laugh with the others. In vain. The mother in her deserted the woman; with all her effort nothing was left of her but a weak, trembling, ghastly, conscience -stricken creature, with breasts throbbing wildly, hands craving their burden, and a heart which all through the dinner and the opera, the champagne and the revelry, had been dragging her back — back to the steps where she had deserted her own flesh and blood.

The men, elegant and discreet, looked before them; the women tittered, whispered, pointed; they were older than she. The crowd carried them all off, leaving her standing by the young pastor.

"Have you put it in an asylum?"

"No! no! no!"

"Take me to it."

He took her hand and led her out, pulling her along for a square or two; then she led him, increasing her speed, as the bad spell on her weakened, faster and faster, until, almost in a run, she reached the bright lights of the broad thoroughfare. She pulled him across it, and on, on, past house after house, to where his little church stood gray and shadowy in the night. Up to the church, to the steps, up the steps to the corner appropriated by the Sicilian Marianna.

"Gone! Gone! My baby gone!" she screamed. She got down on her knees and felt the place with her hands, going over and over it, as if searching for a pin. "Could it have rolled down?" She rushed out in the banquette and looked up and down; she bent over the gutter and plunged her hands in the slime and mud. "My baby! My baby! Gone! I put it here — right here" — laying her hand on the spot — "where the little dago girl sits. She would have found it, taken care of it, nursed it. Every day I've seen her here: she looked like the picture of the Virgin."

"You abandoned it; why should you care for it?" He could not ask the question of her as she stood illogically, inconsequently weeping and wringing her hands, her hat and feathers awry, her long, light, wrinkled gloves wet to the elbow with gutter mud. From all eternity women have been mothers, only faithless momentarily.

"I resisted, I resisted, but the Christmas coming — the noise, the lights, the music, the firecrackers — they called me out, as they called me out of the asylum, out into life, into the world. It was the devil again at me — the devil! My baby! My pretty little baby! She will be sent to the police-station; she will be put in an asylum, to be called out, as I was, by the devil. She will be taken by people who will beat her, by negroes who will degrade and corrupt her. The little dago girl would have been kind to her. I could have seen her every day. My baby! Now I've lost her forever."

Marianna did not wait for the bell from her own fosterling church, for she knew that it was too poor to possess one. But about the time for the other bells to ring, she ran in from her oyster and banana selling to midnight mass there. No crowd, no lights, no music. She slipped through the open door. Was this a church on Christmas Eve?

It could not have been finer in heaven itself than at San Antonio's, their patron saint's, last year. The stable, the oxen, the manger, the Virgin, the Wise Men, and St. Joseph — all life-size and death-stiff. And not even in heaven, unless in the Italian quarter of it, could the candles (great monoliths of wax with orchidaceous efflorescence, only slightly yellow with age), the gilt and silver, the paper flowers and coloring, be excelled. And the votive legs, arms, hearts, hands, eyes — they hung around like the gleanings of a battlefield; and the mental and moral cures, with the printed acknowledgments — San Antonio must surely have thought of the decoration of his own church when he undertook so many miracles. That was a church! Here was nothing, absolutely nothing, but sad green leaves. She knelt down at the altar. If there had been only a bambino for the empty manger! Could not God, who sent bambinos in quantities on the asking, have spared one poor little infant for this cradle? Why did not the patron saint of this church emulate the example of the industrious San Antonio? Not one image! Not one *ex voto*! Not a flower or a gilt leaf! She looked at Pepe in her arms, and at the font. Here was the cradle; here is where the bambino should lie. But Pepe was far beyond the age and cleanliness for the role; his time of dismissal was about come; precocious as he was, he had not learned to crawl a moment too soon. The rich ladies of the neighborhood might have given a bambino, or loaned one of their own.

"Marianna! Marianna!" her mother called. Maria would have sent her voice into the very Vatican when she was in a temper; and the Holy Father himself would hardly have dared defer obedience. The little girl ran by her corner of the steps. Who had been invading it? — her own temper now rising. The bundle fell open at her touch, exposing the contents.

"A bambino! a bambino! God *has* sent a bambino!" A beautiful bambino, clean and white, with naked feet and hands. She dropped Pepe, and carried it in quickly, and laid it on the green couch in the baptismal font in time for the first stroke of the great bell that led the ringing choral, over-ringing her mother's vociferous "Marianna! Marianna!"

"Where are you going?" asked Herbert, taking the girl by her wrist again.

"Nowhere! nowhere! There's no place for me to go on earth. My baby! my baby!" She tried to break from him. "Let me go! let me go! I've lost my child! I've killed her! Let me kill myself, too!"

Her voice was loud and violent. People passing by turned back to look at the desperate woman in struggle with a man.

There was one place open for her and all like her; the host was standing in the door to welcome her. Herbert lifted her, still struggling, up the steps, and carried her, tight and fast in his arms, to the spot where she had fallen prostrate, a broken, helpless creature offering her child to the Saviour. The star shone over the place. Her eyes were quicker than his, but she thought it a

111

fantasy; her poor brain had been so distraught. She had been seeing this baby so long; for weary, weary months; through the glaze of fever at the hospital, through suffering, privation, temptation. She had just been seeing it lost, stolen, ill-treated, dead. She could trust her eyes no more; she closed them on the vision, but they would not stay closed.

He thought her cry was maniacal, and her actions, tearing and scattering the greens from the font.

"I gave her to Him, and now He has given her back to me. See! see! I gave her to Him, and now He has given her back to me." She held the bambino towards Herbert.

With the fear of the committee before his eyes, Herbert replaced, as well as he could, the fontal decorations, artfully trying to suggest in the replacement an impending top-heaviness.

"Where are you going now?"

If he could only have seen the radiance, the sweet holy radiance of her face!

"Home! home! with my baby — my child!"

As they descended the steps a limp figure rolled and lolled over a protesting accordion.

> "Into the light,
> Into the right,
> Christ of . . ."

"Yes, sir! that's so!" The words ended in a snore.

The little church had a grand congregation, a most surprising congregation, for Christmas Day. Everybody who was anybody in the neighborhood seemed to be getting up too late for any but the one church — the gentlemen could not finish their breakfasts in time, nor the ladies dress themselves sufficiently fine, nor the children be made ready, for the fashionable churches uptown. All came. The nobodies of the neighborhood all came, hot from dusting and sweeping and washing up dishes; the cooks ran in pulling down their sleeves, the maids with their caps and aprons; the passers-by stopped in for a prayer or two; and all the roving churchless Christians, who could not pay pew rent anywhere, or who had been dropped by their pastors or shunned by other church officers as irretrievables — the little church gathered them all in; not only them, but their offerings — big donations intended for bigger churches, and the mites which were too small for any church but this one. The young gentlemen from the boarding-house come over at least in time for the plate, and those who could not come sent crumpled bank-bills by their colored waiters.

The music was wretched, every one said, the sermon more commonplace than ever, the reading miserable, the decorations paltry. But it was soon over — a compensating merit fully appreciated by the members of the clubs just around the corner. By twelve o'clock they were all away — all except a tall, burly, shy man and a neat, little, pale, trembling lady, and a long file of children afflicted with irrepressible hilarity, munching apples and whispering their admiration over the agile performances of a lame boy on a new crutch.

"I took your advice last night, sir, and I hope you will marry us this morning, sir. I've got her now, and she sha'n't give me the slip again."

There was no need to answer this, but womanlike the bride would have attempted it if Herbert had not immediately commenced the marriage service. The delighted vestry, with their pocket handkerchiefs tied to bursting over the bills, trade-dollars, halves, quarters, dimes, and picayunes taken up in the collection, acted as witnesses, and gave the bride away in a body, collecting their kisses, however (or they would not have been in the vestry), singly and individually. They shook hands with the groom and tipped the children, from Louisa to Baby.

When they were all leaving the church together, beaming under the load of Merry Christmases they had received and Merry Christmases they had given, who should appear with the greatest alacrity from the corner where she and her curiosity had been concealed but Mrs. Bunnyfeather, note-book in hand, and mindful as ever of her duty as secretary of the Sunday-school chapter. Not one of those little Wiggenses was allowed to depart until the last name, age, and sex had been registered as Sunday-school scholars, membership to commence that very evening at the Sunday-school Christmas-tree, on which, she assured them, Santa Claus had hung a present for each one of them by name. Surprising as it may seem, such really turned out to be the case — not one was forgotten.

In the French Quarter. 1870.

"Now, Margot?"

"In a moment, monsieur;" and Margot's scrubbing-brush proceeded with accelerated force.

The cathedral clock in the vicinity struck the quarter.

"But the time passes, my good Margot."

"In just one minute, monsieur."

The clock rang the half-hour.

"Margot!"

"I am going now, monsieur, at once."

Monsieur Villeminot heard the sound of the floor-cloth really ceasing at the sill of the door, and a last handful of brick-dust fall scattering over the wet boards, and the bucket being carried out.

The room was so small that privacy could only be obtained by standing behind him as he sat in his great leather-covered easy chair, an antiquated "Voltaire," whose flattened springs and stuffing were assisted by pillows and cushions of divers shapes and hues. Margot unpinned the piece of bagging that served for an apron, let down her skirt over her stockingless ankles, and passed a dean calico dress over the soiled damp one she had on. As she had explained to Madame St. Georges only the day before, with a shrug of the shoulders: "Mon dieu, madame! I have not known a more intimate garment than a dress in years, years." She gave a glance of satisfaction over the well-scrubbed floor. "At any rate, it is done now for a week," she said, more to herself than to the occupant of the chair, and shuffled out of the room in her old carpet slippers.

When he heard the door close behind her, the old man among his cushions began as usual to mutter his thoughts audibly, a disconnected, unintelligible monologue, getting more and more distinct with the certainty of solitude. His fine aristocratic language resembled Margot's daily speech as the silken toilets of the ladies in the street resembled her calico homeliness; it was as much out of place in the menial interior of his habitation as the long row of glistening-back books that filled the mantel-shelf. He bent his head forward, listening to his own voice furtively, as he once might have looked at his face in the glass, pronouncing the words and phrases tentatively, interrogatively, scanning his toothless articulation. In his sightless, motionless existence the contracted enclosure of his apartment set no limits to the vast blank space that surrounded him; a space furnished only by the dim scenery of a lived-out past, and with but one certain living reality in it — himself. To-day his words came not, as sometimes, from literary corners or imaginative niches in his memory. Imagination for once was stilled, literature forgotten, phantasms and visions dissolved. The brows over his blind eyes wrinkled and furrowed, his palsied hands clasped and unclasped excitedly the arms of his chair, and his white-haired head, responsive to his own eloquence, rose wrathfully erect. Expressions original in their inspiration fell from his lips, and his voice resounded so firm, so determined in his own ears that, had his eyes been suddenly unsealed, he would have expected to see not a decrepit Octogenarian, prostrate upon the cushions of an easy chair, quartered in a wretched, isolated closet on a servant's gallery; but a youthful, heroic, vigorous figure, aflame with ardor, strength, and patriotism, repulsing by word and blow, in chamber or field, the audacious invasion of his country; the only figure to enclose a French heart, the only heart for a youth born under the star of Napoleon I., the only scene and action for a French patriot in the year 1870! A fit of coughing arrested the resurrection of his youthful self, and he fell back exhausted — back into age, infirmity, and impotence, into the graveclothes and coffin boundaries of his chair.

All the other rooms on the gallery that Margot passed were closed and locked, the lodgers working out by the day. She turned into an open, arched vestibule and went down the contorted, narrow staircase holding the balustrade with one hand, clutching at the wall with the other, and trying to step upon safe places.

The railing was black and greasy from constant handling, and the mortar had been scratched away from the brick all the way down by outstretched fingers. "Ah, the Pagan!" she muttered, "he will break our necks yet some day with his old 'guet-a-peus.'" Had they but have materialized the reproaches and animadversions upon old Grouille, the landlord, they would have incrusted the roof like stalactites.

The landing-place was filled with buckets and tubs, the brick floor was mouldy from dampness, and the fumes of charcoal poured from the Carlins' open room, where a furnace stood in the fireplace heating its load of irons to redness. Margot went in and deliberately removed them one after the other carefully to the bricks. The bed in the corner of the whilom kitchen was heaped with rough-dry clothes; the doorless armoire held heaps of ironed pieces. On the ironing-table was a broken basin of raw starch, a cracked soup-plate of bluing and an unfinished shirt, the bosom drying into wrinkles; Monsieur Wilhelm's weekly shirt it was, marked distinctly with red cross-stitch, for the washing and ironing of which he gave tri-weekly lessons in penmanship to Rougette and Blanchette, the overgrown, but undergifted, sixteen-year-old twin-daughters of the widow Carlin. It was like the Carlins to rush out thus heedlessly from their work at the first cry of news; and Margot's shake of the head betokened as much. She looked into all the other rooms on the ground -floor, but, like that of the Carlins, they were deserted and disordered. She reluctantly crossed the court-yard, pulling at and fastening her dress, and entered the long corridor, the domain of the wealth and elite of the lodging-house.

Even Monsieur Fréjus, she saw, had been seduced away from his post behind his little glass counter filled with an inestimable treasure of red and white coral beads, devotional images and plated silver medals, crucifixes, and prayer-beads.

A volume of mixed voices directed her to "La Rose de France," the shoe-shop of Monsieur Renaudière. There she found them all assembled, the small room quite full. "Papa" Renaudière, in his shirt-sleeves and working apron, was talking and gesticulating furiously, waving and rustling the last "Extra" in his hands; his spectacles pushed back to the bald place on the top of his head, his eyes flaming, his hair and whiskers bristling out laterally from nervous manipulation.

Monsieur Fréjus's head was still moving backward and forward in the melancholy oscillations produced by the first item in the cablegram of the "Extra." *His* spectacles, over his dim, abstracted eyes, looked like the glasses of an unlighted lantern, and his countenance was as dejected as the holy effigies on his crucifixes. He stood with his back to the street, leaning against the show-window where Monsieur Renaudière's misfits were vindictively kept on exhibition; a high -heeled, pointed-toed array of pedal beauty; a temptation and reproach to the slipshod passers-by, and a vaunting advertisement of Monsieur Renaudière's superiority in skill and artistry over bungling, clumsy Nature, and a standing taunt and challenge to her for competition or imitation.

All the Carlins were wedged into the back door of the workshop with the journeymen; the widow's sleeves rolled to the shoulder, and her fat white feet gleaming in the bottom of her sabots; her youthful twin replicas of her honest, handsome face peering over her shoulder. The journeymen listened open mouthed, looking withal askance at Madame Renaudière, who, towering behind her diminutive husband, led the chorus of lamentation with a rank Gascon accent.

"Ah, la pauvre Patrie vas!"

"Pauvre France!"

"Mon Dieu! Mon Dieu!"

"Ah, she has no luck any longer."

"It's a malediction!"

"What will she do now?"

"But what is it? What is it?" asked Margot, eagerly, entering from the corridor.

"Sédan!"

"Sédan!"

"Sédan!"

"Mais c'est dans quoi?"

"C'est dans le desespoir," answered Monsieur Renaudière promptly, in his character of wit and patriot.

"Ah, oui, c'est dans le desespoir." Madame Renaudière rolled out the words as if her mouth were lined with cobble-stones.

"In truth, my friends, it is a great calamity." The mincing accent of the little Parisian flower maker came from the folds of a pocket-handkerchief, behind which her enterprising eyes cast languishing overtures towards old Grouille the landlord. He, unconscious of sympathy or notice, sat on the dainty sofa reserved for customers, holding his bushy head with both hands, excusably as Alsacian as well as Frenchman, giving himself up to those uncurbed demonstrations of grief usually devoted to absconding tenants.

"Sédan, dog of a name!" snarled Jacquet from the "Quincaillerie" opposite. He was Monsieur Renaudière's formidable rival in eloquence, patriotism, and politics, and a fervent red republican, priest-hater, and woman-hater to boot; although there were on-dits and shrugs and winks enough in the neighbor-hood and suspicions enough in his second-hand shop to seriously attaint the loyalty of this last profession of his at least.

"But —" began Margot again.

"Chut!" whispered Anaïs Renaudière, pulling her skirt; "it's the French, the French!"

"The French," interrupted the keen eared Monsieur Renaudière, fiercely snatching her explanation from her. "The French, Madame Margot; France! … "He cleared his throat, which was indeed husky from emotion or prolonged exertion. "France!" all looked up for an expected verbal palliative. "France is — France is — It is a freak of nature! It is an event! It is an occurrence! It! France!" He looked around at them all; he could not say it. "France is eclipsed, momentarily eclipsed!" He launched the word triumphantly. "A cloud is passing over her; a cloud of Prussians. Can the sun, can the moon be destroyed? Well, as they are the orbs of the heavens, so is France the orb of the earth, and" — he was in full course now — "indestructible except by cat-aclysm!"

"Enfant du bon Dieu!" came in naïve awe from Madame Carlin.

"Ha! it is not the end! You think it is the end! But wait, wait for the last word. Your Bice Marque, your Molque, your Quésair …" This apostrophe, dif-ferent in tone and direction, caused his audience to start. "Monsieur Villem!" they exclaimed. Even Monsieur Fréjus's head stopped vibrating at the unfor-tunate apparition of the young German in the door-way behind Madame Margot.

"The Prussians! the Prussians!" screamed Monsieur Renaudière. "I defy the Almighty Himself to create a Prussia that could whip France!"

"But my friends," commenced the young man in a French which was for-eign in clearness and precision —

"Friends! Bah!"

"Friends! Ah, yes!"

"Friends! French and Prussian! Friends!"

"But we are in America; we are Americans!"

"Americans!"

"Ah, yes; Americans!"

"Americans! a la bonne heure!"

"We are to call ourselves Americans, hein? now, when our country is being assassinated?" called out the ebullient Madame Renaudière.

"Americans! vas!" sneered the journeymen.

"Yes, when America was in danger, we were Americans; America was our country, our mother; but France! France! She is before America, she is the first, the source of countries for us; she is the divine incarnation of 'la patrie' as the Virgin, as the Madonna, is the incarnation of womanhood. When I say France," the tears rolled down his face before them all, and his voice broke — "when I say France, it is as if every drop of blood in my body had a voice. Expatriation may change the body, but the blood, the blood, it is always the same, always remains loyal, Gallic! Gallic, my friends; and," with an acute transition from sentiment into anger again, "it is our Gallic blood that calls for vengeance to-day, it is our Gallic blood that blushes to-day at the insult of destiny, and dares to reprove God."

"Gallic blood!" repeated Madame Renaudière, impressed herself and proud of the effect of the high-sounding adjective on others.

"Bravo!" responded Jacquet, applauding the reproof to God.

Monsieur Fréjus hastened out of the room where patriotism was taking a turn inconsistent with his pious trade. Monsieur Wilhelm Müller, the plodding young professor of Greek and Latin, looked round and round in embarrassment, uncertain whether a national or personal explanation would be more appropriate; a deprecating smile on his lips, the color mounting under his thin skin, his simple blue eyes confessing frankly the doubt between grief and anger. He had been fellow-lodger and companion to them for years, a Prussian to them for two months; but there seemed to have been a tacit nullification of all former propitiatory periods and relations. From each familiar face black flags and martial accoutrements waved and bristled now to his peaceful overtures; even from his scholars Rougette and Blanchette, even from Anaïs.

The shoe-upper Anaïs held in her hand shook and quivered, dancing the glistening, pendent needle at the end of a long, black, silk thread. Her head was tossed back, her chest heaved turbulently; in her eyes rose up the whole terrible calamity of Sédan; those shy, alluring black eyes, his paradise and temptation! For the first time they avoided the sweet intoxication of a rencontre with his. As for Margot, she stood stupid and silent, neither daring to hazard another question, nor return without more definite information to her husband.

The women's voices, which had been modulated in woe, began to rise shrill and sharp in reflections and insinuations against their elected foe, Wilhelm, now in full retreat. Margot hastened after him through the damp corridor as fast as her slippers would allow.

"Monsieur Willem! Monsieur Willem! For God's sake, tell me what it is all about! I can't understand a word, no one will explain — the patron waits, he is agonized to hear the news. It is a perfect gombo."

The sharp snapping of his finger-tips ceased, and he turned around, "Sédan!"

"But that's what I say! C'est dans quoi?"

"It's another battle."

"What! Only another battle! All that fuss about a battle! Mon Dieu! I thought some one had been killed!"

"Tell Monsieur Villeminot that his nation is whipped, his Emperor a prisoner, his army surrendered! eighty thousand men, eighty thousand cowards! ..."

"Tell Monsieur Villeminot that! tell 'mon patron' — oh. Monsieur Villem!"

"I am as big a fool as the others," the German exclaimed. He looked down on the little woman with her patient, earnest face raised to him, and the unbecoming, ireful gleam in his eyes faded away. Her feet in his own cast-off slippers; her colorless blond hair, her sallow skin, her tired, faded features; as if she had worn away her natural outfit of good-looks with her clothes, and life had only second-hand or cast-off supplies to grant to her poverty. Her figure, in the pitiful manner of overtired women, bent back as if in search of support; but her eyes looked at him from it all, with all their original expression of trust and confidence.

"If he could read it for himself, if some one else could tell him, but me! Mon Dieu!" she explained.

"No, I will not speak to any one of them! not one of them!" the young man broke in resentfully at the sight of the Carlins crossing the yard in his direction. "I shall come in this evening myself, Madame Margot; I shall bring the paper and explain. Do not you say anything. Tell him it's a mistake, the news has not arrived yet. Monsieur Villeminot shall not be grieved. Tenez! I had almost forgotten the coffee and the picayune for milk for to-morrow morning." He put a small, fragrant, brown -paper parcel and a coin in her hand, and hurriedly walked through the corridor into the street.

The cathedral bells rang out their welcome or illcome intervening hours, measuring their second century of time and high and low masses to the clockless, watchless humanity of the city in the French quarter; chiming slowly and deliberately through the bright, fleshy days of the young, and most cruelly prolonging the fretful impatience of Monsieur Wilhelm, who awaited eagerly for the stroke which was to make or lose a day in his eternity. But hurrying echo, close upon stroke, linking sunrise to sunset in an ever shortening chain to the old — this seemed to make but moments of the diminishing, flitting, ghost-like days of the blind old man convulsively grasping from his Voltaire chair after but life enough for one more item of earth news:

the viaticum of defeat or victory to his country! hoping, despairing, expostulating, wrestling with Fate, trafficking with some far-off phantom of infantile Faith, conjuring up a belief in immortality, that he might barter or wager it for the proud privilege of continuing the triumphant traditions of a stalwart period, and so provide delusions still for his — French corpse.

It was nine o'clock ringing. The gas, an alternate mode of illumination by the economical city, was being turned off. The unpunctual moon was, however, behind time; only the silvery clouds, blown by a light breeze across the segment of heavens above the court-yard, warranted the reliability of the almanac, and told of the distant brilliancy in store.

"Mademoiselle Anaïs! Anaïs!"

Monsieur Wilhelm walked close to the wall under the gallery, and tapped with the merest tip of his finger on the glass door of the shoemaker's work-room. He could see the light through the gathered dimity curtains, and he knew that the circle of radiation inside held a head wound around with thick black plaits; a *gentille* little head bending over button-hole making in French kid *bottines*.

"Mademoiselle Anaïs! Anaïschen."

The tap and whisper were accentuated by his ardent heart. He knew she was there; there was never any one else in the workroom at that hour. Later in the season, yes, in midwinter when the carnival was crowded with balls, then it would be different, there would then be bustle and noise enough behind the curtains. The ponderous, noisy old sewing-machine would be stuttering and stitching through bewildering varieties of slippers, Monsieur Renaudière would be volubly ordering and directing, Madame Renaudière no less volubly disobeying and contradicting. There would be no little quiet moments like this then!

"Anais!"

Sometimes his finger barely touched the door before it flew open. If she were not sitting there making button-holes, she was standing by the table comparing, perhaps, some rejected shoe with original measurements; rehearsing plausible excuses for visible differences, protestations against invisible ones, and polishing up her elocutionary skill for special pleading on the morrow against obdurate toe twinges; shrugging her shoulders, raising her eyebrows, and gesticulating with her long-nailed fingers.

Oh, he had seen her preparing often enough, the coquette!

It was very necessary to reconnoitre before knocking in front, for the menage Renaudière was in as constant a state of revolution as a Central American republic. There was always a struggle for domination going on between the stronger and weaker sex, freakishly reversed in the husband and wife, but whichever party was victorious, the costs of revolution never failed to be extracted out of Anaïs and the younger children. Of seven children Anaïs was the eldest, and step-sister to the rest. It was a moment after one of these reckonings which had betrothed them. The good God had sent him through the corridor and Anaïs out of the door, there to dry her eyes, at the same instant. One little moment, but it had been repeated and repeated whenever their glances met. Only, the white eyelids of Anaïs would always waver a moment too soon, and the heavy lashes would always fall just in time to hide the confession coming, always a thought too late, from the frightened little heart; the tardy flush alone arriving to remain unconcealed, and burn eloquently of hidden motives to his eyes. Wilhelm's dream was some day to stay those eyelids but long enough for the blush and confession to meet.

The water trickled and dripped from the mossy green cistern behind him which filled an angle in the galleries and screened him from the rest of the yard. He sat down on the bench against it, upsetting the tin cup hanging over the faucet.

"Qui va là?" (Who's there?)

He heard Madame Renaudière bound from her bed. Her threatening tones fell from the window-shutters on the gallery above him.

"Who's there, I say?"

The heavy hooks dropped from the windows, and she came out on the gallery, hastily pulling on her blouse-volante.

"Who's there? If you don't answer I shall call my husband!"

This was intended for the ignorant, mal-intentioned ones, who supposed that Monsieur Renaudière stayed at home of evenings attending to his business, instead of discussing the war with Jacquet and others at the "Quincaillerie."

"Passe, chat! Passe!" she called, after a pause.

"It is only I, Madame Renaudière! Margot! I must have made a noise coming through the corridor, it is so dark."

"You, Madame Margot? So late!"

"It is only a little after nine, Madame Renaudière."

"Ah, I thought it was cats!"

"The pests, they are dreadful! I cannot sleep for them myself at night. 'Dieu vous benisse!'" Margot called promptly as a violent sneeze shook the gallery above.

"Ah!" feeling instinctively for her snuffbox, "I am catching cold! Well, goodnight, Madame Margot."

"Good-night, Madame Renaudière. No chance of getting in without your knowing it; vas!" she grumbled as she passed on in the direction of her gallery. She stopped at the door to return to Madame Carlin the bonnet and shawl borrowed for the occasion, and proceeded up-stairs to her room.

Monsieur Wilhelm, busy even in waiting, fixed his eyes upon the obstinate glass doors and fell mechanically to repeating the different classifications of English adverbs, marking them off on his fingers by an original system of mnemonics. The voices in the yard all died away, the different rooms one by one retired into darkness, nothing but the prowling cats disturbed the sleeping silence all around. His thoughts passed on to certain subtle deductions by which he hoped to classify lucidly obscure similarities between the German and English languages, looking to the ultimate establishment of some rule for the regulation of the pronunciation of the vowel sounds of both. But it all went abruptly out of his mind with the light behind the curtains, and he stared blankly at the place where she had shone in the room, as she shone in his heart. No mental exercises, knowledge, or experience, had ever prepared him for this event! He almost forgot to breathe.

"Thou forgetful! Thou heartless one! Thou ..." He abandoned his conscientious efforts at English self-communication. "Thou unwomanly one! Knowing only too well who was waiting outside, thou couldst yet extinguish that light! Without pause, without hesitation, nay, without remorse!" There came over him the violent bitterness of disappointment and the stinging humiliation of slight, insult, and a resentful reversal of all the flattering epithets which only a moment before had fitted his love so sweetly. "So! it is Sédan still! So! it is Bismarck and Napoleon and Prussia and France! So! it is not two living and loving hearts, but two inimical nations in our bosoms!"

He jumped from his seat and stamped his foot on the ground, this time driving the meddlesome tin against the house; but the madame had long been lulled to sleep by the rival and perpetual serenades of the "Marseillaise" and "Wacht am Rhein" of recurring organ-grinders at the different street corners within hearing. He strode across the yard, and, regardless of the treacherous pitfalls of the staircase, mounted boldly to the gallery, sought his room, and, with a reckless extravagance of matches, lighted his lamp.

His blond hair glistened like a silver nimbus around his red face, his light eyes were frankly infuriated. He broke into a voluble, passionate soliloquy, getting farther and farther away from his trained pedagogical German as his indignation increased, and lapsing deeper and deeper into the provincialisms and vulgarisms of expression and pronunciation of his peasant home.

"So! That is it! She will not open the door to me! She will not come out to me! She does not love me! She wishes to rebuff me! She hates me! That is enough, she is French, I am Prussian — to put out the light in that heartless way. O thou! So snail-slow to love, so lightning-quick to hate!"

He looked around his diminutive chamber. It had been large enough to contain such a world of ideal happiness; all in fragments and ruin now! "O thou female Samson!" On the table were piled the fool's cap copy books for correction; his nightly task, the flotsam and jetsam from the oceans of Greek and Latin ignorance in which God had willed he should travel through life. And there, ranged in file for use, were the red ink and the blue ink and the black ink with their symbolical values of meanings, and the smeared, rumpled copy-books of Rougette and Blanchette, the blotted currency with which he paid for his washing.

He would never have known he was a man if Anaïs had not grown into a woman; grown right there before his eyes, nay, publicly, before the eyes of the whole world. So quietly and imperceptibly at first, as if to slip into it befo.re they knew it, but with an exotic rush at the last. Into a woman! That little girl running around in short clothes when he first came to the house. In the dull, dingy, damp court-yard where plants were coaxed to grow and no flower cared to bloom, amid the clothes -washing, the shoemaking, the step-motherly assiduities, and paternal vexations, the great miracle had been accomplished. The transformation of her, and of him, too! For through the Greek and Latin bricklaying of his monotonous life visions and dreams had come to beautify his future, and novel thoughts to beset and tempt him, and in his breast a spring of poetry had been unlocked to gush and flow at the mere thought of her name. Napoleon III. could have conquered Prussia and passed it through a mill and not have eliminated Anaïs from his heart!

And she had turned the light from it all — deliberately, determinedly. It was to be all darkness henceforth, and grovelling work. He was to come through the corridor evening after evening, tired, heart -hungry, and pass straight on....Their eyes were no more to meet. ... "Nein, und wieder nein!"

He closed his lips, dragged his trunk from under the bed, and with desperate energy began to throw into it all his possessions, everything, pellmell: books, clothing, copy-books, pens, pencils, shoes. He stayed his hand at the ink-bottle, which he carefully corked and put into his pocket, took his umbrella, turned out the lamp, and, as if he were starting out on his daily routine, shut and locked the door behind him.

"Is anything the matter. Monsieur Villem?"

He had not noticed Madame Margot, standing in the far corner of the gallery.

"No, nothing at all. I am going away." He passed on as resolutely as if she were Anaïs.

"Going away? Mon Dieu!"

He awed her with his far-away, determined manner.

"But stop a moment, Monsieur Villem! Your coffee, your picayune, I shall return them."

Unfortunately, she belonged to the sex of Anaïs; his tone was brusque and ill-tempered,

"What do you take me for? If you do not want them, throw them into the street. I shall not touch them!"

She looked after him with her characteristic helpless docility,

"Well, good-bye, Monsieur Villem,"

"Good-bye, Madame Margot," groping his way down the steps.

"Monsieur Villem! Monsieur Villem!"

He was nearly to the landing. Looking up through the dark funnel above, he saw her bending over the balusters peering after him, the moonlight falling through the archway behind her, all over her head and shoulders. Her whisper was sharp and distinct.

123

"Remember, one teaspoonful of 'sirop de violettes' in a cup of 'tisane de bourrache' boiling hot."

"Thou dear God!" Tears came into his eyes. The strong fragrance of the violets came over him, and the suave consciousness of maternal solicitude, and the delicious sensation of awakening from pain and seeing Madame Margot with a steaming delft cup in her hand, standing at his bedside. Oh, those wintry nights of loneliness, homesickness, orphanage, and pneumonia!

"Thou dear God! It is the best Thou hast done, after all — the mothers! Happily for us men Thou stationedst them all through life. Thine own hospitals! heart sanctuaries!" He ran back to embrace his deputy mother, descending the steps again slowly.

The moon had at last reached the yard, and was poised full overhead, pouring down generous largesse of splendor on the humble scene below; transfiguring the most sordid detail with heavenly light and loveliness. Tire leaf plants in the little gallery gardens glistened and shimmered in the heavy September dew, pranked with a thousand diamonds, in default of the inert blossoms that could not be caressed out of their stems. From the great, rounded-top central window of the main building, old Grouille's vine fell in long, uneven fringes over the defaced stucco. A pang, which in its acuteness might have come from his delicate chest, shot across Wilhelm's anger at the thought of leaving the old caravansary that had housed him so long; that had lent to the lodging contract the kindly grace of hospitality, and so well concealed the pecuniary nature of their relationship. How bravely and pathetically the building rose in the moonlight, with its rooms full of tired, sleeping, homeless lodgers! Itself an aristocratic outcast, exiled in poverty, trading its shabby beauties, its comforts, the shelter of its roof, for a mere pittance. The skeletons of former romances, and the ghosts of former sentiment, seemed yet to flit across the galleries, look from the windows, and lurk in the dark corners.

The cathedral clock preluded midnight; was every one asleep? Asleep and unconscious of the sound of the hour and the sight of his going? Every one? No, there was old Grouille, his heavy foot descending step after step, from the third storey gallery, his candle flaring up to his nightcapped head, coming down, as usual, to close and bolt the heavy porte cochere. Wilhelm hastened through, just in time to escape unperceived.

Madame Margot, still on the gallery, crossed herself as if midnight were the angelus, and listened until the last musical stroke died away in the cool, damp air. She took out a book from under her sacque and held it closer and closer to her eyes. The mottled paper cover, the red morocco back, and the lurid gilt title stood out clearly enough, but the words that filled the inside pages were all uniformly unintelligible. Just as she was on the point of making one out, they all seemed to sink back into the white paper purposely to evade her. How was she ever to read it? She turned the soft, flimsy pages over, one after the other, carefully with her rough fingers, so many of them!

and all filled with words! She screwed her eyes almost close; but they were still too blunt to see through the fine, thin moonlight medium.

She was determined to read the book, to read it for herself. That was the result of all her winter's interviews with Madame St. Georges, of the --- Convent, that and the little colored picture of St. Roch in her room, and the candles to burn before the altar. She stood and thought, holding the book. She could not get out of the circle of what she had told Madame St. Georges and what Madame St. Georges had told her. More particularly what she had told Madame St. Georges, for that had excited her most. It was strange the way she talked then, she who never could talk. The words came all of themselves. Even now, at the remembrance of an expression or a tone of the reverend Mother's, the same words rushed again to her lips, her heart getting warm, and her eyes moist, just as they did then. It was Madame Carlin who had done it all. It would never have come into Margot's head to think of such a thing, and she would never have done it for herself, only for Monsieur Villeminot. Madame Carlin was a notorious gossip. She had talked to Madame St. Georges about Monsieur Villeminot, she had induced Margot to go to the convent after Monsieur Villeminot was asleep evenings, and she had persuaded Margot to take surreptitiously all the volumes from the mantelpiece, one after the other, to show to the reverend Mother; volumes written long, long before she and Monsieur Villeminot had come together in the sacrament of marriage. And it was Madame Carlin who had suggested that Monsieur Villeminot was blind, and would not miss them. Madame St. Georges was the Superior of the convent, where for the last five years a succession of Carlin girls had been making their first communion. It was well that Monsieur Carlin had not lived any longer, if a widow was the only support he intended leaving his children, and girls the only estate provided for his widow.

Fleurs Erotiques, Les Tropiques de l'amour, Vies Poetiques, Statistiques du Coeur, Romances Fantastiques. Proud and confident Margot had carried them all across the consecrated portals; a deception 'tis true towards her "patron," but then . . . the admiration, the appreciation of the reverend Mother, the homage when she had read — and who knows what ensuing services and worldly comforts? And in New Orleans, *her* New Orleans, who had more power, wealth, and influence than the Sisters? Oh, *they* could do anything!

"My good woman," said Madame St. Georges at the end of it all that very evening, "have you ever read any of these books?"

Read! Read Monsieur Villeminot's books! The idea! She had hardly dared handle them to fetch them to the convent! The very Sacred Host of literature to be enshrined on a mantel! and worshipped with unexamining faith and reverence.

"Oh no, reverend Mother! Not one of them."

"It is well. They are of the evil one! Pollution! Corruption! Infectious with vice and crime! Destructive of soul and body. Moral and physical poison. Burn them, burn them; destroy them! Remove the taint from the world! Remove, if possible, by prayer and sacrifice, the taint from the soul of the author! It is such books that make a hell of earth!"

"Grand Dieu, Seigneur!" Margot turned from her pious attitude of admiration before the case of scapularies and religious embroideries, and looked at the metamorphosed, pale, calm Sister in supreme amazement.

"Sin, vice! Evil one! Burn them. Monsieur Villeminot's books! Save his soul, Monsieur Villeminot's soul! The reverend Mother herself must be possessed."

"My poor woman, how came you to marry such a man?"

"I marry him, madame? I! I! I have that presumption? No, thank God! He married me. Ah, no, madame, you do not know him. My 'patron' is a gentleman, an aristocrat, a 'man of letters!'"

She drew herself up in rehearsal of the scene just as she had done then, only now she was barefooted and without the Widow Carlin's bonnet and shawl.

"What does the reverend Mother take me for?" she had pursued, reproachfully. "His wife should have come from the ladies up there; way up there. 'Bien en haut!'" Not meaning the pictured canonized ladies on the walls at which she was looking, but those who had the earthly precedence of dressing in silks and satins and riding in carriages to the opera. "It is only misfortune that drove him to me, poor man!"

An inspiration came to her to exonerate Monsieur Villeminot, and in a humble way to palliate her own conduct.

"There was a poor old gentleman sick in the little corner room on the gallery where I lived. Ma foi! they called him old ten years ago! He was poor, because it was the smallest and cheapest room in the whole house. No one knew him; you see he was above every one else in the yard, a gentleman in fact; an aristocrat, an 'homme de lettres.'" How she loved to pronounce the three words! "They only know he was sick because he ceased going out to work. He worked in a printing-office. As for me, I never had seen him in my life. I sewed by the day for Piton, at the 'Bon Marche;' made blouses by the dozen. But I am that way, madame," explanatorily. "When I hear of sickness, I cannot keep away, I suppose the good God gave me the vocation to be a sicknurse; I do not know. One day I was just passing the door with my bundle of work, and the impulse came to go in and see how the poor old gentleman was, and I stayed; in fact, I never left him day nor night. It was a long time — weeks; he suffered enough! Naturally he could not pay his rent; how could he, madame? Fever, rheumatism, and God knows what all! Old Grouille was for putting him in the street; sick! a gentleman, an aristocrat, a man of letters! Ah, that was too much! Well, the old miser! One room was enough for both, thank God! One day he thought he was getting well, and the idea took him; he sent for a priest and married me — Mon Dieu! there has been misery enough in this world for him!"

She had forgotten the book, and was looking straight before her with a smile on her lips, filling out from memory the *précis* of what she had given the Sister, rounding, amplifying, beautifying, and sublimating the prosaic facts as women will do about their marriage; counting over her own secret little hoardings of looks, caresses, thrills, and tremors — the precious private coin of love.

The time passed. How suddenly it had grown dark! She looked up in astonishment for the moon. No cloud hid it; it was only slipping away along the smooth heavens, drawing stealthily its silver light and loveliness away from the sleeping world as gently and easily as a mother withdraws the covering from a sleeping child. The tall chimney of the next house cut a great notch in the full round globe.

She was in despair. How could she manage it now? In the daytime she had her task of sewing. If the moon had but stayed longer she might yet have sharpened her eyes sufficiently. The blind need no light or she might have had one in her room; although there *was* one there, in the farthest corner behind the bed, standing on a backless chair. It was neither hers nor Monsieur Villeminot's; it was St. Roch's — Madame St. George's donation; a spiritual disinfectant in behalf of the old author against his own works; dedicated to consume its substance away in acts of grace before the picture of the saint. Could she, dare she read by it?

The moon disappeared entirely behind the chimney. St. Roch's candle or not? She took her slippers in her hand, passed into the room, and stood before the improvised altar cogitating. Who would ever know of it but the saint and herself?

"St. Roch, priez pour moi!

"St. Roch, ayez pitié de moi!

"St. Roch, daignez me secourir!

"Enfin, he is a man, he will understand!"

There was not the same difference between him and other men as between the Sisters and herself. The transparent, waxen Sisters, they embarrassed her with their pure eyes and lips, their unsoilable hands, their immaculate bodies. Spouses of the Holy Ghost, any one could see that! not of craving, ailing humanity.

She knelt at the chair and repeated her prayers interrogatively, looking timidly to the armed knight for some sign or token of disapproval. Then, an apprehensive glance for other lurking presences all around the chamber, then — a pause to listen to the sleeping respiration of her husband, then — slowly and stealthily she put her hand behind her, drew a book from the floor, and opened the pages of *Les filles de Lucifer.*

The wick neither flickered nor winced, but shared its rays fairly and indiscriminately between the gaudy beatitudes of the saint and the chastely printed type of Monsieur Villeminot's luxurious imaginings.

127

"Les filles de Lucifer! But who are the daughters of Lucifer?" She tried to remember if her knowledge of womankind had ever contained them. Alas! her schooling had been of the shortest, surrounding only the year of her first communion, distant now and dim.

"Lucifer? his daughters? Mon Dieu! I did not even know he had any."

It was hard to read words she was unfamiliar with; still harder to recognize her own every-day intimate expressions in such service as was needed to portray the charms and characteristics of the ladies in question. Whole pages vanished before her into the unintelligible, descriptions remained sealed to her limited understanding. The open spaces and short sentences of dialogue, however, were loop-holes into the fiction which, in her simplicity, she mistook for reality, and at last she comprehended.

"Mon Dieu! mon Dieu!" she murmured, from time to time, under her breath. She bent her perplexed brows nearer to the book, as if her heavy eyes were attempting to deceive her. At intervals she raised her head, clasped her hands, and looked in dispassionate appeal to the miniature saint. Once a blush mounted under her thick, sallow skin, and her heavy fist fell on the passage, burying it from his sight and from hers.

"And you," apostrophizing St. Roch, "you all up there, you know all this, you see all this, and do nothing! great God!"

The cocks in the neighboring bird-store began to make stifled guesses at dawn from their imprisoned cages, the candle was nearing the socket, when the last pages were reached and the book fell to the floor. She stood up and held her forehead tightly. Her plain, work-a-day eyes burned from the pandemonium of light dancing before them. Perfumes and flowers, music and wine, and the intoxicating glamour of idealized passion confused and staggered her. She groped her way to the bed, 'les filles de Lucifer,' houris, sultanas, sirens, joyous nights, nocturnal days, orgies, fêtes, nudities, rhapsodies — the whole saturnalia of life, with grotesque lasciviousness passing and repassing in her brain.

As she Stood grasping the post the blackness faded into gray, the gray lifted like a mist, and the bed slowly emerged from obscurity — the tossed-up draperies, the indented pillow bearing the white-haired head, with the long beard hiding the sunken cavity of the toothless mouth, the thin hands, and the body. The body that had disported youthful passions and graces for the daughters of Lucifer — what had become of it under the sheets? A bare outline!

He lay, the unconscious author, in the heavy torpid sleep of the aged, moving his hands uneasily, as daylight approached, muttering, muttering incessantly in his own private, aristocratic language:

"A gentleman, an aristocrat, and an 'homme de lettres!' the biographer and companion of 'les filles de Lucifer!' If it were not so, why should he write it? — why write such lies? If it were so, God and St. Roch help him!" The past of St. Roch himself had not been more above suspicion.

She bent over him as she had bent over his book — doubting, questioning, confused. Only her same old Monsieur Villeminot — her same old, blind patron. Not an infirmity, not a distortion, not a wrinkle missing, thank God!

"Madame, never a cross word, never an ungentle tone, never a complaint."

Her own words recurred again, enveloped in the same mist of tears that had blurred the Mother Superior from her eyes. "And blind, hopelessly blind." How clear and well-scrubbed her own humble, uneducated past had been!

"O God! why didst Thou make men so? or why didst Thou not protect Monsieur Villeminot?"

And again the unforgetable in her life came to her and held her, while the gray light of dawn broadened its streaks in the crack of the door and crept down the window, shutter by shutter.

"Enfin, God knows best. She is the Mother Superior of the convent, I only Margot! Husband for husband. He has given her the Church; but to me He has given Monsieur Villeminot." ...

Absent-mindedly, she made and carried the habitual cup of morning coffee to Monsieur Villem's room. It was not until after repeated knocks on the door that she realized his departure of the night before. The little flowermaker was just going out to her work, "tirée à quatre épingles," as usual. A suspicious character she was, in her tight-fitting, flounced dresses, kid gloves, and diminutive capote, tied coquettishly under her chin with bright ribbon.

"Ha, the lazy one! Still asleep!"

"Mon Dieu!" answered Margot, with a sigh; "he is not there at all."

The flower-maker's malicious eyes twinkled knowingly as she minced out:

"Ah, le brigand! but that is the way with young men!"

"He has gone away, mademoiselle, forever."

"Gone away forever! But where? but why?"

Margot's shrug of the shoulder left the answer to the inventive powers of the other one.

"Tant mieux!" shrugging her shoulders also; "one enemy less here; one more to kill over there."

There was a general excitement in the yard among the lodgers over the news; and the satisfactory feeling of elation that France had been so promptly vindicated by them continued until old Grouille made his appearance with his greasy bunch of pass-keys, and marched lugubriously up-stairs, followed by a porter.

"Now, if the steps would crack under him — hein!" the women whispered; "that would be a judgment!"

Prussia and the little black trunk were incontinently carried ignominiously out of the corridor, pursued by witticisms and patriotic jests, which culminated in boisterous hilarity as the bandy-legged, staggering porter finally disappeared, Anaïs, returning from early mass, knocked against him as he stepped onto the banquette. It was only Wilhelm Müller, painted in white letters on the trunk, that she saw, not Prussia; and the tender sentiments of repentance which were now making her heart eloquent with contrition took one bound into remorse — dumb, agonized remorse. Margot waylaid the man at the corner, and detained him until a message translated into his native Creole had been reiterated into intelligible conveyance on his part.

The war travelled all the way down the street from Canal to Esplanade; zigzagging like a streak of lightning from banquette to banquette, to separate friends from foes in all the little shops and industries, neighbors for decades; playing havoc with trade, blockading sociability, and laying waste whole quarters of human affections. From every German signboard victorious Prussian armies seemed contemptuously to issue with cannon, flags, sabres, and insults, to besiege an opposite or proximate French heart, which was daily fighting, starving, freezing, despairing, mutinying, with Paris enshrined in its very core.

In "La Rose de France" misfits accumulated beyond the capacity of the show-window; orders diminished below comparison with any previous era, and Anaïs, to her stepmother's vituperative indignation, was discovering a vocation for the cloister. The world had become manless for her; all her growing and blooming, dressing and coquetting useless and distasteful; her dreams, plans, and musings out of place and inappropriate. She had to learn a different language from the moonbeams and flowers. Her ears misinterpreted the strains of music. Her heart bounded and started on false scents and trails. Her lamp burned long and bright behind the curtains. How often the doors opened to illusory taps!

The news from France? What were battles and invasions? She, she alone, could tell what real misfortune, real pain, were. The phenomenon was that life could continue at all under the circumstances; that the sun could shine, and the people pass in front of the shop day after day, just the same. Yes, it was evidently God's will to make a nun of her…Was there, could there be, a greater tragedy than hers in His world, among His people?

Either France or the shoe business had to suffer, and Monsieur Renaudière was too good a patriot to hesitate in such an emergency between his workroom and Jacquet's "Quincaillerie," where the war was being diligently supervised and the Government vigorously reconstructed in nightly seances of midnight duration.

As Napoleon waned, Jacquet waxed, and his cottage rose in direct importance with the adversities of France. Trade was never brisker. The high-pointed tile roof over his shop seemed hardly able to hold down the plethora of wares underneath. The front room was in a constant state of overflow into the back room, which in turn disburdened itself onto the unpaved yard in the rear, where were huddled together old cartwheels, primitive sugar boilers, millstones, yellow water jars (retired into desuetude by increasing use of cisterns), chains, cannon-balls, and rusty heaps of mingled odds and ends, leaving barely space enough in the centre for a half-dozen chairs to mortise themselves comfortably in the soft earth, under the reverberative periods of Jacquet's hyperbolical eloquence. Here, evening after evening, under sunsets, twilights, moons and star risings, royalty had been guillotined, religion suppressed, priests extirpated, palaces and churches fired, dejected imperialists coerced into red-republican acquiescence by the fiery iron-monger, and "la patrie Madonne," coifed and costumed for the third representation of that drama, whose fifth act this time, according to the author, was to be a permanent denouement of victory and peace. But constant defeat and the protracted siege had driven the little coterie into despair and into the house, as winter succeeded to autumn, and it was finally in the dimly-lighted back room, surrounded by the shadowy forms of Jacquet's favorite metal, a prey to sinister noises and fancies, listeners to the stolid rejoicings of foes outside and the indifferent gayety of neutrals, that the compatriots suffered the full bitterness of their expatriation and humiliation. At the end of hope and patience, on the point of reacting vindictively into royalism, they sat one night, alas! and waited for the last news from Paris the terms of surrender.

"It is with a sword in the hand of a republic."

The word was, as usual with Jacquet, misfortune; instead of silencing his tongue, appearing to license it.

"Boutique!" (Shop!)

An old carafe to be sold, or a broken cup to be matched, or five cents of nails to be bought on time, or the shiftless Carlins redeeming or pawning necessary or useless flat-irons; and the Government had to be suspended, and the priests allowed a breathing-spell until, not satisfaction (for that, even in a second-hand condition, was not to be found in Jacquet's shop), but agreement was arrived at.

"It is iron, 'le fer, le fer, le fer,'" beating down as he spoke on a newly-polished stove.

"Shop!"

"Au diable la pratique!"

And they all listened listlessly to a tedious rigmarole of chaffering over a coffee-pot.

"And that is the last price. Monsieur Jacquet?"

"All that can be called 'last price.'"

"Mon Dieu! how dear these things are!"

"Cré nom! if I gave it to you for nothing you would still call it dear, you women!" and he commenced closing and bolting his shutters, for it was ringing nine o'clock.

"It is not that it is dear, Monsieur Jacquet, but money is so scarce." The voice sounded of an empty purse.

"There is no law to compel you to buy a coffee-pot, saperlotte!"

"And times are hard, mon Dieu, harder than in our war!"

"Si! the times are hard, but no harder for you than for me, par example!"

"Well, it's no use; I had better have the old one mended. Good-night, Monsieur Jacquet."

"Good-night, Madame Margot."

His voice was acrimonious and disgusted enough; he bolted the door noisily against the intrusion of any more customers.

"Va-t-en, imbécile! idiote de femme! dear, dear, dear!" whining in imitation of her tones. "She could not tell the truth and say she had no money; the truth from women; ha, bonjour! I guarantee she had not a picayune in her pocket. Ah, good God! what fools women are! He knew what He was about when He made them so. But it is not the men who should complain of it, nor her old patron — Hein, Madame Margot! Madame Margot!"

She was nearly through the corridor, but his voice arrested her in time and brought her back.

"But come in. Don't be a fool. What are you afraid of? Here, for God's sake, take it for a picayune, on time, anything, only don't talk any more about it. Here, go make the 'patron' his coffee; bon soir! En — fin," as he sharply shut the door behind her. "Poor wretch, if he has the coffee to make. He is a Frenchman also, her 'patron.' He will not want for misery and disgrace to-morrow morning! Blind and infirm — it is very little, after all, a coffee-pot! A gentleman, an aristocrat, and a man of letters, too, according to that great cow of a Widow Carlin and her two heifer daughters. Pests of the earth, with their flat-irons! Oui, messieurs," returning to the back door, "it will come hard upon him; he dates from the time of the great Napoleon when there was a Franca to gurround (g-r-r-r-ound) the Prussians under her heel. Ha! The time will come again! We must begin again as they did. ... As I was saying, the republic. . . . But what is the matter? You are all going?"

He had been too busy with his own soliloquy to hear the conference of the others. Old Fréjus had been, the orator this time; he who had sat obstinately silent during the autumn and winter debates of his compatriots, from whom neither guillotines nor petroleum could evoke more than increasingly melancholy shakes of the head and increasingly dejected arrangements of feature, whose tongue had refused to participate even in the allowably desperate prophecies and surmises of the hour; he had found a text in the dialogue between Margot and Jacquet for a sermon, and the language — poor old silent Fréjus! — of a Dominican in Passion Week to deliver it in. Not that his friends, being Frenchmen, needed more than a suggestion to kindle their hearts into generosity and sympathy. He buttoned up his overcoat and tied a bandanna over his head, still talking along in his tearful, complaining tone, as if his tongue could not cease all at once the unaccustomed impetus and motion; his words falling through the red and yellow folds, being twisted around mouth and neck.

"Humanity! Christianity! A good, pious woman! In poverty! No friends! Companions! All Frenchmen alike! Conquered by Prussians! Blind; alone; infirm! Weather so cold! A gentleman; an aristocrat; a man of letters! Poor woman, no money, no coffee! And we sitting here spouting! spouting! spout-ing! with — hé, my Saviour! — full stomachs and warm bodies — we let Frenchmen die of hunger and want! The Prussians kill them. We are more brutal than Prussians."

It was a short speech, but the longest he had ever made in his life; and it was more effective than any of Jacquet's or Renaudière's, for it left no minori-ty. "En avant, mes amis!" commanded Jacquet. All the overcoats were but-toned up, all the handkerchiefs knotted, and all stood outside the door and shivered unanimously, while Jacquet hunted for the key-hole with his pass-key in a darkness that seemed assembled en masse to quell forever the im-pertinent efforts of gas. They crossed the street, slipped against and stum-bled over each other in the corridor, traversed the yard, and directed their steps to the stair-way, each one silently conning some Gallicism of respectful homage and love. Renaudière held back. Fréjus absent-mindedly or unself-ishly mounted the rotten stairs first, and was miraculously followed in safety by all the rest.

The aroused Carlins peeped through their door at the astounding deputa-tion filing past, and all, old and young, followed on tiptoe after; but they were not half-way up the stairs and darkness before they were overtaken and star-tled into suppressed screams and ejaculations by the lightshod Anaïs, who, also peeping, was also driven by curiosity into following the procession.

Fréjus discreetly tapped, then waited a while, then softly opened the bat-tened doors, and all the heads came together to look through the glass case-ment inside. Oh, the battle of Sédan had been followed by defeat, bloodshed, and humiliation enough to have cracked the panes as the concentrated ha-tred of their gaze fell on what they had accustomed themselves to regard as the physiognomical expression of Prussian avarice, cruelty, and oppression — the mild face of Monsieur Wilhelm Müller. Rage at the sight of him swept like a blast all the soft impulses away from their hearts and the pretty speeches a-making in their brain.

"He had not gone away, then, the liar! He was not fighting with his coun-trymen, the coward! He had remained rather, vilely to creep and spy among the unfortunate French under the cover of darkness! Bribing and corrupting poverty pinched French patriots into disgraceful social intercourse! That was like a Prussian. Sitting, laughing in his sleeve at them! After they had put him out; cast him and his trunk into the street, he was mocking them! Despising them! Ah, they would show him! They might be beaten in France; but here in America, in New Orleans, there was still something to be said, to be done. Did he take them for children? For babies?"

Serenely unaware of the muffled heads, red noses, and vindictive whispers of his mortal enemies outside, the young German seemed in the dim room to be pursuing an amusing, if hesitating, narrative; reading from time to time from the telegraphic columns of a newspaper he held in his hand. Renaudière alone could catch the drift of it, for he, sacrificing vision to hearing, was bent over, holding an uncovered ear against the key-hole.

"But what is it? What is it?" demanded Jacquet. "What lies? What infamies?"

"Sacré!" A laugh, actually a laugh through the orifice, to be reported by Renaudière. A pleased, easy, complacent laugh by the old man in the chair to stick and quiver in their hearts. A laugh by a Frenchman, at this fatal hour, and before a Prussian!

"He reads telegrams," continued Renaudière, and then opened his lips for no more items; for, though he glued his ear to the key-hole, he knew that the words which he heard could only have emanated from his own diseased brain. "French triumphs — Prussian defeats — despair of besiegers — courage and fortitude of besieged. In all probability peace with glory and success to France! Paris..."

Was he (Renaudière) crazy, or they?

"Ha, ha, ha, Prussians repulsed again! Still holding their own? Ah, my brave Frenchmen, my brave Parisians. My polished lions! Starvation, shells, snow, prrut!" A cracked sound of his youthful expression of contempt. "They are fighting now for Paris, mon ami, for no government, no man, but for Paris! Ah, you don't know what that means! I do, I do! it will make them indestructible. Paris surrender?" He strove, but could not hide the tremulous vacillation from confidence to apprehension. The others merely stared from the outside, waiting for some event to enlighten them or prompt future action.

Margot, alas, for the easy descent of it! was kneeling on the floor before the picture of St. Roch, but only to hold the new coffee-pot over the flame of the votive candle. Her face was turned away from her task towards Monsieur Wilhelm, whom she was prompting by nods and signs and smiles of encouragement. The flames played over the sides of the unsteady tin, blackening and smoking it, and sending little waves of shadow over the whitewashed walls. The men outside nudged each other as the red and gilt backs of the books lightened and darkened on the mantel,

"Look! his books! it's true, a famous author; a man of letters."

"Paris surrender! Paris surrender!" The shrill voice came through the key-hole to Renaudière. "Never! Why, her paving-stones are the very bone, her sewers the veins, of the French people. Surrender to Prussians! Before the last soldier, the last man, the last woman, the last gamins from the streets had perished in her defence? Before the generale had been beaten throughout the whole world and the last French heart securely sleeping under foreign flags roused? Never! never! To arms! To arms! Her cry would go from city to hamlet, from hamlet to family, from the family to the distant wandering sons in mountains, swamps, and prairies. Country in danger, my children! To arms! To arms! Who — who of us would hold back? On! On!"

He was hidden by the cushions. They on the outside could hear nothing, but they could see his fingers creep along his chair. His white head came into view bent forward in blind intensity of expression, his thin, long beard agitated by the excited utterances.

"Paris in danger! To the rescue! All! all! — Ranks, Politics, Religions, Oriflammcs, Fleurs-de-lis, Tricolor! My country! We come! We come!"

The gaunt form sprang electrified from the chair, and made a step forward, an extended hand grasping an imaginary banner, the faded dressing-gown falling (as if to free him of infirmity and disease) from the bent shoulders. "We come! Yes! All! all!"

He swayed, tottered, and fell like a clod back into his cushions.

They threw open the doors and rushed in, trampling over the prostrate form of Renaudière. The coffee-pot fell from Margot's hands, upsetting the candle and splashing the coffee over the floor, Margot, Monsieur Wilhelm, but, most vociferously, Renaudière, interposed, and before a word could be uttered by the uninitiated, excited ones, they all stood committed to the supposititious triumphs of France, the supposititious successful defence of Paris, and were made by signs the confidants of Monsieur Wilhelm's nightly stolen visits, his generosity, his "bonté divine," his un-Prussian good-will. Jacquet lighted the candle and placed it with a bow of national politeness under the saint again, and then Margot shoved them all out into the darkness and cold of the gallery, entangled with Carlins, incoherent of speech, and distorted from prolonged shrugs of the shoulder.

"Mais, que diable! that woman, eh, she is never going to allow Paris to be taken," grumbled Jacquet.

Renaudière, after several mistakes in the obscurity, finally seized the right man, Monsieur Wilhelm, by both hands.

"Mon ami, you are great, you are noble; don't say a word, I understand, I appreciate. As a Frenchman, you see, I must detest you; as a man," suiting the action to the word, "I embrace you."

Old Fréjus had not been missed until he reappeared with arms filled: crucifixes, beads, pictures, and candles, a complete installation from his showcase for the proper, fitting service of the knightly, handsome St. Roch.

And she, who waiting in despair for one more chance, one more tap on her window, thought herself drifting towards the convent? There was no moon to gild the heavens above her, and the water dripped into icicles from the cistern behind her, but her vigil was neither long nor cold, although the cathedral clock was striking midnight before she caught him slipping past into the corridor — his nightly martyrdom, slipping past love and happiness, into a cold, deserted, denuded world.

She caught and held him — "Wilhelm!" And it was as if there had never been war or discord in the world; as if, indeed, there had never been a world but for them, for that moment. Only a moment, but it was sufficient — only a moment, because old Grouille was promptitude itself in bolting and barring the gate of the lodging-house at midnight.

The End.

www.ingramcontent.com/pod-product-compliance
Lightning Source LLC
Chambersburg PA
CBHW021923170626
46807CB00007B/2961